SPIRIT OR MAN?

The crash of thunder came at almost the same instant as the flash of lightning, illuminating every rock and twisted tree in sharp detail. And standing not twenty yards from him was the savage who hunted him, *Stone Hand*.

In the frozen moment of brilliant lightning, the man appeared to be more spirit than mortal. And though it was for no more than an instant, the image of the infamous killer was seared into Jason's brain.

Jason reacted immediately. He rolled over behind the carcass of his horse, his pistol ready, and prepared to shoot when the next bolt of lightning flashed. When it did, he could see no sign of Stone Hand. The man had disappeared. Like a spirit . . .

Vision or reality, spirit or man, it didn't matter. Jason was ready to deal with whatever Stone Hand was.

STONE HAND

CHARLES WEST

A SIGNET BOOK

SIGNET
Published by the Penguin Group
Penguin Putnam Inc., 375 Hudson Street,
New York, New York 10014, U.S.A.
Penguin Books Ltd, 27 Wrights Lane,
London W8 5TZ, England
Penguin Books Australia Ltd,
Ringwood, Victoria, Australia
Penguin Books Canada Ltd, 10 Alcorn Avenue,
Toronto, Ontario, Canada M4V 3B2
Penguin Books (N.Z.) Ltd, 182–190 Wairau Road,
Auckland 10, New Zealand

Penguin Books Ltd, Registered Offices:
Harmondsworth, Middlesex, England

First published by Signet,
an imprint of Dutton Signet,
a member of Penguin Putnam Inc.

First Printing, March, 1998
10 9 8 7 6 5 4 3 2 1

To Ronda . . . who else??

CHAPTER 1

Jason Coles stepped down from the saddle and dropped Henry's reins. He stood and watched for a few moments while the horse drank from the tiny stream, really just a trickle through the soft rock of the hill above him. It was a long way between water holes in this part of the territory and Jason let the horse drink his fill. He knew Henry would not take on more than he needed. He was an Indian pony.

Jason had traded for the horse with an Osage scout two years before. He had cost Jason a Henry rifle, so Jason thought it appropriate to name him Henry. It had been a good trade for both of them, the horse and Jason. Henry had turned out to be the stoutest horse Jason had ever ridden. The Osage hadn't treated the horse well, so it turned out to be a better deal for Henry, too. Jason had another horse that wasn't exactly a slouch either. A little mare named Birdie, she had black stockings on her forelegs and a little white patch in the middle of her chest that looked like a bird in flight. Both horses were unshod. In his business, it was safer to leave unshod hoofprints in case a war party happened upon his trail.

He stretched hard to pull some of the stiffness out of his muscles. He had been riding since sunup and he still had two days' riding ahead of him before reaching Camp Supply, although the going would be easier once he hit the main trail. He didn't ordinarily like to travel stage roads, but it had been four years since the Cheyennes moved onto the reservation at Camp Supply and there had been no real hostile activity in this part of the country. It was still considered hostile territory, however, because of a few scattered bands of renegades, so Jason was careful to maintain a sharp eye.

In the saddle again, he settled into Henry's easy gait and let his mind rummage through the events of the past couple of days. The message he got from Colonel Holder, summoning him to Camp Supply, held an urgent connotation although it offered no details as to the employment the colonel had for him. Jason had worked for Holder before, in the summer of '69 on a campaign that set out from Fort McPherson, Nebraska, headed for the Republican River. The expedition was accompanied by a whole battalion of Pawnee scouts but Holder had wanted Jason to go along as his own personal scout. Jason went but he didn't have much to do with the Pawnees. He preferred to work alone. It wasn't that he thought he was any better scout than the Pawnees. It was just his way. He had always relied on his own intuitions and intuition was as big a part of scouting as reading sign.

He was jolted from his thoughts by the sharp crack of a rifle, army carbine by the sound of it. It was followed by a series of shots, some of them from a muzzle loader. He figured it had to be an attack on a settler's wagon because he was less than a mile from cutting the trail to Camp Supply. Somebody was in trouble. He prodded Henry gently and the pony immediately took up a canter. By the time he emerged from a treeless ravine and climbed to the top of a rise, the firing had subsided to an occasional shot from the rifles. Below him, in a stand of cottonwoods, he saw what the shooting was about.

It appeared to be an army ambulance, half hidden from his view by the trees, and three, maybe four, soldiers were shooting from under it. Their attackers, some dozen or more Indians, were shooting at them from two sides. Jason took a moment to assess the scene before he took any action. Evidently the Indians had ambushed the ambulance when it entered the trees. It was Jason's guess that the raiders were after guns and ammunition because there was only one old musket between them and it was misfiring half the time. The rest of the raiding party were using bows. It didn't look like much of a raiding party to Jason. He wondered why the troopers didn't go out after them. They had rifles. It wouldn't take much to discourage that bunch.

"Hell, Henry, I reckon we'd better root 'em out of there or them poor soldier boys will lay under that wagon till they run out of ammunition."

Keeping low behind the rise of the hill, he circled around behind until he had a clear field of fire. Then he left his horse and crawled up to a point behind a fallen tree. From there it was a simple matter to bring his Winchester to bear on the attackers and he methodically began to pick off one after the other, taking out three of the party before they figured out what was going on. In a matter of five or ten minutes, the rest of the raiders were scrambling to get to their ponies and, taking their dead with them, quit the fight. Jason stood up and watched until they disappeared over the horizon.

"They were a pretty sorry-looking lot," he muttered to himself. "Renegade Cheyenne, I expect. They look like they've seen better days." Glancing back toward the trees, he saw a soldier crawl out from under the ambulance, looking first at the departing Indians, then back at Jason. Jason called out, "I'm coming in. Hold your fire." He turned to retrieve his horse.

"Well, sir, I'm mighty glad you come along when you did." The man who spoke wore the uniform of a sergeant, with the insignia of the medical service. Behind him, two privates crawled out from under the ambulance. They were followed by an officer dusting the sand from his uniform. By the insignia on his lapel, Jason saw that he was a doctor. In a glance, Jason summed up the situation, a doctor and his orderlies. What, he wondered, were they doing out here away from the post? It was lucky he came along. No doubt they would have laid under that wagon and shot up all their ammunition. Then the renegades would have walked in and scalped the lot.

"Looks like you folks were in a tight spot," Jason said. "What in hell were you . . ." He stopped in midsentence, his thoughts interrupted by the appearance of a figure behind the wagon wheel. Crawling on her hands and knees until she cleared the wagon bed, she then stood up and began to vigorously brush the dirt from her riding skirt. Jason was stunned. She glanced up briefly and smiled at him, more interested in removing the dust from her skirt.

Jason watched, fascinated. It had been some time since he had seen a white woman. This alone, in a place like this, was enough to leave him speechless for a moment. Even allowing for that, this woman was as out of place as if she had come from the moon. It was not her outfit alone, attire more suited for a canter in the park in Philadelphia perhaps. It was more than that. Her face was alive with the sparkle of youth and her skin as fair as a spring morning. Jason hardly heard the surgeon's words as he expressed his appreciation for Jason's sudden appearance.

"I want to thank you, sir, for coming to our aid." Jason nodded, and he continued. "We were in a desperate situation. I'm Captain John Welch. I'm on my way to Camp Supply—temporary duty to set up a field clinic."

Jason shook the outstretched hand. "Jason Coles," he replied, his gaze still fixed on the vision that had appeared from behind the wagon wheel. Her skirt now thoroughly dusted, she approached him.

"We are certainly in your debt, sir." She smiled and extended her hand. Jason clutched it awkwardly. "I'm Sarah Holder."

"Jason Coles," he blurted. Her smile warmed him like sunlight. He had to lecture himself to wipe the foolish grin from his face before the lady marked him for an idiot. He didn't know why he seemed struck dumb by the appearance of this splash of original beauty in this drab territory but he knew he'd better come back down to earth. "I'm pleased to meet you, Miss Holder." Then he paused. "Holder? You wouldn't be kin to Colonel Holder, would you?"

"He's my father. I'm on my way to visit him now."

"Well, I'll be . . ." He didn't finish, somewhat surprised that Lucien Holder would permit his daughter to come out to a desolate place like Camp

Supply. It was hardly the kind of place a man would want his daughter, especially if she looked as genteel as Sarah Holder. Well, he decided, it wasn't his business. "Camp Supply," he stated. "That's where I'm heading. Your daddy sent word he wants to see me."

"Good," the doctor chimed in, "maybe you'll ride along with us."

"I reckon," Jason answered, noting the smile his reply brought to Sarah Holder's face.

Jason was immediately taken by the young woman. There was something about her that struck a chord deep within him, a chord that had been mute for years. What was it about her that aroused long-forgotten feelings? It was more than the natural loneliness that was common baggage for life on the western frontier. Then it struck him. Sarah Holder bore a striking resemblance to a young girl of eighteen who would always occupy a small corner of his subconscious mind. Her name was Kathy and she had loved him and they were to be married when she returned from a visit with her grandmother in St. Louis. Only she had never returned to Kansas, where he had waited. He had long ago decided that she had been too perfect for this world and that was why she was taken from him. There had to be a reason for her to be taken at such a tender age. Her death was so sudden and unbelievable—a rock slide had caused the stage she traveled in to venture too close to the edge of a deep ravine. The driver escaped by leaping from the coach as it tumbled over the side. Kathy, her mother, and father, all three were killed.

He shook his head as if to clear the memories from his conscious mind. He had tried to make it a rule never to dwell on what might have been. Even though more than ten years had passed since that fateful day, he still found it painful to recall. Sarah Holder had brought back thoughts he had sought to forget. Things happen the way they're supposed to, he told himself. Looking now at the smiling face of Sarah Holder, he thought, if I were a few years younger, I might give that dashing young doctor a run for his money.

Once the party was under way, Jason pulled up alongside the doctor. "Captain, what in hell are you people doing out here with no escort?"

Captain Welch shrugged. He made no attempt to hide the sheepish expression on his face. "It was my understanding that the Cheyennes were at peace and had been for several years. We were going to have to wait three more days at Ford Cobb before a military escort was provided. Miss Holder arrived at the fort and was anxious to see her father. So I figured it would be all right to escort her myself."

"Didn't anybody tell you there were still raiding parties out here?" Jason found it difficult to believe they were permitted to set off across the territory with no more protection than one doctor and three orderlies, none of whom appeared to be the least bit familiar with the rifles they carried. It was the answer to a renegade Indian's prayer.

"We were warned, but I guess I underestimated the danger." He shrugged off the responsibility for his rash judgment. "We are supposed to be at peace with the Indians. Anyway, it turned out all right. You showed up in the nick of time."

"If I hadn't, your scalps would be flying on a Cheyenne lance right now, except for the woman's. She'd be on her way to a Cheyenne camp."

"But you showed up," Welch insisted.

"I reckon," Jason replied. The doctor was oblivious to the consequences that might have resulted from his naïveté, consequences that should have resulted from an action so stupid.

"Mr. Coles."

Jason glanced up when he heard his name called. He was checking Henry's right front hoof for sign of a stone bruise. He had crossed through a rocky region a few days before and he thought there might be the possibility that his horse had caught a sharp edge. Henry appeared to be all right. He dropped the horse's hoof and straightened up. "Miss Holder?"

"I wanted to tell you we have plenty of food and you're welcome to join us. Captain Welch brought enough provisions for three more days and, since you say we'll make Camp Supply by tomorrow afternoon, we have enough for a banquet. That is, if you can consider salt pork and biscuits proper fare for a banquet."

He returned her smile. "Why, ma'am, that sounds like a real feast to me."

"Good. There's no sense in your sitting over here by yourself when we're all traveling together."

Jason blushed a little as he fumbled for an explanation. "Well, I didn't want to impose myself on you folks. I know I don't look too presentable after being in the hills for the past six months. I don't reckon you see many half-wild men back East in . . ." He hesitated.

"Baltimore," she filled in the blank.

"But, if you don't mind my scruffy appearance, I'd be delighted to join your party. First I'm gonna take a little look-see around our camp to make sure we don't have any guests without invitations."

After satisfying himself that the Cheyenne raiders were no longer in the area, Jason unsaddled Henry and joined Sarah and the doctor at their campfire. The three enlisted men sat off to one side, nursing their own campfire, a fact that amused Jason. There they were, six souls, out in the middle of the Oklahoma territory, and protocol dictated separate fires for the officer and the enlisted men when there wasn't much firewood to be found in the first place.

"If you don't mind me asking, ma'am, does Colonel Holder know you're coming to see him?"

"Well . . ." She hesitated, a hint of a guilty smile parted her lips. "It's going to be a surprise."

Jason thought this over for a moment before replying. "It sure is," he said.

"Do I detect a hint of disapproval in your tone, Mr. Coles?" Her voice held a touch of amusement. It was apparent that she was unconcerned with what others might think regarding her actions.

"Oh, no, ma'am, not in the least. It sure ain't my place to approve or disapprove of what anybody does. But you sure will surprise your daddy. I know that for a fact."

"Oh? Is there some reason I shouldn't be going to see him? Camp Supply is a military post. Is it not?"

"Well, I guess some folks might call it that," he allowed. "Injuns, maybe. But I'm afraid you might find it offers rude accommodations for the fair sex. Camp Supply ain't much more than a field camp and a Cheyenne reservation."

"I'm sure my father will be happy to see me," she insisted. "And I don't need genteel accommodations, Mr. Coles. I'm not as fragile as you may think."

He had to smile at that. "Yes, ma'am. I didn't mean to be rude. I was just surprised you were going to Supply, that's all. I'm sure you can handle it."

Sarah Holder was not a woman easily impressed by just any man she happened to meet. She suspected that there might be something more to this seemingly simple man than he openly displayed. Possibly, he was justified in questioning her judgment to journey unannounced to see her father but it didn't worry her. Though young and only recently graduated from finishing school, she was none the less secure in her self-knowledge and confident that she was fully competent to make her own decisions. This was probably a result of having a father who was absent from home most of her life, stationed in some remote wilderness like Camp Supply. Constance Holder had been a loving, almost doting, mother until pneumonia claimed her life two weeks before Sarah's seventeenth birthday. Her aunt, though a willing substitute for Sarah's mother, was no match for her headstrong young niece. Consequently, Sarah did pretty much as she pleased. And at this point it pleased her to go to visit her father at this desolate outpost on the frontier. She was to begin her tenure as a teacher in Baltimore in the fall and thought this the best time for a visit with her father before she embarked on a career. Aside from a desire to visit her father, this would probably be her best opportunity to see the frontier. She and her friends had often wondered what it must be like to actually see wild Indians in their rugged homelands. The thought never failed to excite her and on a sudden whim she had decided to make the trip that summer while she had the time.

She had no thoughts regarding marriage at the

moment. There had been opportunities but none
that provoked even a spark of serious consideration. Though it may have frightened most girls her
age, she was not concerned by the thought of facing her twenty-first year without any prospects of
marriage. Marriage would come, she was reasonably certain. But when it did, it would be of her
choosing and not from fear of becoming a spinster.
Besides, there was a desire on her part to taste at
least a small sample of life outside the protected
womb of the classroom and her mother's house.

Already her impulsive journey to Oklahoma Territory had provided adventure unimagined by her
friends back East. Traveling alone with an army officer and three enlisted men would seem shocking
to her girlfriends at school. Sarah saw nothing
wrong with it. The three soldiers were distant and
respectful and Captain Welch had behaved gal-
lantly. The surgeon was obviously taken with her
beauty and charm. Of that she had no doubt and
she had to admit that she had a more than casual
interest in the young surgeon. He did present a
rather dashing figure in his captain's uniform. But
for now, she simply enjoyed his attention to her.
She was not prospecting for romance.

And then there was this strange creature who
had appeared out of nowhere to save them from
the savages, this Jason Coles. What was she to
make of him? A wilder-looking man she could not
imagine . . . little more than the wild Indians he had

driven off, judging by his appearance. She couldn't resist wondering what he would look like without the face full of whiskers and the worn buckskins. He was obviously younger than she had thought at first glance. She felt a strong desire to peel away the rough bark to see what was beneath. She knew one thing for certain, she felt a great deal safer with Jason Coles along.

By midafternoon of the following day, the rough structures of Camp Supply came into view. The little party made its way directly toward the rows of tents some distance apart. The headquarters tent was easily identified by its size and the flagpole in front.

Sergeant Major Maxwell Kennedy emerged from the large tent, coffee cup in hand, and took a few steps in their direction as they approached. "Hello, Jason. I see you still ain't lost your scalp yet." He eyed the ambulance with open curiosity. "What have you got there?"

"How ya doing, Max?" Jason turned to follow the sergeant major's glance as Captain Welch helped Sarah Holder from the wagon. "A little surprise for Colonel Holder," he said. "A pleasant surprise I hope."

The sergeant major stood beside Jason, saying nothing more, waiting for the explanation that would account for the unexpected appearance of an attractive young lady in the midst of his raw military world. Maxwell Kennedy was a patient man who had lived the army life since he was a boy of eighteen. His was the patience that comes with twenty-four years of unexpected and unexplained events. He watched with some interest as Captain Welch graciously saw to the young lady's comfort before concerning himself with reporting. Kennedy looked the young woman over, unabashed, obviously evaluating her qualities. Sarah, in return, stared back at him, favoring him with a warm smile.

Satisfied that Sarah was safely dismounted from the ambulance, Captain Welch stepped up before the sergeant major. "Sergeant, I'm Captain Welch. I'm to report to Colonel Holder."

"Yessir," Kennedy replied, unimpressed. He offered the captain a halfhearted salute, the coffee cup still in the hand he saluted with. "You're the sawbones we were told we were getting. We didn't expect you till next week."

"I know. I decided to come on earlier to escort Miss Holder."

This caused a spark of interest in the sergeant major, evidenced only by the slightest raising of one eyebrow. "Miss Holder? I thought she must have been your wife."

Sarah stepped forward. "I'm Sarah Holder, Colonel Holder's daughter." She extended her hand. "You must be Sergeant Major Kennedy. My father has mentioned you in his letters."

"Yes, ma'am." Kennedy's weathered features relaxed into a broad grin. "Why, I'm right glad to meet you." He transferred the coffee cup to his other hand and took her outstretched hand in his. "So you're the colonel's little girl. Well, I'll be . . . Does the colonel know you're coming? He ain't said the first word to me about it." He didn't give her space to answer before adding, "How did you come to be traveling with a renegade like this?" He gestured toward Jason, his grin indicating that he was joking about the renegade label.

Jason had been standing by during the introductions, mildly interested in the sergeant major's reaction to his surprise visitor. He barely grunted in response to Kennedy's jab. Sarah favored him with her generous smile.

"Mr. Coles came to our rescue when we were attacked by savages. If it wasn't for him, we might not be here." Realizing at once that she might have injured John Welch's pride, she quickly added, "Although I'm sure Captain Welch and his men would have been more than a match for the savages."

Kennedy shot a quick glance in Jason's direction. Jason answered with a faint smile. Turning back to the captain, he said, "The colonel's over at the agency. He'll be back pretty soon." His eyebrows raised a little. "I reckon he might want to talk to you about bringing his daughter out here without a proper escort." He didn't give the captain time to respond. "As for you, young lady, he might want to spank you for coming out here." His smile told her that he was amused by her obvious spunk. "I'll have you a place fixed up. It won't be like you're used to back east, but it'll be out of the weather." He turned to signal an orderly. "Johnson, take these folks over to the mess tent and tell Sergeant Ortiz to find 'em something to eat."

Jason stood silent while Kennedy issued orders to find accommodations for the new arrivals. When the others left to go to the mess tent, he spoke. "Max, what does the colonel want with me?"

A wry smile creased the sergeant's weathered features. "Now, Jason, you know the colonel gets a little testy when I talk about his plans. I'll let him tell you." The grin widened. "But, if I was you, I wouldn't get too comfortable with garrison life."

"I never have been," Jason replied. He knew Kennedy could have told him why he had been summoned. His curiosity was not so great that he would badger the sergeant to find out. From Kennedy's brief comment, he could guess that he was going to be asked to go on a scout of some kind. But he had assumed that from the beginning. He hoped it wasn't for a general troop campaign. He worked better alone. "I'm going to take care of my horse and then maybe see if I can get something to eat. I'll see the colonel when he gets back."

A short time later he saw the colonel ride back into camp but he remained where he was, using his saddle as a backrest. The mess sergeant had rustled up some coffee and biscuits for him and he was in no hurry to finish his repast. Anyway, he figured Colonel Holder was going to be so damned irritated to find his daughter waiting for him that he wouldn't want to talk business until he had a chance to simmer down. Jason smiled to himself when he thought about the lecture the young surgeon was bound to receive for bringing Sarah Holder through mostly hostile territory with no more protection than a doctor and three orderlies.

It was almost dusk when Jason ambled into the headquarters tent. He nodded briefly to Kennedy. "You reckon the colonel is ready to see me now?"

Kennedy grinned. "I reckon he is." Without getting up from his desk, he called over his shoulder. "Colonel, sir, this no-good renegade scout is here to see you." His grin expanded as the blanket that served as a divider parted and a tall, rawboned man plunged through.

"Jason Coles! How the hell are you?"

"Colonel," Jason responded. He smiled and took the outstretched hand.

"I knew you'd show up. Jim Riley said he thought you'd retired from Indian fighting. But I figured you'd show when you got my message."

Captain Jim Riley commanded a company of Pawnee scouts. Jason had ridden with him out of Fort Cobb the previous spring. "Well, I was getting pretty tired of hunting and you went to a lot of fuss to find me so I figured I was curious enough to see what you had on your mind."

Colonel Holder beamed at the scout, genuinely pleased that he had responded to his call. "I understand I owe you a word of thanks already for seeing my daughter safely to the camp."

Jason shrugged. "I just happened along and we were all going to the same place so I came on in with them."

Colonel Holder expected the tall scout to downplay his part in the action. "Well, I appreciate the fact you just happened along." His smile faded for a moment and his face reflected a fatherly concern. "That girl is bound and determined to get herself killed. She had no business at all coming out here. And that damn fool doctor doesn't have any more brains than to . . ." Realizing he was berating a fellow officer in front of an enlisted man and a civilian, he broke off and collected himself immediately. "But enough of that. Did you get something to eat?"

"Yessir."

"Good. All right, let's get down to it then. Coles, I need your help. I've got a problem I can't seem to solve with a regiment of cavalry." He pulled a stool up under him and settled his lean frame. "For the past four years, ever since Custer's Washita campaign, we've been chasing small bands of Cheyenne and Arapaho raiding parties. Most of the tribe has come in to the reservation but there are still a few renegades out there and they are raising a lot of hell on the settlers and stage lines." He paused to offer Jason a cigar. After they both lit up, he continued. "Now, my boys are a pretty good bunch, all seasoned and tough as nails, and we're gradually wiping out most of the hostiles. But, dammit, there is one red son of a bitch that has me buffaloed and that's why I sent for you." He glanced at Sergeant Major Kennedy before continuing as if for confirmation. "His name is Stone Hand and he's a damn loner, even with his own people. But he raises more hell than all the rest of 'em put together, raiding, stealing, murdering. If I could get my hands on him, I'd hang him in the middle of the Cheyenne camp. Like I said, he's a loner, always raids by himself. The trouble is, the rest of the damn Indians have come to think he's something special, superhuman. Some of them are starting to think he can't be killed, he's some big medicine. I'll say this for him. He's one wily son of a bitch. We can't even figure out where he is or where he's gonna hit next because he's just one man. He can go where he wants, when he wants."

"And you think I can catch him for you?" Jason interjected.

Holder hesitated briefly. "Well, if *you* can't, then I don't reckon anybody can." He studied Jason's face intently, waiting for his response. Jason said nothing. "I figure one man who knew what he was about might be able to get on his trail and stick with it where a troop of cavalry couldn't. What do you think?"

Jason scratched his head while he thought it over. "Where did he hit last?"

"Twelve miles from where we're standing." There was a strong hint of disgust in his tone, "Last Tuesday."

Jason smiled faintly. "He don't show a whole lot of respect for you soldier boys, does he?"

"The son of a bitch." Holder snorted. "And, as long as he keeps getting away with it, he just gets bigger and bigger in the eyes of the young bucks on the reservation."

"I'm surprised none of the young ones haven't jumped the reservation and joined up with him."

"Hell, they're afraid of him, too. I tell you, Coles, there's something basically evil about this one."

Jason stroked his chin thoughtfully. "Why does he hang around so close to the army if he doesn't want to get caught?"

"My scouts tell me that he has his own personal vendetta against the army. That son of a bitch is dedicated to one thing, killing as many white men as he can. He prefers killing soldiers. But anybody white will do in a pinch. I swear, I believe if he ran out of white men, he'd start killing Indians."

"You're telling me that this man comes to the reservation whenever he feels like it? Why can't you send a troop of cavalry into the reservation and take him?"

"I wish it was that simple. The trouble is we don't ever know when he's there. He's got his own people so damn scared of him that nobody will tell on him. He's big medicine. And the son of a bitch uses disguises half the time, rides right by our patrols."

Jason glanced quickly at Kennedy then back to the colonel. "And you want me to catch him? This big medicine killer?"

"Will you do it?"

"Well, as long as the army wants to pay me for it, I reckon I can try."

"Good man. I knew I could count on you. We get rid of that bastard and it'll make my job a lot easier around here. You'll be saving a lot of lives to boot."

"Hold on, Colonel. I said I'd try to catch him. It don't sound like it's gonna be an easy job."

Holder's face relaxed into a satisfied smile. "I feel a helluva lot more confident with you on the job. Let's have a drink on it. Sergeant Major, break out that bottle in my trunk."

Jason held the small shaving mirror up close to his face so he could evaluate the job he had just completed with his razor. He had let his beard get a little ragged during the last few weeks, having no incentive to keep it neat. It was time, he decided, to shave it off and start a new crop. He did not try to deceive himself by thinking the presence of Sarah Holder had nothing to do with it. She was a fine-looking woman and her arrival on the scene had caused him to feel some discomfort in his appearance. Although he harbored no illusions that there was even the faintest of sparks between them, he at least wanted to present his more civilized side.

"Well, I've seen worse," he decided and replaced the mirror in his saddle pack, along with the razor. He was invited to have the evening meal with Colonel Holder and his daughter. The doctor was also invited. Jason hoped his manners would be polished enough to dine with a young lady from back East. "That's the best I can do." He sighed and, after pulling his clean shirt over his head, he headed for the colonel's tent.

Jason was the last of the party to arrive. Colonel Holder turned to greet him as he entered the large tent. "Well, my God, I didn't know who you were at first, Jason." Jason blushed. "We were just having a little drink before supper. Can I pour you one?"

"I reckon not, Colonel. Maybe later." He grinned at Sarah Holder and added, "Miss Holder and I will stay sober so we can enjoy that hindquarter of deer I saw roasting on the spit out back."

Sarah returned his smile. She had been studying the transformation that had taken place. "I must agree with Daddy. I almost failed to recognize you, Mr. Coles." Her remark caused Jason's blush to deepen, a fact that Sarah did not fail to notice. It pleased her that her presence caused some awkwardness in a man noted for his cool demeanor.

She took a moment to reevaluate her impression of the Indian scout whom her father had praised so highly. There was definitely something about him that sparked her interest and, while she was not willing to pronounce his face handsome, he was not unattractive when he was clean-shaven. Of the two men, the scout was no competition for the surgeon when it came to social niceties. Captain Welch was polished and well-spoken and obviously well schooled in social graces. And there was no denying the man was handsome, almost to a fault. When she compared the two, it brought to mind the contrast between a sleek, well-groomed polo pony and an untamed mustang. Still, she admitted, the mustang held a certain fascination for her. Her thoughts were interrupted by the steward's announcement that the meat was ready to serve. Captain Welch was at her side instantly to offer his arm. She smiled graciously as she accepted it and he escorted her to the table outside under the tent flap. Jason and the colonel followed.

During dinner, Sarah took charge of the conversation, charming her male companions with the effortless grace of a young woman who was very comfortable as the center of attention. Even her father's complaining about her unannounced visit to this frontier was disarmed. Listening to the charming young woman's rambling conversation as it skipped along over a field of trivial topics, like a butterfly in a spring meadow, Jason realized that Sarah was playing her part as the colonel's daughter. He concluded that she was no more interested in what the ladies in Baltimore were wearing this season than he was. There was a gleam in her eye that told him she was performing for the men, being Daddy's little girl. Jason glanced first at the doting Colonel Holder, then at a totally mesmerized Captain Welch. Welch in particular made no effort to hide his fascination for the handsome young woman. He hung on her every word, as if he were vitally concerned about the cotillion she was to miss because she had elected to come to visit her father. Once during the evening, her glance had held Jason's gaze and there was a flicker of communication between them. She smiled, as if having been caught at playing a game and then, in an instant, darted off on another topic. Jason decided then that there was more to Sarah Holder than she exhibited for their amusement. Too bad she was going back East, he decided.

"How long are you planning to be with us, Miss Holder?" Jason asked during a rare lull in the conversation.

"I think about a week, maybe two." She looked at her father for his reaction.

"Oh, I hope it will be longer than a week," John Welch blurted.

"We shall see." She beamed. "I really don't have to be back in Baltimore until the fall."

Her father's stern expression gave indication enough to inform them of his opinion of the situation. "You really had no business coming out here in the first place, young lady, and you're going back with the first troop movement to Fort Cobb. This is no place for a lady."

"Why, Daddy," she teased, "what about the sergeant major's wife? I'm sure you don't mean that Mrs. Kennedy is no lady."

The colonel almost sputtered his response. "That's different," he stammered, then regained his composure. "You know what I mean. Cora Kennedy and the other three wives in garrison are damn near as hard campaigners as their husbands. They weren't raised in Baltimore like you were. At any rate you are going back at the first opportunity."

Sarah said nothing in reply but her smile told them that she would probably return to the East on her own schedule. Jason found himself hoping she would stay longer than a week also, even though he would be unable to find enough excuses to remain in camp himself. The girl held a certain fascination for him. He had to admit that. Why he even bothered with the thought was a mystery to him. Even if he held romantic interests for the girl, he could see himself as no competition for the dashing young surgeon who was so obviously overwhelmed by her. Still, he admitted, it would be nice to have her around for a while.

While the colonel and his daughter entertained their guests, less than ten miles from the camp a

lone, menacing figure sat, silently watching the
evening activities of a cavalry patrol some fifty feet
below the ledge he perched on. It was a small patrol, no more than a dozen troopers. Still, they
would be at small risk of attack from any of the
roving bands of hostiles in the territory. It was their
misfortune, however, that this was no ordinary
Cheyenne renegade silently watching and waiting
for the camp to settle in for the night. He sat pa-
tiently, his rifle cradled across his arms as he noted
the horses hobbled off to the left of the bivouac and
the single guard posted there. He watched the two
perimeter sentries as they finished their coffee and
left the campfire to take up their posts. Only three
of the twelve were on guard while the others rolled
up in their blankets. Typical, he thought, and a
faint smile creased his face.

CHAPTER 2

Jason stood over the mutilated body of the horse guard while the sergeant related the events leading up to the previous night's raid. "They must have been positioned on three sides of the camp," the sergeant speculated. "Near as I can figure, all three must have been hit at the same time."

Jason didn't say anything for a few minutes. Then he turned to the sergeant and quietly announced, "There was only one man." His scout around the perimeter of the campsite had told him that the raider had acted alone. There was one set of prints, one horse. He had come down from the bluff overlooking the small stream where the patrol had carelessly made their camp. Jason would never have picked the spot himself. It offered cover on three sides to anyone inclined to attack the camp. It could not have been more inviting to the renegade. Still, it took more than the average man to accomplish the three separate killings of the guards as well as the theft of a half dozen of their horses. All this happened without waking the rest of the camp. Jason did not have to be told that this could be the work of only one man, Stone Hand.

So at last he was confronted with the task that lay before him. Colonel Holder had dealt him no pat hand. He was going to earn his money on this one. He bent down over the mutilated body to examine it more closely. He had noticed it on the other two bodies. This Cheyenne had a signature. The left eyebrow of each man was slit with a single stroke of the scalping knife. It had to be intentional, there being no reason for it beyond a deliberate sign to let the army know that it was the work of one man. "Well, he's telling us he did it and he's daring us to catch him." He glanced up at the sergeant who was watching him examine the body. "He's an arrogant bastard."

"You think it was that damn devil they call Stone Hand?"

"That's my guess." Jason sighed. "Well, I guess I'd better go to work." He whistled up Henry and mounted, nodded to the sergeant, and rode off to follow the trail Stone Hand had left.

There was no effort on the Cheyenne's part to disguise his trail for a mile or so. It was a simple matter to follow the trail left by the seven horses. Stone Hand obviously felt no concern that he would be followed until morning so he loped along at his leisure. Jason was able to make good time as the trail led him through the scrub and over the hills toward the Cimarron River. It was reasonable to assume that a loner like Stone Hand would not keep a string of horses. He'd leave too wide a trail. So he would undoubtedly get rid of them as soon as possible and that meant he would have to be heading to some renegade village somewhere north of Supply. Jason urged Henry on. Maybe this Indian was not as clever as he had been led to believe; maybe he was even lying around somewhere in a Cheyenne camp gloating over his raid.

After following the obvious trail for over an hour, it occurred to him that the Cheyenne might be luring him into an ambush. He had to discard that as a possibility because Stone Hand would not know he was being tracked unless he stuck around to see. And the trail was old enough to indicate he didn't. Jason kept his senses sharp anyway, carefully studying every likely site for ambush. Then he topped a slight rocky rise and the trail disappeared.

He pulled Henry up short and looked around for some indication of a trail. Jason held himself as a pretty fair tracker and he didn't see how he could lose a trail left by six shod horses. He dismounted and searched the rocky ground for dislodged pebbles or broken scrub. It appeared that the Indian and his horses had simply vanished into the air. "I must be getting crazy," he mumbled. Leading his horse, he backtracked to the point where he had last seen tracks leading into the rocks.

He had to come out somewhere, he thought, and

he searched the rocks until he found what he was looking for. He stopped here, he decided. He took the horses on short rein, in a tight bunch. Jason suddenly smiled. "That son of a bitch," he said softly, "he wrapped the horses' hooves with rags or something and changed directions on me. He ain't heading north at all." It took another thirty minutes or so but he finally found a faint print leading toward the west. The land was rocky and it was difficult to pick up a trail, causing Jason to lose valuable time searching for sign. About a mile from the first print, he came upon a stream. Studying the sign around the stream, he determined that the Cheyenne had removed the wraps from the horses here and had followed the stream south.

After several miles, the trail left the stream, leading once again toward the west. He followed the tracks until late in the afternoon when the sun was low in the sky. It would be dark soon when it dropped below the hills directly before him. So he started thinking about a likely place to camp. He was in uncertain territory now, Commanche country. There was no telling how many independent bands of renegades roamed this territory.

Just before darkness set in, he crossed another small stream and decided he had better camp while he could still see what he was doing. He allowed himself a small fire in a hollowed-out bend of the stream to boil some coffee to add a little spark to his cold supper of dried jerky. Afterward, he banked the coals of the fire, hoping to save at least a spark for morning. Then, as was often his custom when camping in hostile country, he arranged his saddle pack near the fire, making it look like a sleeping man. That done, he took his blankets and rifle and lay down under Henry, some fifty feet away from the fire. It would take an awfully good eye to see that little fire from any distance but he saw no sense in taking chances. He felt safer sleeping under Henry. The horse had never stomped on him yet and would wake him if any horse-stealing Indians tried to sneak up on him.

Along about dark the next day he caught first sight of the camp. He worked his way along a ravine until he reached a point of woods about three hundred yards from the northernmost lodges. He counted twenty-three tipis along a bend in a shallow river bed. A nice little hornet's nest, Commanche, he thought. I wonder if Colonel Holder knows about this bunch.

The colonel had been concerning himself with the tracking and hunting down of the many small groups of Cheyennes, usually a half dozen or so renegade bucks. This, on the other hand, was a sizable band of Commanches. The colonel would want to know about any congregation of hostiles this size. One of the army's major concerns was to keep these little bands from joining together into any sizable fighting force. Jason knew, if that were to happen, there would be a steady stream of young men leaving the reservations to join them. For his own part, he knew also that if he were a young Cheyenne he'd be damned if he would rot away on a reservation. What puzzled him most was why the Indians didn't break out now. No man should have been born to reservation life, white man or Indian.

Well, he thought, it ain't for me to say. My job is to catch one murdering renegade. He looked around for a way to crawl up closer to the camp for a better look.

After making sure there were no lookouts posted, he worked his way up to the edge of the camp, no more than twenty feet from the outermost lodge. He lay flat behind a slight rise in the riverbank, his rifle close up against his side, watching the camp settle down for the night. The cookfires were dying out as heavy darkness crept in among the lodges. Satisfied that all was peaceful, he rose to his feet and made his way around the lodges to the horse herd. Even in the darkness it was a simple matter to find the stolen army horses. They were bunched together, still not ready to mingle with the Indian ponies. Stone Hand was here all right. But there was little he could do about it. He sure as hell wasn't going to go into a Commanche village to look for him. He would have to wait and hope for a chance to take him alone, maybe in the morning. There was no way he could be certain but he had to figure that since Stone Hand was a loner he wouldn't hang around long socializing with the Commanches.

More than likely he would move on in the morning and that would be Jason's best chance to get him.

He made his camp that night some two miles from the Commanche village. In the darkness, he led Henry down to the water and let him drink before riding back up into the hills for the night. He didn't worry about the possibility of Henry's tracks being discovered by the river since the horse was unshod and would be indistinguishable from the Indian ponies. It was a cold camp that night since he deemed it prudent to do without a fire.

Shortly before dawn, Jason was out of his blankets and in the saddle. He rode back to the point of trees at the head of the ravine where he had watched the Commanche camp the night before. He hobbled Henry and positioned himself where he could watch the Indian camp as it came to life with the rising of the sun. It appeared to be a peaceful camp. He was tempted to say nothing of its existence to Colonel Holder when he got back. But he knew he had to. That was part of his job, to report any renegade bands of Indians he discovered. Jason didn't like that part of his job. These Commanches seemed to be peaceful enough, just trying to live free, as they had done for hundreds of years. He knew if he were an Indian he would not go peacefully to live on a reservation. But his task that day was to hunt one particular man, he reminded himself, and the people of the village were harboring him.

He spent the entire day watching the comings and goings of the village. There were a few young men who left the camp in small groups to hunt, one old man on a broken-down pony left around midday, leading a packhorse. Women worked around the river and lodges, children played. But there was no sign of anyone that even suggested the description of the infamous Stone Hand. Jason scanned the camp constantly with his field glasses. After a while he began to doubt his instincts. Maybe the man was not there. But he was certain of the trail he had followed. Still, there was no indication that Stone Hand was in the camp. When could he have left? During the night? Jason doubted that. Why would he? He'd just arrived. He had horses to trade. He couldn't be aware of the white man stalking him or he would have had the whole camp out looking for him.

When darkness approached once more, Jason had to conclude that his man was not in the camp. With his field glasses he carefully scrutinized each member of the small hunting parties when they returned. He was sure Stone Hand was not among them. Feeling that he had wasted his time and had been bested in this first encounter with the notorious outlaw, he had to figure Stone Hand must have ridden out with one of the hunting parties and did not return to the camp. Disgusted, and with no trail to follow, he decided he might as well head back to Camp Supply.

A half day's ride away, what at first appeared to be an old man slumped under a blanket and riding a broken-down pony slid off the pony and cast the blanket aside. He rubbed his long hair briskly with his fingers, shaking the ashes from his braids until the gray turned into a deep black. For a few minutes he stood watching his back trail until he was certain there was no one following. Then, without emotion, he drew his long scalping knife and calmly slit the neck of the broken-down horse he had ridden from the village. That done, he jumped on the horse he had been leading and continued his journey.

Stone Hand was not always so cautious and deceptive in his comings and goings. But when his senses told him there was cause for caution, as they had warned him that morning, he always obeyed. His were the instincts of the hunted and his spirits told him there was danger close by. That morning, before daybreak, when he went to relieve himself, he was startled by the sudden flight of a blackbird. The bird did not fly straight away but circled and reversed its flight, a clear sign to Stone Hand that it would be wise to disguise his trail that day. Now as he looked back over the rolling prairie and found it empty of enemies, he gave thanks to the spirit of the wolf and the hunter. He then kicked his heels into the ribs of his horse and rode off toward the Arkansas River. There was a settler's cabin there and it looked like a good day to kill.

CHAPTER 3

He was not always called Stone Hand. His father had named him Black Eagle and he had lived with his parents until his fourteenth year. They belonged to Black Kettle's village and Black Eagle was much like any other Cheyenne boy of that age. That is, until one cold and frosty morning in the year of 1864.

They had descended upon the sleeping village just after sunup. Sweeping in from the south, their horses thundered across the sandy stream bottom and through the narrow ribbon of water. Steam from the horses' nostrils formed a ghostlike fog on the crisp November morning as the first line of troopers splashed through the shallow water and up toward the unsuspecting village. Many in the camp were still sleeping, only a few were up and about. One of the women had discovered the presence of the large body of soldiers shortly before daybreak and came to alert Chief Black Kettle. As the troopers came into sight, a group of men, women, and children gathered before the chief's lodge and watched the advancing cavalry nervously. Black Kettle told them there was no danger. Major Anthony had told them to camp here.

A bugle blast pierced the peaceful silence, minutes later becoming a dull background strain as the soldiers opened up with their rifles. Soon, the entire village was drowned in an explosion of continuous gunfire. Unprepared and without warning, the men of the village were helpless to defend their women and children. Following instructions from Major Anthony, most of the young fighting men were off to the east, hunting buffalo to feed their people. What had been a sleeping village moments before, had become a killing ground as the cavalry made sweep after sweep through the tipis, burning and slaughtering.

A boy no more than fourteen summers stumbled from his bed and out into the cold of the late November morning, his bow and quiver the only possessions he had time to take. He took no notice of the cold as the scene that met his eyes would endure in his mind for the remainder of his life. In the horrible confusion that swept over the village like a tidal wave of fire and gunfire, he stood there for a moment, uncertain which way to run. He did not understand the attack. His village was at peace with the soldiers. Suddenly he was aware of his father's voice yelling for him to run for the river. His mother and father, running close behind him, were cut down by the blistering rifle fire that had somehow missed the boy. When he turned to help his parents, he was horrified by the sight of his mother's forehead splitting open as another rifle ball found the mark. They were finished, there was nothing he could do for them. He must save himself now.

He ran, dodging the slashing sabers and hastily aimed carbines of the soldiers until his path was suddenly blocked by a trooper who had been chasing a group of fleeing women. The trooper and the Indian boy saw each other at almost the same time and the soldier wheeled his horse around to cut off the boy's escape. He had been trained to become a warrior since he was a small boy but he had never killed a man. The soldier spurred his horse. His saber drawn and held high, he bore down on the Indian boy. The boy was calm. He felt no fear. He deliberately fit an arrow onto his bowstring and drew it back. Waiting until the charging horse was almost at his feet, he released the arrow and calmly stepped aside to avoid the animal's hoofs. His arrow buried itself deep into the man's chest. His first kill and there was a feeling of deep satisfaction. More than that, there was a rush of blood through his veins, a feeling he had never experienced before, and one that he wanted to feel again.

Making his way along the dry creek bed, he joined a group of his people who were running toward some sandpits where the banks were some ten feet high. One hundred people, mostly women and children, they made their stand, holding the troopers at bay with their bows and the few guns that some of the men possessed. Here they prepared to fight to the death, defending the few survivors of the massacre. Frantic men and women clawed desperately to dig rifle pits in the sand in an effort to gain some form of protection from the stinging rifle balls that filled the air around them. Many people were killed. All about him the bodies of his friends and relatives lay in the sand. The boy shot all his arrows. It was now left to the men with guns to hold the troopers at bay. They fought for most of the day until a short while before sundown when the soldiers withdrew, losing stomach for the fierce engagement with the embattled survivors. It was less risky to return to the burning village to pillage and mutilate the wounded.

As evening approached, the people were able to leave the sand pits and escape up the wide creek bed, carrying their wounded on the few ponies that some of the men had managed to catch. The rest of the people walked. They made camp ten miles from the site of the cowardly attack and took care of their wounded. Cold and hungry, they gathered dry grass to build fires, for there was no wood to burn. All during the night stragglers wandered in by twos and threes, looking for warmth and food and asking about the fate of relatives. When morning came, they would start for the Cheyenne camp at Smoky Hill, some fifty miles away.

This, then, was what was left of Black Kettle's village on Sand Creek. Black Kettle, the peaceful chief, had brought his people to the fort on Sand Creek to sue for peace with the soldiers. He had gone into the fort to talk with the soldier chief, Major Anthony. The soldier chief said that he did not have the authority to make a treaty with Black Kettle but his people could camp there under the protection of the fort.

Upon hearing that a great body of soldiers was advancing toward their camp, Black Kettle assured the group of men, women, and children who had gathered around his lodge that morning that there was no danger. The village was peaceful and under the protection of Major Anthony. To emphasize the camp's peaceful disposition, Black Kettle had raised a large American flag on a pole in front of his lodge and had told his people to stand around it. Had not the soldier chief, Greenwood, given him the flag and told him that as long as he stood under the American flag no soldier would shoot him? Still his people were frightened. As an added precaution, he had raised a white flag beneath the American flag so there would be no misunderstanding. Still the people were uncertain. Even when the soldiers had come into sight, advancing steadily toward the Cheyenne camp, Black Kettle had continued to counsel patience. "We are not at war with the soldiers," he said. "Do not fear." The people heard him. He was their chief. Had not the governor in Denver sent word for the peaceful tribes to come into the fort so the soldiers would know they did not want war? Had not Major Wynkoop, a trusted friend to the Indian, given his word that Black Kettle's people would be protected? Still they were afraid. Most of the camp had not even come from their tipis at the time. Only a few cookfires were started when the bugle sounded and the first line of soldiers charged into the village, rifles blazing.

The people of the village on the Smoky Hill River joined their brothers in mourning for their dead and wounded at Sand Creek. The warriors were angry and demanded that restitution be exacted from the whites. The chiefs sat in council to decide what action should be taken. After much discussion it was agreed that they would send messengers to the Sioux camp on Solomon Fork and extend an invitation to join them in a war against the whites along the Platte. From Solomon Fork the messengers were to visit a band of Northern Arapahos camped on the Republican River and extend the same invitation. The Sioux and the Arapaho both accepted the invitation to smoke the pipe with their Cheyenne brothers and the three factions agreed to join forces to punish the whites for their outrages.

Among the most eager of the young men to go on the warpath was the fourteen-year-old boy whose parents had been slaughtered before his eyes at Sand Creek. The events of that frosty morning in the shadow of Fort Lyon would never fade from his conscious mind. His eternal hatred for the white man was spawned on that day and it would remain a constant flame that consumed him in his lust for revenge. In the crucible of terror and slaughter, the youth became transformed into an instrument of vengeance who vowed to kill white men until his hands turned to stone. As a symbol of this pledge, he announced to the council of elders that he would take the name of *"Stone Hand."* And from that day on this is the name he would be called.

Along with his Cheyenne brothers, Stone Hand traveled to meet with the Sioux and Arapahos where they had agreed to camp, on Cherry Creek. There, a raid by their combined forces was planned on the stage station at Julesburg. The Indians left their camp on Cherry Creek on a cold January morning and set out to the northwest toward Julesburg. Since the Sioux had been offered the pipe first, they were in the front of the column, led by their chiefs, Pawnee Killer and Spotted Tail. Stone Hand rode behind his chiefs in the middle of the column. Cheyenne Dog Soldiers rode on either side of the march to make sure none of the young warriors became impatient to fight and raced ahead of the main body. The chiefs did not want to give warning to the white men that there were Indians close by. The most impatient of the young men was Stone Hand. They knew of his hunger to take the first scalp and he was watched carefully by the Dog Soldiers.

After two days' march, they camped south of Julesburg in the sand hills and prepared to attack the following day. Their plan was to send a few warriors to show themselves outside the small army post at Fort Rankin to try to draw the soldiers out so they could be led into the hills and ambushed. After they had killed the soldiers, they could then attack the station at Julesburg. All during that night, the camp was guarded to keep the young warriors inside. No noise was permitted. The secrecy of the raid was to be protected at all costs.

Stone Hand went to talk to Big Crow, the chief of the Cheyenne Crooked Lance Soldiers, and asked to be one of the warriors sent to draw out the soldiers from the fort. Big Crow said nothing for a moment while he studied the face of the young warrior.

"For our plan to work, we must make sure the soldiers are drawn all the way into the hills. It will be of no use to us if you try to fight them as soon as they come out."

"I understand this," Stone Hand replied impatiently.

"Will you have the patience to lead them away from the fort and into our ambush? Your lust for blood is a known thing among our people."

Stone Hand scowled. "Do not worry. I will not kill all the soldiers. I will leave some for you."

Big Crow studied the arrogant young brave for a moment longer before deciding to ignore his sarcasm. "Very well, you will go with the others I have picked."

So when the sun rose the next morning, Stone Hand, along with four other Cheyenne warriors and two of Pawnee Killer's Sioux, rode out toward the tiny fort. Upon reaching Fort Rankin, the men paused to watch the post for a while before exposing themselves. The fort was small but it was well fortified with a high stockade all around. It was about one mile from the fort to the Julesburg station. They would be able to hear the shooting from there, but after the soldiers were taken care of there would be no need for stealth.

Stone Hand was impatient. "I will sit here no longer. Come if you want, or stay here and I will bring the soldiers out." Without waiting for a reply, he kicked his pony hard and rode out toward the gate of the stockade. The others had no choice but to follow.

Stone Hand pulled up before the gate and yelled defiantly at the fort. "Hairface cowards! Killers of women and children! Come out if you dare! Come out and I, Stone Hand, will hang your scalp on my lance!"

The sentry on the front guard walk, surprised at the sudden appearance of the wild ranting savage, could not understand the words hurled in his direction but he did not mistake the flavor of his message. He raised his rifle and fired. The rifle ball barely missed its mark, leaving a crease across the left side of Stone Hand's face. The wound only served to infuriate the young warrior. He charged toward the fort, fitting an arrow in his bow as he rode. The sentry fired again, missing this time. He did not have time to fire again before ducking behind the log stockade to avoid the arrow that imbedded itself in the soft wood. When he looked up again, he discovered six more hostiles riding toward him while the one who had charged the fort rode out of range before wheeling around defiantly.

The small band of raiders circled in front of the fort and fired at the soldiers on the wall until the commander of the fort, Captain O'Brien, led a body of soldiers out to attack them. According to plan, the Indians retreated into the sand hills, followed closely by the cavalry.

Hidden in the hills, waiting, the main body of Sioux, Cheyennes, and Arapahos could now hear the shooting. The chiefs cautioned their braves to be patient, not to expose themselves until the soldiers had been led further into the hills. Some of the young warriors were impatient to ride and the Dog Soldiers and Crooked Lance Soldiers had to restrain them. Finally, a group of young warriors, unable to wait any longer, broke through the Dog Soldiers and raced toward the sound of fighting. The chiefs had no choice but to follow with the main body.

Captain O'Brien, upon first sighting the horde of savages that appeared over the rim of the hill, immediately gave the order to retreat. His detachment turned around and galloped for the safety of the stockade.

Stone Hand was furious. The foolish warriors had given away the ambush, allowing most of the soldiers to escape. He turned his pony and rode after the retreating soldiers. His horse was tiring rapidly but he was closing in on the rearmost trooper. The soldier turned in the saddle to discover Stone Hand gaining on him. He fired several times with his pistol but Stone Hand ignored the bullets and steadily reduced the distance between them. The trooper holstered his pistol and concentrated on urging his horse on, but he was rapidly falling behind the rest of his troop. Stone Hand whipped his pony mercilessly. He would kill the beast if necessary. Gradually, the Indian pony closed the gap until his neck was abreast of the other horse's flank. The trooper, frantic now to escape, looked back at the menacing face of the savage, the blood from the crease in his cheek blended with the red and black war paint, the result an eerie countenance of undiluted fury. The soldier panicked. He fumbled to draw his pistol again, trying to spur his exhausted horse at the same time. When he turned to fire at the demon, even now almost at his back, he dropped the reins and the two horses collided, sending horses and riders into a crashing ball of hooves and bodies.

Stone Hand hit the ground rolling over and over. In an instant, he was on his feet and charging toward the dazed trooper. He was still on his hands and knees when the young savage grabbed his hair, and pulling his head back sharply, scalped him. As the soldier screamed in agony, Stone Hand took his time taking his pistol and retrieving his army carbine from the saddle. After he examined the rifle for a few moments, he calmly walked over to the trooper and shot him in the face.

Over the next four years, the Cheyennes raided the farms and outposts along the South Platte, terrifying the settlers of that area. During that time, Stone Hand was a fierce and tireless fighter. His name soon became legend among the Cheyenne and Sioux and was well known in the outposts along the river road. He stayed on to raid and kill after his own village left to move south. Black Kettle was still in favor of peace with the whites and he decided to move his people back south to the

Oklahoma territory to disassociate themselves from the warring tribes. Stone Hand was contemptuous of his people for seeking peace with the soldiers. Black Kettle counseled that it was futile to fight the invasion of settlers, miners, and railroads that was rapidly consuming the land, land Stone Hand insisted belonged to the Cheyenne long before the first hair-faced mountain man plodded uninvited into their hunting grounds. So he watched Black Kettle and his people leave, preferring to remain with the Sioux and the Cheyennes of Pawnee Killer.

As the years passed, Stone Hand's hatred for the white man increased with each scalp taken. His thirst for vengeance tended to turn his anger inside until, gradually, he became a loner. Many of the young men of the tribe hated the white man and sought to avenge the atrocities perpetrated upon their people. But with Stone Hand the hatred was a passion that burned like a live coal deep in the pit of his stomach. It was a constant fire that never cooled and while he was a welcome member of any war party he had no friends among the men he rode with. Soon, his only reason to live was to kill. It was inevitable that his reckless and bloodthirsty style of fighting would eventually build a wall between him and even the fiercest warriors of his own tribe. He held a complete disregard for his own safety. Arrogant and defiant, he openly challenged the enemy, so much so that the other warriors became concerned for their safety. Stone Hand became almost suicidal when in battle. The fact that he was never wounded, in spite of his recklessness, fueled his reputation until he became a legend to the Cheyenne—a spirit almost. Some thought an evil spirit and, before long, most of his people avoided him even though they held a grudging respect for him.

During the winter of 1868, the raiding on the Platte declined with the presence of more and more soldiers and the arrival of cold weather. Out of sheer boredom, Stone Hand decided to journey south to join his own people for a while. He had heard that Black Kettle had moved his village to the Washita, so he gathered his weapons and horses and rode south.

Upon hearing that Stone Hand had returned to the village, Chief Black Kettle was at once concerned. Stone Hand's reputation had spread throughout the southern tribes and, although still a young man, most of the men feared him. Crow Foot, who brought the news of Stone Hand's arrival to the chief, expressed his concern that the renegade's presence in their camp might jeopardize their peaceful profile.

Black Kettle spoke. "Have you talked with Stone Hand? Why has he returned to our village?"

"No. I haven't seen him myself. Lame Elk has spoken to him. He said Stone Hand has gone to the tipi of his uncle, Little Hawk. He does not know why Stone Hand has returned."

Black Kettle considered this for a few moments. "This is his village, the village of his mother and father. It is only natural that he should return to the village of his people. Perhaps he has tired of the killing. We will wait and see."

In the days that followed, Stone Hand rested, and when he grew restless again he walked out among the people of the village. He had expected to be given a warm welcome by the people of his father and mother, a hero's welcome in fact. He had killed many of their enemies. Instead, he found a camp still petitioning for peace with the white soldier chiefs. And while he was treated with polite respect, he sensed that the people avoided him. His reaction to this sense of atmosphere was one of contempt, contempt for what he considered his brothers' weakness.

Five days after Stone Hand returned, Black Kettle and three of the elders met with the soldier chief, Hazan, to plead for a treaty. Stone Hand was outspoken in his contempt for their actions and when the chief returned to report on the meeting, Stone Hand was openly critical. He rose to his feet to speak in the council lodge.

"My brothers, I think it is foolish to talk to the soldiers about peace. I look around me in this camp and I see men who were once warriors, now weak and foolish, waiting for the white father in Washington to claim them as his children. Why do you try to make more treaties? Has the white man ever honored a treaty before? There will be no peace for the Cheyenne until all the white men are dead. Then there will be peace! I, Stone Hand, say this. I will give the white man peace with my scalp knife."

When he finished, he turned and strode out of the lodge, leaving a low murmuring of voices behind him. One of the young men rose to speak. "What Stone Hand says may be true. The white man has broken every treaty before."

Black Kettle quickly responded. "We must be careful whose counsel we heed. Stone Hand has drunk of the blood of vengeance. His words are blind with the hatred he bears. We must think of the future of our people. If we are to survive, we must be at peace with the white man. He is too many. We must have food. The buffalo are gone. The antelope and deer are disappearing. Our only hope for survival is to make peace with the soldiers. Hazan has promised to talk with the white father in Washington. We must wait."

As he did in Big Crow's camp, Stone Hand withdrew to himself, preferring to be alone. He left the village to hunt or raid by himself, often staying away for two or more days. The people became accustomed to his absences and his return, often with the bloody scalps of his raid. Black Kettle grew more and more worried that Stone Hand would become a thorn in his side. He feared he would seriously jeopardize his peace efforts. Finally the old chief called his elders to council to decide what must be done about this mad dog in their midst.

All agreed that it would only be a matter of time before the soldiers would seek retribution against the whole village for the sins of one man. Stone Hand would surely bring the soldiers down upon them. So, on that day in early November, 1868, it was decided that Stone Hand must be asked to leave the village on the Washita for the sake of the people.

Stone Hand sat before his fire, intent on the scalp he was drying on a forked willow branch. It was an unusual scalp. The hair was a golden maize with scattered strands of darker brown. He held it up to examine it, turning it to view the morning sun's reflection upon it. She had been a young girl who had the misfortune to be with her father in the stage station when Stone Hand struck him down with his war ax. The fact that the scalp was that of a little girl did not bother Stone Hand. As far as he was concerned, she was little more than another variety of the lice that had infested his land. He glanced up at the three men approaching his campfire.

Black Kettle spoke. "I see that you have raided again." He eyed the blond scalp Stone Hand was admiring. "Why do you not make war on the Pawnees with the other young men of the village?"

"The white man is my enemy," Stone Hand replied without emotion.

Black Kettle glanced quickly at the two elders who accompanied him before returning his gaze to the young warrior. "We are now at peace with the white soldiers but we cannot make this peace if our warriors are still raiding and killing white people."

Stone Hand looked up at the old chief, his gaze hard as flint. "You are at peace with the white man. Stone Hand will be at peace with the soldiers when they are all dead. What good is your peace? The soldiers want you to go to the reservation but you do not go because the land is dead and the water bitter." His eyes were still intent on the scalp he was admiring. "They will not let you stay here in peace. They will come to kill again. It is their way. I will not be fooled by their lies."

Black Kettle exchanged glances of frustration with the two elders. "It is as we have talked. This man is determined to push us all into war. He will have us all dead." He turned back to Stone Hand. "The people have decided to make treaties with the soldiers. It is the only way for the village to survive. If you are to remain with the people, then you must lay aside your weapons and smoke the pipe with the soldier chief."

Stone Hand's response was bitter and he spat his words at the three old men. "I will never smoke the pipe with the white man. I will leave this village of women and toothless old men and go to the north to join the Sioux. Maybe their men still walk upright and refuse to crawl before the soldiers like camp dogs."

Black Kettle ignored the angry young man's insults. "Yes, that is best for the people."

So it was that the violent young warrior, whom the army wanted to capture more than any other, rode away unmolested, while behind him Custer's cavalry was already advancing toward the peaceful village on the Washita.

The massacre of Black Kettle's village created no sorrow in Stone Hand's heart. It merely served to strengthen his hatred for the soldiers. He was contemptuous of Black Kettle's peace efforts from the first and Custer's cowardly attack on the village only confirmed his opinion of the white man's intentions to slaughter all Indians, peaceful or otherwise.

When he left Black Kettle's village on that morning, Stone Hand rode to the Cheyenne camp on the Red River. It was here he learned of the massacre on the Washita when, several days later, a few survivors of the raid straggled into camp. The news of the raid caused great fear and concern among the people. They were afraid that the soldiers would come there next. A council was called to discuss their options. Like Black Kettle, they, too, had refused to go to the reservation, still hoping to make peace with the soldiers while remaining free on their own hunting grounds.

Stone Hand sat back away from the front of the council lodge, listening to the wailing account of the surprise attack that had killed most of his father's people. One Elk, his arm badly shattered by a rifle ball, was speaking now. He told the council that the white soldiers were too many and the people were starving. It was time to go to the reservation. The old ways were gone. It would be foolish to continue to resist. When One Elk sat down, there was much discussion over his words. Yellow Hand agreed. It was suicide, he said, to defy the soldier chief's demands that all Indians must return to the reservation. Stone Hand grunted and all heads turned to hear his words.

"I am sick to my stomach of this talk. I have just come from a village that made the same talk and most of them are dead now. Since when has a Cheyenne warrior decided that to live as a slave is better than to die in battle? I do not know these words. I do not want to hear them. The reservation is death. It is much better to die quickly, in battle, than to rot away like the slaughtered buffalo carcasses on the prairie. I will make no peace with the soldiers." He stood up and glanced at the circle of elders around the council fire. "I will go to my campfire now. If you decide to surrender to the soldiers, I will fight them by myself."

A few days later, a messenger came to the villages on the Red River. He brought word that a Colonel Holder was coming to the village. The people should know, the messenger said, that he was coming to talk, not to fight. Two days later, a troop of cavalry was sighted, approaching the village. At the head of the column, sitting ramrod straight in the saddle, his slate gray beard trimmed neatly to a point directly above the top button of his heavy blue coat, rode Colonel Lucien C. Holder.

Stone Hand watched the approaching column with bitter interest. The soldiers were riding under a white flag. As he sat on his pony, watching from a small bluff by the river, he was tempted to send a rifle ball to meet the gray beard sitting so militarily rigid in the saddle. The only reason he resisted the urge was the havoc it would bring down upon the village. He did not trust the soldiers so he watched from a distance, his weapons about him, ready to make an instant escape if necessary. He fully intended to live beyond this day to kill many more white men.

True to his word, Holder asked to talk with the chiefs. A pipe was smoked and then the Colonel told them that the great white father in Washington wanted his children to come to the reservation at Camp Supply. There they would be fed and cared for. There would be no need for the Cheyenne men to hunt. Beef cattle would be provided for them. He added that if the Cheyenne people did not come into the reservation, he would bring many soldiers to punish them.

After much talk, One Elk told the colonel that his

people would put themselves under the great white father's care. They would go to Camp Supply.

"Good," Holder replied. "This is a wise thing you have decided." He smiled at the chief as an uncle would smile at a child. "There are some conditions that must be satisfied before the white father will welcome his children. First, you must give up any white captives that are living with the Cheyenne." One Elk nodded agreement. The colonel continued. "Secondly, you must turn over all firearms in your possession." Again One Elk nodded. "And third, my scouts tell me that the renegade, Stone Hand, is in your village. You must turn this man over to me now."

One Elk shrugged. "I cannot do this. Stone Hand came to my village as a guest. It would not be right to do this."

"I want that son of a bitch and I mean now!" The colonel's nostrils flared with his anger.

"I cannot," One Elk replied and turned to point toward a distant rise in the prairie.

Colonel Holder turned to see a lone rider disappear over the rise, the feet of his pony kicking up small clouds of white dust.

"Damn!" Holder spat.

His adjutant, Captain Horace Sykes, leaped to his feet. "Shall I send a detail after him, Colonel?"

Holder sighed. "No, Horace. It would be a waste of time. You'd never catch that son of a bitch with the lead he has. We'll get him another day."

CHAPTER 4

Sarah Holder emerged from the tent prepared for her just as a rider approached the camp. She watched, disinterested at first until the rider began to take on familiar characteristics. "Jason Coles," she announced silently as she identified the easy way the man sat in his saddle. Man and horse seemed as one, rocking in rhythm as the horse picked its way over the uneven banks of the stream. Something about this rough-cut Indian scout fascinated Sarah, something she found difficult to explain. He was by no means a handsome man, at least not in the sense John Welch was. But there was a wild beauty about him, much like the striking beauty of the rugged mountain ranges to the west. Her father thought a lot of the man. That was obvious in the way he talked about his knowledge of the land and the Indians. She decided to find out more about this genuine Indian fighter. Her friends back in Baltimore would be fascinated to know men like Jason Coles really existed.

Jason unsaddled Henry and turned him out with the army's horses before reporting to Colonel Holder. The colonel was seated on a camp stool in front of his tent while an orderly trimmed his hair and whiskers.

"Hello, Coles. I didn't expect you back right away. Don't tell me you caught our renegade already."

"Not likely," Jason replied dryly. "I did cut his trail but he gave me the slip. He ain't gonna be easy to catch." He pulled up a stool and sat down opposite the colonel. "But I reckon that's why you sent for me in the first place."

While the colonel's orderly finished with his barbering, Jason recounted his actions of the previous two days and his discovery of the Commanche camp.

"How many lodges did you say?"

"I counted twenty-three," Jason answered.

"That would be Lame Dog's band, I suppose. We had reports he's been raiding along the Canadian River. He must have worked back in this area again. He's probably figuring to pick up some of the Cheyenne from the reservation."

"Is this official business? Or can anyone join in?" Sarah Holder swept into their discussion.

Jason rose dutifully to his feet and nodded to the young lady. "Miss Holder," he said.

The colonel remained seated but his face was immediately transformed into that of a proud and doting father. "No, no, darling. Come on in. Mr. Coles and I were just having a little conversation about some hostiles he found."

She turned to face Jason and smiled warmly. "That sounds exciting. Were you in any danger, Mr. Coles?" She quickly added, "I suppose, being an Indian fighter, you are accustomed to living in danger."

Jason looked embarrassed. He looked at the young woman for a long minute before answering. He wasn't quite sure how to take her question, whether the girl was teasing him or simply naive. He wasn't sure he liked being called an *Indian fighter* at any rate. After searching Sarah's eyes for a moment, he decided she was not being snide and his own expression softened as he explained. "No, ma'am. I don't think I was in any danger. I just saw the camp and watched it for a while."

"Weren't you afraid, though? I mean, what with all those savages, and you by yourself? I would think being an Indian fighter is a dangerous occupation."

Jason flushed, embarrassed by the openly childish remarks. "I'm not an Indian fighter. I mean, I'm not an anything fighter. I just do what I can for the army." He glanced quickly at the colonel to rescue him, only to find her father enjoying his embarrassment.

"My, how modest! But I see I'm embarrassing you. Perhaps I should have said army scout." She turned abruptly to her father. "Is Mr. Coles going to join us for dinner?"

Jason stammered, "Why, I don't think so. I just came off the trail. I don't reckon I'm fit to sup with a lady."

"Nonsense," Colonel Holder interrupted. "Of course Mr. Coles will eat with us. I insist."

As before, Jason was not the only guest to dine with the colonel and his daughter that evening. Captain Welch was also in attendance. Jason stood back and watched, amused, as the young doctor maneuvered to gain the chair next to Sarah. Jason, his clean shirt tucked neatly into his one pair of good trousers, settled into a chair beside the colonel. Captain Welch lost no time in enlisting Sarah in some light patter about the weather, whether or not she was enjoying her visit, and offering his services for whatever she might need. Jason and the colonel looked on with amusement as the young officer launched an obvious campaign to charm the colonel's daughter.

Colonel Holder, for his part, squandered not a second of concern, for he was confident his headstrong daughter had a mind of her own and could handle the likes of the young doctor. Sarah was not easily impressed by handsome young army officers. On the other hand, a girl could certainly do worse than marrying a career army officer, and a doctor at that. So he let the captain have free rein and directed most of his conversation toward Jason and the possibility of trouble from Lame Dog's band of Commanches.

During a lull in the conversation, Sarah interjected. "Father, Captain Welch has invited me to go on a picnic outside the camp. Is that all right?"

Colonel Holder glanced up at the young surgeon and Captain Welch quickly explained. "Just down at the willows, sir, by the creek . . . if that's all right with you, sir."

The willows he spoke of were a small stand of a half-dozen trees no more than five hundred yards from the colonel's tent. Holder shrugged. "I don't see any harm in that. I wouldn't want you to go any further out of camp though."

After dinner, Jason and Colonel Holder walked outside to enjoy a drink of the colonel's brandy and smoke a cigar. Captain Welch remained to entertain Sarah with his charm. It was after nine o'clock when Jason excused himself and retired to his blankets.

Shortly after sunup the following morning, Jason saddled Henry and rode out to the Cheyenne village on the reservation. He had learned from Colonel Holder that an old acquaintance of his, Sam Running Fox, was living with a Cheyenne woman on the reservation. Jason had worked with Sam two years before when Sam was a member of Colonel Forsyth's Cheyenne Scouts. They were not close friends, merely acquaintances, but Jason felt there was a mutual respect between them that would ensure some honest information about the man, Stone Hand.

Jason never felt comfortable visiting any Indian reservation. Call it conscience, or guilt felt for all the atrocities committed upon the red man by the whites. There was a pall, like the carcass of a dead spirit, that hung over every reservation he had ever been in. It was a sin what the U.S. government had done to these once proud and free people, breaking every promise they had made in their many treaties. He himself was not without blame. He rode with the army. He had killed Cheyenne, Kiowa, and Commanche. But he wasn't proud of the fact. It was just the way the cards had been dealt.

He felt the stares of the people as he rode slowly through the Cheyenne village. The lodges were laid out in a half circle around the agency building, a rough log affair that housed the agent and doubled as a warehouse for the provisions that were meant to sustain the people of the village.

Jason didn't like what he saw. To him, this camp displayed a village of broken spirits. The women and children stood by the lodges, watching him with eyes vacant with boredom. Some of the men were gathered in an idle group near the agency building. They appeared to be doing nothing more than passing time, perhaps remembering earlier times when they would be out hunting. There was no game to hunt in this sorry land. Jason felt a tension running through the entire camp. This was no way for a young Cheyenne brave to live. He wondered how long it would be before they simply exploded and broke out. It was bound to come. Sam Running Fox confirmed his intuitions.

Jason pulled Henry up before a lodge decorated with paintings of buffalo running before a band of hunters. A short, barrel-chested man emerged from the entrance flap. He was wearing a breechcloth and leggings. He wore no shirt, a necklace of bear claws the only adornment of his upper body.

"Jason Coles," he said matter-of-factly. "What the hell you doin' here?"

"Howdy, Sam." Jason stepped down.

"I ain't seen you since I don't know when. You still working for the army?"

"I wasn't for a while, but I reckon I am now." The two men shook hands. "Colonel Holder said you were living out here with a Cheyenne woman. You must be getting soft, living on a reservation."

Sam smiled. "I reckon I got a craving for a good woman to cook for me and keep me warm at night."

"I never figured you for reservation life. I thought you'd be more likely to hightail it for the mountains."

Sam's face took on a serious expression. "I'll tell you what's the truth, Jason. If I was a little younger, I'd of done been gone. This place is a dead place."

He gestured toward the group of men talking behind the agency building. "I'll guarantee you them young men are talking right now about whether or not it would be a good idea to leave this place. They done found out there's no steel in a white man's word. I swear, if I was younger, I'd go. I'd rather die from a bullet than waste away like I'm doing here. I might go yet." His eyes hardened. "I just might do it, Jason." There was a long, awkward silence, then Sam's fierce expression relaxed and he asked, "Anyway, what brings you here?"

"I'm needing some information. What can you tell me about a renegade buck named Stone Hand?"

Sam grunted involuntarily, "Huh." A wry smile creased his face. "Stone Hand . . . so the army's got desperate enough to call you in to try to catch Stone Hand. I ain't surprised. Well, Jason, I'll tell you this. It ain't gonna be easy. This ain't no ordinary reservation buck you're chasing. Stone Hand is big medicine and, if you don't watch your hind end, he'll be chasing you."

Jason grunted. "If he's as bad as everybody says, I might just better run off somewhere and hide."

Sam laughed. "It would be the smart thing to do, I swear." Then his face went dead serious and he looked Jason straight in the eye. "Jason, you better watch your back for sure. This buck is bad. He's got all the other men of the tribe spooked. Some says he ain't even human. I don't know about that but I do know he's big medicine and the only thing he cares about is killing."

Jason's face creased with a faint smile. "I swear, Sam, you sound like you really believe all that. I expect he's one smart Injun, but I reckon he's human enough."

"Dammit, I'm just warning you, that's all." Sam was becoming impatient with Jason's lack of concern. "He talks with the spirits and they tell him things." Sam looked around anxiously as if he might be overheard. "He comes and goes on the wind. I mean, he won't be nowhere around and then you turn around and he'll be standing behind you. I'm telling you, Jason, he's powerful medicine and you better watch your backside, especially if he finds out you're chasing him."

"I will, Sam. I appreciate the warning." Jason wasn't ready to accept the idea that he was chasing a ghost but he could see that Sam was dead serious. But then Sam was half Cheyenne, so he was thinking with his Indian half. "I was hoping you could tell me a little bit more about him so I can recognize him if I cut his trail. I need to know what he looks like."

Sam, his face still a mask of concern, replied, "You'll know him. I guarantee it. If you see Stone Hand, you'll know it's him. If you ain't sure, he's got a scar running across his left cheek where a bullet grazed him."

Jason was beginning to lose patience with Sam's

obvious reverence for this one Cheyenne warrior. "You wouldn't know where he might likely be, would you?"

"No, I wouldn't," Sam replied smugly. "But he was here last night."

"Here? You mean here in the village? On the reservation?"

Sam nodded.

"Why that . . . He's a gutsy son of a bitch! You're telling me he was right here under the army's nose last night?"

"He goes where he pleases," Sam said stoically.

"Where did he go? Did he say where he was heading?" The thought of the brazen renegade rubbing the army's nose in it was enough to get Jason's blood hot.

"He never says. Only Stone Hand knows where he goes."

"Aw, horse manure, Sam. He's got you people believing he's some kind of spirit." Jason was tired of playing the game. "Did you see which way he rode out?"

"Yessir, I did. He rode out to the south, if that helps you any, but I doubt you'll have much luck trailing him." He watched Jason climb up into the saddle before he added, "Jason, I ain't no personal friend of Stone Hand, nobody is. I can't tell you much more than what I see. And I reckon if he found out I told you anything at all, you might see my hair hanging on his lance."

"I appreciate it, Sam. I reckon I'll go see if I can catch a ghost."

"You better watch your back."

Stone Hand wasn't the only one who rode out to the south that morning. There were tracks of a dozen or more ponies leaving camp in that direction, hunting parties looking for the little game that could still be found. Counting on the stories he had heard, that Stone Hand was a loner, Jason followed the common trail, disregarding trails that branched off showing two or more ponies. He stayed with the trail until he came to a small stream where one set of tracks crossed over to the other side and headed east. He was riding on a hunch that his man was not leading a packhorse. Stone Hand seemed the type to prefer riding one horse to death and then stealing a replacement. It seemed like a long shot but Jason had little else to go on so he stayed with the trail. He was to have no better luck than the first time he had trailed the Indian. After spending most of the day tracking Stone Hand, Jason was stopped cold when the trail petered out at the edge of a steep ravine.

"Well, damn. Did he just take off and fly?" he muttered in disgust and backed Henry in an effort to see if the Cheyenne had backtracked on him. If he did, he had been too clever for Jason to catch him at it. Jason, frustrated, spent the rest of the day scouting in a circle, trying to pick up the trail. Finally, he had to give up and admit another defeat at the hands of the Cheyenne warrior.

When he returned to Camp Supply that night, he learned from Max Kennedy that a settler and his wife had been murdered over on the Arkansas River. A patrol discovered the bodies that afternoon and reported that they were badly mutilated and the cabin burned to the ground. Out of curiosity, Jason asked if the victims had a slit through the left eyebrow.

"As a matter of fact, they did. How'd you know that?"

"Just a hunch," Jason replied. To himself he thought, Well, now I know where he was yesterday.

Jason was greeted by Captain Horace Sykes, Colonel Holder's executive officer, when he reported in that night. The colonel had decided to go on patrol, an overnight march, with B Company to Lame Dog's camp. Had he known Jason would be back that night, he probably would have waited for the scout to lead the patrol. As it was, it was after nine when Jason returned. Sarah Holder had retired to her tent and John Welch was sitting in the headquarters tent talking to Captain Sykes.

"Well, Mr. Coles, how is the hunt for your renegade progressing? I'm surprised to see you back here. I thought you'd be out trailing him."

Jason looked at the young surgeon for a moment before answering. "The hunt isn't progressing very fast," he replied, "and I'm back here in camp because that's where the trail leads."

Captain Welch was confused. "I don't understand. You think he's here in Camp Supply?"

"Well, he was last night. I don't know where he is tonight but he seems to want to stay close to the army, I reckon to show us he can go where he damn well pleases."

"I guess I should keep a close eye on Miss Holder then, if what you say is true."

"Yeah, I reckon," Jason responded. In his mind, he wondered what good the doctor would do for Sarah Holder if Stone Hand was around. He was pretty sure Welch would keep a close eye on Sarah even if there wasn't a savage within fifty miles. He said good night to the two officers and retired to the far edge of the camp where the horses were grazing. Before settling into his blankets, he told the trooper on horse guard of his presence. He didn't want some trigger-happy guard stumbling over him in the middle of the night.

He was awake the next morning with the first rays of the sun. He didn't get out of his blanket right away, preferring to lie there for a few minutes and consider his options. Where to start his search again, he could only guess. Stone Hand was too unpredictable to try to establish a pattern. The only thing that approached a constant was the man's audacity and his penchant for sticking close to his en emies. Jason was beginning to think Stone Hand believed in his invincibility as much as his fellow tribesmen did. Maybe he should go back to talk to Sam Running Fox again. It made little sense to ride out to the settler's cabin on the Arkansas. He needed a fresh trail to follow and he didn't have any idea where to search for one.

He rolled over on his side, preparing to get up when his eye caught sight of something on his saddle beside his head. At first he thought it was a caterpillar. It was hairy and approximately that size. But it didn't look like any caterpillar he had ever seen before. He sat up to examine it more closely and then realized what he was looking at. It was no caterpillar or worm of any kind. It was a human eyebrow. He bolted out of his blanket and looked quickly around him. There was no one near him. He looked toward the herd of horses grazing peacefully by the river bed. All seemed peaceful. Off to his right the usual sounds of an army camp awakening indicated nothing out of the ordinary had happened.

His initial reaction after that first startling discovery was anger, anger at himself. The brazen son of a bitch had sneaked right up on him and left his gruesome calling card. Jason was not a heavy sleeper. He could be fully alert at the sound a crow makes walking across a grassy meadow. It was a characteristic necessary for survival in his line of work. How then was this man able to walk right into an armed camp and lay this piece of flesh and hair right beside him without waking him? More than anger, it caused an unsettled feeling in his mind and he couldn't help but recall Sam Running Fox's words about the man he hunted. He wondered no more than a moment about why he was still alive. That was easy to answer. The savage was playing with him, letting Jason know he knew he was being hunted, daring him to come after him. He showed his contempt for the white scout by not killing him and counting coup on the sleeping man. The thought of that savage standing over him, watching him as he slept, vulnerable and helpless as a baby, infuriated Jason. This was no ordinary maverick Indian. This renegade amused himself with mind games. His message was clear—he could take the army scout anytime he wanted.

At least the two men had an understanding now, and Stone Hand, by his actions, let it be known that the game was on, if the white man still had the stomach for it. Jason gathered his blankets and picked up his saddle pack. He noted with some chagrin that his visitor did not even steal his rifle. "Well, that might have been a mistake, mister," he muttered. "You might better wish you had shot me while you had the chance."

After Henry was saddled, Jason scouted around his bed, looking for sign that would tell him how the renegade had approached. It didn't take long because the tracks were obvious. There was no attempt to disguise them, another show of contempt on Stone Hand's part and an obvious indication that the Cheyenne wanted Jason to know that he had simply walked right by the sentry and stood over the sleeping form of the Indian scout. Jason had a feeling that he wouldn't have to worry about tracking the Indian all over the territory. No, this rebel was a breed apart. His ego, or arrogance, or whatever, would dictate that he stay close to Jason, taunting and tempting until he tired of the game and decided to kill him.

Recovered now from his initial anger, Jason was able to look at his situation with more rational thought. He even had to smile as he realized that the game was on. Sam Running Fox thought Jason was trailing a spirit but Jason didn't think so, and as long as he was mortal Stone Hand was as vulnerable as any man to be bested. "All right, Big Medicine, we've dealt this hand. We'll just see who's the best poker player."

CHAPTER 5

The morning was fresh and bright, a perfect day for a picnic, she decided. The thought of spending the afternoon with Captain John Welch was a pleasant one. She had tried to remind herself that she was not looking for involvement with any man, especially on a brief visit to the frontier. Still, she was reluctant to admit there had been a quickening of her heartbeat when the dashing young officer rode up, leading a horse for her. God, she thought, he is a handsome devil. She could see that any young girl might be mesmerized by the finely chiseled features and the regal mane of dark black hair that never seemed out of place, even in such crude surroundings as Camp Supply.

Her first impression of the young doctor, that he was a harmless flirt, had been somewhat tempered in her conversations with him over the past few days. He seemed to be genuinely taken by her and she had to admit that she found it to be more than a little disturbing to her sense of control. Was she at last beginning to feel the amorous stirrings that preceded infatuation? I must sweep such thoughts out of my mind right now before I start wondering what it would be like to be in his arms, she told herself.

"Sarah, you look as bright as the morning sun. Are you ready to go?"

She favored him with a warm smile and replied, "Why, thank you, sir. Yes, I'm ready." He helped her up in the saddle and they rode out across the rough parade ground toward a small clump of willows that lined the banks of the shallow stream, no more than a quarter of a mile from the command tent.

What happened that day, in the balmy shade of the willows, came as a complete surprise to Sarah Holder. She had no plans to fall in love with the handsome young army surgeon. Her thoughts of him, up to that day, had been mere flights of fantasy, solely to amuse herself. John Welch, on the other hand, had thought of nothing but the wooing and winning of the colonel's daughter. In his eyes she was the perfect candidate for a career officer's wife . . . beautiful, vivacious, educated . . . and the daughter of a colonel.

Though somewhat calculating in his thoughts of capturing the prize that was Sarah Holder, still he had to admit that he was totally charmed by the young lady and might have sought to woo her even had she not been the colonel's daughter. He had already decided he was in love. Sarah had yet to discover her infatuation. After the horses were tied to a willow, John spread a cloth beside the stream. He selected a spot just below the rise of the bank so as not to be in constant view of the camp.

"I'm afraid it's not what you might call an elegant lunch," she commented cheerfully. "But I think Sergeant Ortiz did a wonderful job under the circumstances." She held up a biscuit for him to see. "It could be a crumpet if you exercised your imagination a bit."

He laughed and reached to take it from her, his fingers brushing hers. "It is the most elegant of picnics if only because I'm sharing it with you."

She blushed. "Why, Captain Welch, are your flirting with me?"

His expression sobered and he reached out and took her hands in his. "No, Sarah, I'm not. It's far beyond that. I'm in love with you."

His blunt declaration of love sent her senses reeling. She had not been prepared for it. The shock must have shown in her eyes because John recoiled as if he had been rebuked. He quickly stammered, "Please, I don't mean to be too forward. I hope you'll forgive my bluntness but I hope you feel . . ." He didn't finish the statement. "I'm sorry. Have I offended you?"

The concern in his eyes melted her heart. "No, John, I'm not offended. I'm just a little surprised, that's all. That's quite a mouthful, combined with Sergeant Ortiz's biscuit."

"Damn. I really feel like an ass . . . a simple schoolboy." He released her hands. "Do you want me to take you back?"

She reached out, taking his hands in hers. "No, of course not. I don't want you to take me back. I want to stay here and talk and have our picnic."

Encouraged, he pressed her for an answer. "Do you feel anything at all for me? Or am I in this thing alone?"

She laughed. "This is all a little too sudden for me." Before his face could cloud up again, she added, "But, yes, I feel something for you."

At once his smile returned and once again there was hope in his eyes. "Oh, Sarah, I do love you and if you'll give me the chance, I'll make you love me." He did not wait for her to respond. "You know, I won't be assigned to this godforsaken outpost for long. We could go back East. If the army won't transfer me back, I'll resign my commission and go into private practice."

Sarah could not help herself. She could feel herself being caught up in the excitement of his proposal and had to force herself to remain in control. She looked deeply into his eyes, seeing a new image of Captain John Welch, one that she found desirable. "Let's not rush into anything. You haven't even given me time to catch my breath."

"Do you love me?" he asked bluntly.

"I don't know." She hesitated. "Yes, I love you." She blushed, surprised by her own answer.

He pulled her closer to him. He kissed her. She let him, passive at first and then she returned it, having found the passion that she knew was in her but until that moment had never been permitted to surface.

The midday sun was warm as it embraced the two lovers lying on the army blanket beneath the willows. John was eager to love her and she responded to his passion. He drew her closer and closer to him until their bodies were pressed together as one. The young doctor was intoxicated with the magic of the moment. His fire engulfed her and she was swept away in the tide of his passion. She had not thought to let it go that far. The afternoon ended all too soon.

"Let's just keep this our little secret for awhile," she said when it was time to go back.

"Whatever you say, darling. I'm just the happiest man in the world."

Afterward, when she was alone in her tent, thinking of the incredible change that had taken place on that day, she found it almost too much to believe. Had it really happened? It must have. She could still feel the fire that had raged through her thighs, leaving her weak and warm. But was she really in love? Or was it the passion of the moment? Possibly the surroundings she found herself in inspired a disproportionate balance between infatuation and genuine love. And John Welch would not have overwhelmed her so had the location been in the park in Baltimore instead of this isolated outpost. Mrs. John Welch? Could it be possible? I guess it could, Sarah girl, she told herself. You could do a whole lot worse.

"So, Mr. Coles, I see you're still with us. I thought you might be riding out after your renegade."

Jason turned to see Sarah Holder approaching the mess tent where he stood drinking a cup of coffee. "Morning, Miss Holder." He watched, amused, as the colonel's daughter glided through the group of men standing around the tent, causing them to jump to attention, stumbling over one another to get out of her way. She graced the assembly with her smile and thanked Sergeant Ortiz for the cup of coffee he had hastened to fetch for her. It was her nature, Jason decided, to shun the privacy of her tent and ignore the breakfast no doubt delivered there for her convenience. The cook, expecting a complaint and consequently a dressing-down by the colonel's daughter, fumbled for words.

"Can I help you, ma'am? Was something wrong with your breakfast? I can sure cook you some . . ."

"Oh, it was fine, very good." She didn't let him finish. "I just thought I'd like some more coffee." Her smile put the flustered man at ease.

"Yes, ma'am," he answered.

Jason, enjoying the havoc the little lady could wreak just by showing up in the mess tent, said nothing until she turned to face him again. "You better be careful with that coffee. That tin cup will blister your lips." He figured the coffee served with her breakfast might have been sipped from a china cup.

"Thanks for the warning but I've had coffee from an army cup." She settled herself on a camp stool and smiled up at the tall scout. She said nothing for a few moments, her smile seemingly frozen on her face and Jason realized that he was staring at her . . . and she was aware of it.

"Well," he blurted abruptly, "I reckon I better get to work."

"You're always running off someplace, Mr. Coles. I declare, I believe I must have that effect on you." She flashed her smile again and pretended to be offended.

Jason considered her coquettish gesture for a moment before answering. "No, ma'am, I wouldn't say that. I figured Captain Welch was taking care of the social activities for you."

His remark brought a twinkle to her eye. It pleased her that his thoughts were running along that vein. Maybe he looked upon the surgeon as competition. Was it possible this rough-hewn frontiersman was not as indifferent to her charms as he had taken pains to show. She pretended to concentrate on the hot cup of coffee in her hand as she studied the rugged face that under her gaze seemed to appear slightly flushed. She could not deny a keen fascination for the man her father had described as more Indian than some full-blooded Cheyennes. She decided to probe his intentions a bit further.

"We had a delightful picnic in the willows yesterday. Captain Welch arranged for a basket from Sergeant Ortiz, and I must say, it was surprisingly elegant." She watched his face closely for his reactions. "I wish you could have joined us," she added.

Jason began to fidget. He was uncomfortable with the conversation and he realized he was being drawn into a childish game with a girl barely out of her studies. "Thank you, ma'am, but I don't reckon I'm much on picnicking."

She pursed her lips, pretending to pout. "I may tell my father that you are neglecting me," she teased. Something about the rough-hewn scout made her want to tease him. He was so obviously uncomfortable with her playful attempts to embarrass him.

He grunted. "Huh, I reckon your daddy might want to spank your bottom for even talking to the likes of me."

"Why, Mr. Coles"—she pretended to be offended—"what a thing to say to a lady." Her face, a stern mask for a moment, quickly broke into a mischievous grin. "I think I'm going to insist that you take me on a picnic."

Jason laughed. "I think you ain't only gonna get your bottom spanked. I think you're gonna get me fired to boot." In spite of her flirtatious conversation, he knew better than to think the young lady had any interest in a man as unrefined as he. She was playing with his emotions, like most young girls, he figured. It was the second time he had been teased that day and the sun wasn't even high in the sky yet. Although he had to admit that this time was not as gruesome as the episode with the eyebrow. He gulped down the last few swallows of his now-cold coffee and handed the cup to a private behind the table. "Much obliged," he said. Nodding to Sarah, he said, "Enjoyed talking to you, Miss Holder. I hope you have a pleasant day."

His common sense told him there was nothing between the young lady and himself. Still he could not put the flirtatious conversation out of his mind. Now, almost an hour later, he found himself riding past the little stand of willows where Sarah and John Welch had picnicked the day before. For no reason he could explain, he dismounted and walked over to the stream. The grass was still depressed where they had spread the cloth and sat to have their picnic. He could not help the sinking feeling in his heart when his trained eye told him the grass was flattened a little more than normal if two people were simply sitting and eating. He did not want to let his mind pursue the thought. He wasn't sure why he was wasting his time there, or why his thoughts were of a melancholy nature. Maybe Sarah's presence in camp, and more specifically her tendency to flirt just a bit, had triggered a need in him that he had managed to suppress until then.

His was a lonely life. There was no regret, however, He had chosen it. In fact, he realized he could live no other way. The freedom he possessed was more than a preference for him. It was essential, for he had found early in his life that he could not tolerate a crowd of people for very long. For that matter, he was almost certain he could not tolerate but one person for a long period of time. And that one person had been taken from him more than ten years ago when that coach had careened over the side of a mountain. For that reason, he had never even considered the possibility of marrying.

Now this young girl, fresh as a spring morning, comes into his life and awakens troublesome emotions within him, and with no more than a few harmless comments that he chose to interpret as flirting. He stood silently staring at the fading impressions in the grass. "Wake up!" he scolded, "standing here like a damn fool!" Why, he wondered, would a young thing like Sarah Holder even look at a rough-shod grizzly like himself? Shaking himself mentally, he discarded his foolish daydreaming and told himself he had let his imagination run away with him. He decided to put the girl out of his mind and get back to the business he was being paid for, to track down a murderer.

It was by pure accident he noticed it, one bent branch of a willow. Even then it would have escaped his sharp eye if he was not naturally alert for signs. He stopped to examine it and then he decided to take a look further down the bank. Barely twenty yards from the picnic site, he found a footprint. A more thorough search revealed several prints, enough to give him a vivid picture. The moccasin prints were about a day old. There was no doubt in his mind that they were Cheyenne and he was dead certain they belonged to one Cheyenne in particular, Stone Hand! Jason recreated the scene in his mind. The savage had watched the afternoon picnic of Sarah and Welch from no more than a few yards away. Once again the boldness of the renegade shocked Jason as he formed the picture of the girl and her escort, eating and talking, unaware of the rattlesnake leering at them. Sam Running Fox's words echoed in his ears. Stone Hand goes where he wants.

But why did he not act? Jason asked himself. The man lived only to kill as often and as many as he could. Why did he spare these two? The thought of Sarah chatting gayly, mesmerizing the young doctor with her lilting laughter while no more than a stone's throw away a dark and menacing killer silently watched, sent a shiver down his spine. Stone Hand could have easily slipped in and cut both their throats. But he didn't. Why? The more he thought about it, the more he was struck by the complexity of the man he hunted. The man's ego was enormous. He was playing another game. And Jason was convinced that he was Stone Hand's chosen opponent in that game. Looking over the tracks again, he began to see more than the obvious evidence that a man had stood watching the young couple. It was too obvious, certainly for a man who could make a trail of seven horses disappear. Stone Hand intended for Jason to find his tracks. He was telling Jason once again that he could go anywhere he chose, when he chose. It still didn't explain why he had not killed them, unless it was just another mind game he was playing with Jason. Stone Hand most likely knew Sarah was the colonel's daughter. If he wanted to cause as much injury to his white enemies as possible, stealing the colonel's daughter was the way to do it. This was the way an Indian would think, to bring personal distress to an enemy was better than killing any number of nameless troopers. Jason was sure now that the savage meant to kidnap Sarah Holder. But first, to satisfy his sadistic ego he felt the need to flaunt his intentions in Jason's face, daring him to stop him. At once there was an urgency to act. Jason knew Stone Hand would strike soon. He had to warn Colonel Holder.

CHAPTER 6

Colonel Holder was clearly alarmed although he didn't say anything at first. He was a man accustomed to facing unexpected situations but Jason's warning hit squarely in his own family. In spite of his immediate concern, there was never a moment of panic. When he spoke, it was with great resolve. "That devil is as brazen as they said he was. We've got to act fast, Jason. If what you suspect is true, Sarah's in danger right now."

The colonel moved quickly, summoning the sergeant major and ordering him to mount a patrol immediately. While in the process, he explained to Jason that Sarah was not in camp. Captain Welch had invited her to accompany his medical team on a visit to the agency clinic. Sarah, anxious to get a closer look at the women and children of the reservation Cheyennes, accepted with enthusiasm.

"Damn!" Jason exhaled. "When did they leave?"

"Just after breakfast."

She must have left right after he had talked to

her at the mess tent. He found it irritating that, moments after teasing him with her playful chatter she had ridden off with Captain Welch. He immediately reprimanded himself silently for thoughts of such a petty nature in the face of the serious business at hand. "I'm going on ahead," he said over his shoulder as he hurried to his horse. He didn't express his entire feelings to the colonel, no need to add to the man's distress. But he knew in his gut that Stone Hand had given him a warning at the scene of the picnic. And now Sarah could not have cooperated more with the savage in his deadly game.

Sarah Holder was both fascinated and appalled at the conditions she found at the agency. She had heard many exciting stories of the proud and fierce Cheyenne people. She was not prepared for the pitiful appearance of a people in captivity. There seemed to be no purposeful activity in the Indian camp. The men stood in groups, talking. The women sat silently before their tipis, some mending clothes, some making corn cakes from government-issued meal. They stared with empty eyes as she walked among them. John seemed impervious to their plight as he walked along beside her, carrying on a constant chatter about his clinic and how the Indians were like children with no practical knowledge of modern medicine. It was clear to Sarah that the doctor saw himself as some sort of medical savior to these people. She couldn't help but feel troubled that he gave no consideration to the obvious fact that they had somehow survived for centuries before he arrived with his white man's medicine.

"Will you be all right for a little while?" He stood with her while his men erected a tent to be used for a field clinic. "If you like, I can have a blanket spread for you in the front of the clinic."

"No thanks, but I think I'd rather look around out here. You go on and tend to your patients. I'll entertain myself."

"As you wish. But, Sarah, don't stray far from the clinic."

She answered with a smile and the doctor excused himself to see to the needs of the small gathering of people awaiting him. Sarah occupied herself by watching a group of children playing a game behind the tent. It was a spirited game and it captured her interest immediately.

After a short while, she glanced over as an old man appeared on the opposite side of the circle where the children played. He was bent and gray, a blanket draped over his shoulders. Sarah gave him no more than a fleeting thought. He seemed to be watching the children at their play with some interest.

The children had a ball of sorts, fashioned from hide, and they were indulged in a spirited effort to knock it about with sticks. It appeared to Sarah that the children themselves were knocked about more often than the ball. There was a great deal of laughter and excited cries and while she was unsure of the object of the game she became fascinated with the intensity of the players. When she glanced up at the old man again, she noticed that he had moved around the circle, closer to her. He seemed to be as intense a spectator as she. She was distracted for a moment when she heard her name called and turned to see John standing outside the tent.

"I just wanted to make sure you were all right," he called out. "I hope you're not too bored. I'll be a while yet. Then we'll have lunch. I had Sergeant Ortiz prepare a picnic basket for us."

"I'm fine," she called back. "See to your patients. I'll amuse myself."

"All right then, just stay close to the clinic." He disappeared around the corner of the tent.

The events that took place during the next few seconds happened so fast and with such suddenness that Sarah had no time to react. A powerful hand was clamped tightly over her mouth and she was lifted off her feet by an arm that crushed the breath from her lungs. Everything went black and she lost consciousness without ever having made a sound.

When Jason galloped up before the agency building, he was met by a scene of confusion bordering on chaos. He didn't like the look of it, knowing at once that his worst fears had been realized. He was too late. Captain Welch was pacing back and forth, ranting before a stoic group of young Cheyenne men. His orderlies were searching frantically from lodge to lodge. The Cheyenne women and children stood passively by, watching the confusion. Jason did not need an explanation. He knew what had happened and his only concern at that moment was a dread that he might find Sarah's body. He had to count on a feeling that Stone Hand's inclination would run more toward abduction than murder, for no other reason than to extend the anguish of his enemy. When a thorough search of the entire village turned up nothing, he assumed his hunch was correct and there was a small measure of hope that the girl was still alive.

"Goddamn, Coles, I swear I don't know how it could have happened! She was right behind the tent here, watching some children playing. I just checked on her to make sure she was all right, just a few minutes before she disappeared." Welch was grief-stricken and more than a little bit concerned about his responsibility for the safety of the colonel's daughter. "Find her, Coles! For God's sake, find her!"

Jason wasted little time in hearing out the doctor's justification for his lack of protecting Sarah. He knew he was already losing precious time. A quick scout of the area painted a vivid picture of what had occurred. Stone Hand, it could be no other, had snatched Sarah from behind and carried her inside a nearby lodge. There he undoubtedly had tied her up and then carried her out behind the lodge where his horses were tethered. The trail led off to the west.

Welch mentioned that there had been no one around Sarah except the children and an old man who was also watching the game. Something jogged Jason's memory and he recalled that when he had watched Lame Dog's camp he had seen an old man, bent and gray, ride out alone. Coincidence? Maybe, but he remembered Colonel Holder remarking that Stone Hand often wore disguises. As he stood, gazing out in the direction the tracks led, he glanced over to discover Sam Running Fox standing nearby. When Sam caught his eye, he walked over to Jason.

"Like I told you." Sam stated the obvious, "Stone Hand goes where he pleases."

Jason didn't answer right away, staring at the half-breed for a full minute before he spoke. "Sam, can you give me any help on this?" Sam simply shrugged. "Where will he likely take her? Any idea?"

"No. Who can say what is in Stone Hand's mind?" He watched Jason's reaction and he could see that the girl was important to the tall Indian scout. "Stone Hand is big medicine. He has no friends. He talks to no one. It is best you leave this one be, Jason, or you'll be next in line to decorate his scalp stick."

Jason considered this sober advice for no more than an instant. Then he climbed into the saddle and turned Henry's head to the west. "Well, I aim to give the son of a bitch a chance at this scalp and I'll tell you this . . . he damn sure better be a spirit . . . because, if he's a mortal man, I'm gonna hang that devil." Henry sensed the urgency of his master and Jason had to hold him back a moment, long enough to call out to Captain Welch. "I'm going after them. Tell the colonel I've gone on ahead." He started to leave when Sam grabbed Henry's bridle and held him.

"Wait. I'm going with you."

Jason was startled. "What? I thought you said it was no use going after him. Aren't you afraid he'll kill you?"

"I'm already a dead man," Sam replied stoically. "He knows I talked to you the other day." He turned to get his horse and weapons, pausing to give one more comment. "I'd rather hunt than be hunted. Maybe we might get lucky."

The trail led to the west for what Jason figured to be about ten or twelve miles where it turned to the north, following a small stream. Stone Hand was traveling fast. Jason had sought to gain ground on the renegade but they were unable to shorten the distance between them. He had hoped that having

Sarah with him would slow the Cheyenne down. At least he could be reasonably certain that the girl was still unhurt at this point because Stone Hand was traveling hard. She was no doubt bound hand and foot. He and Sam remained hard on the trail until daylight began to fade. Darkness found them close to a low butte, dotted with an occasional tree. There was nothing they could do at this point but wait until first light to pick up the trail again. Theirs was a cold camp that night.

Sleep was not easy. Thoughts of the girl weighed heavily on his mind and he found it impossible to avoid envisioning possible scenes of Sarah's fate. Her survival depended solely upon Stone Hand's moods and what he planned to accomplish with the kidnapping of the colonel's daughter. Although he and Sam were the pursuers, he was mindful to keep a cautious eye for attack from the Cheyenne. He felt that Stone Hand knew he would be coming after him . . . wanted him to, in fact. And he just might double back on them. Sleep finally came in spite of the many thoughts racing through his brain and he awoke to the sound of Henry's noisy grazing on the sparse grass around his head.

They didn't waste any time in getting under way again. After a couple of hours' ride, they came across Stone Hand's campsite. In spite of the urgency to keep going, Jason stopped briefly to scout the campsite. There was not a great deal of sign to tell them what took place during Sarah's first night of captivity but there was enough to form a picture in his mind.

"The girl put up a fight here." Sam's fingers brushed over some crushed blades of grass. "She got beat or mounted, or both. Can't tell."

Jason's face was tense. "I hope she just got beat," was all he said.

Sam detected a deeper message in Jason's tone and realized that the girl might mean more to the scout than the simple fact she was the colonel's daughter. He tried to ease Jason's mind somewhat. "Probably just a couple of smacks to let her know not to give him any trouble. Stone Hand don't usually mount white women. He don't think they're good enough to breed with a Cheyenne."

Sam's comments did little to ease Jason's mind. He decided he had better not dwell on thoughts of that nature and climbed back in the saddle. Nudging Henry with his heels, he took up the trail again.

Toward midday they determined that the signs were fresher and they knew they were gaining on Stone Hand. He urged Henry on. As he rode, his eyes constantly searching, it dawned on him that the trail was too easy to follow. Possibly Stone Hand felt he was safely out of danger by then. Something cautioned him that the man they followed was smarter than that and he realized there was another possibility to consider, one that was more likely. Stone Hand had traveled fast the first day, maybe to distance himself from the cavalry patrol he knew would follow. But he made no effort to disguise his trail. Now he slowed his pace, possibly to allow Jason and Sam to catch up. Sam agreed that that was more likely what he was thinking. It fit the devious mind of the renegade. The game was on again. Stone Hand was inviting them to catch him if they could.

Late afternoon found Sam and Jason approaching a low line of hills that stretched out across the horizon for miles, disappearing into a brown haze in the western sky. This could mean trouble, Jason thought. It would be no more difficult to trail Stone Hand through the hills as long as there was not too much rock. But there would be many more opportune places for ambush. He looked back to signal Sam to pick up the pace.

Darkness came once more, Sarah's second night of captivity, and while he was sure they were closing the distance between them, still they had not gotten close enough to get even a glimpse of Stone Hand on the horizon. As he settled in for the night, he wondered how far behind them Colonel Holder might be—by now, possibly a full day. They had been traveling fast. His concern now was for the horses. Henry was as stout a horse as he had ever seen. He was a match for any horse on the plains. But he was beginning to show signs of fatigue, as was Sam's paint. Stone Hand would ordinarily ride his horse till it dropped but under these circumstances he would be forced to rest his horses, too.

This might be the time Stone Hand made a move. Jason and Sam took turns standing watch that night. There seemed little sense in taking chances.

Morning came without incident and they took up the trail once again. Midday found them traversing one low ridge after another, watching the trail before them and to both sides, alert to any sign of ambush. Jason unconsciously eased his rifle a little in its boot to make sure it was free and quickly available. The summer sun hammered the rocky trail they followed up yet another ridge of scraggly brush and twisted trees. They were moving slowly now in order to follow the tracks across a rocky point. Up ahead of them, the trail closed to a narrow gap between two small cliffs . . . a spot made for ambush.

Jason stopped and waited for Sam to pull up beside him. "I don't like the looks of that. Whaddaya think, Sam?"

"If I was looking to ambush somebody, I couldn't find no better place than that." He stood up in his stirrups and looked to both sides. "We could ride around, pick up the trail on the other side."

Jason looked out to both sides of the gap. To skirt the steep draw would mean a loss of precious time and add the possibility of not being able to pick up the trail again. The hills on both sides were steep and rocky. It might be difficult to pick up a trail that could go in any direction on the other side of the draw. And if they didn't find a trail that might mean Stone Hand was still in the draw and they'd have to go in to find him anyway. "Hell," he finally said, "I'm sticking with the trail." He nudged Henry forward.

"What the hell," Sam muttered and followed.

They moved slowly, eyes darting back and forth, searching the sides of the draw from rock to rock, looking for any obvious ambush position. Once within the narrow walls of the draw, there was no sound to break the leaden silence except the muffled padding of the horses' hooves in the dust. It seemed that all living things in the canyon were holding their breath, watching the two men. Jason could feel the weight of the silence, his body tense, waiting for the rifle shot that would tell him that he had been a fool. There were hundreds of ideal ambush spots in the silent boulders that lined the walls of the canyon. Still there was nothing to break the silence by the time they reached the halfway point. Now he could see the far end of the passage and the open hills that lay beyond. Were it not for Sarah, he would have gone around. Only a fool rode willingly into an ambush. What purpose would it serve if he got himself killed while trying to save a couple of hours' time? It was useless to worry at this point, nothing to do but keep going and keep his eyes peeled.

Another fifty yards, they were almost through the draw. If he had the luck to pick up the glint of sun on a rifle barrel, he might be able to react in time. He knew that, behind him, Sam was thinking the same thought. They could see the end of the passage now. Jason could see a small stream crossing the trail ahead where it trickled down from the hills to form a shallow pool. Beyond the stream the land was rolling again. If they could get to the stream, they would be out of the ominous threat of ambush.

At last they emerged from the draw. They had been so sure of ambush while in the passageway that it was almost a letdown when nothing happened. He glanced at Sam and the half-breed made an exaggerated sigh. He began to wonder what was in Stone Hand's mind, why he did not attempt to rid himself of his pursuers. Could it be that he really wasn't aware of the two men tracking him? Jason gave that thought no more than a second. He knew all right, the son of a bitch knew.

As if reading his thoughts, Sam spoke. "He's playing with us. He wants to make us sweat some."

Jason grunted. "Well, he's doing a damn good job of it."

Whatever the reason, Jason was able to breathe a little easier. He checked Henry up short for a few moments while he surveyed the little valley before them. Satisfied that all was peaceful, he pushed on to the shallow pool and continued to scan the hills around them while the horses drank. He decided that Stone Hand had figured he would not follow him through the narrow draw. Probably didn't figure me to be a damn fool, he said to himself. They pushed on, climbing into the hills, following a trail that was still very much obvious, until darkness called an end to the day's march.

A moonless night settled over the tiny valley, spreading a dark blanket over their camp. Thousands of stars pierced the heavens with pinpoints of light. It was the kind of night that under other circumstances would be quiet and peaceful. "You want to take the first watch or the second?"

Sam answered. "I'll take the second if it's all the same to you."

Jason took his blanket and wrapped it around his shoulders and positioned himself with his back to a large boulder where he could see anything that moved. Sam turned in and was soon asleep. The hours passed slowly but without incident and along toward midnight, Jason rose stiffly, shook some of the kinks from his muscles, and took a walk around their camp. When he was sure that everything was all right, he woke Sam. Sam was reluctant to wake up but Jason finally roused him.

"Everything all right?" Sam asked.

"Yep. I took a little walk around. Everything's quiet."

"I swear, Jason. I'm gittin' too damn old for this. My bones are aching." He picked up his rifle and moved over to the boulder Jason had sat against. "I'll see you at sunup."

Although he was not sure it would be possible, Jason was sound asleep in seconds. His sleep was filled with dreams of Sarah and John Welch and Colonel Holder. It seemed that the colonel was telling him that he could not let him marry Sarah, that Jason was too rough-edged to marry a colonel's daughter. John was in his dream, charming the girl with elegant speeches. Then the three of them laughed at Jason in his buckskins. He looked at Sarah, laughing, and then it wasn't Sarah laughing at him but Stone Hand. He was faceless but he knew it was Stone Hand.

He was awakened by Henry nuzzling close to his back, grazing on a few thin blades of grass beneath the scrub he had placed his blankets under. He lay there emotionless for a few moments until he could shake the cobwebs out of his brain and determine what time of night or day it was. When he realized it was already sunup, he bolted upright and crawled out of his blanket. He looked across at Sam, who was sitting against the boulder. Jason could tell at once that Sam was not awake. "Helluva sentry," he mumbled. "Stone Hand could have walked right in and killed us both." He stood up and took a few steps away from the remains of the small campfire and relieved himself. When he finished, he walked over to Sam and stood directly over him, waiting for some response. There was none. Finally, he said, "I hope me walking around ain't disturbing your sleep." Sam didn't move.

Jason reached down and shook him. Only then did he notice the bloody shirt under Sam's blanket. Stunned, he drew his hand away quickly. Sam slid over on his side in the dirt. The long open gash across his throat opened slightly to form a grisly smile that seemed a grim reminder that Stone Hand's deadly vengeance could strike whenever and wherever it pleased him.

"Jesus!" Jason stepped backward a couple of steps. His rifle up, he looked from side to side. There was no one in sight. He looked back at Sam. "Jesus!" he repeated. Then he noticed the slit across Sam's left eyebrow. "The son of a bitch . . . the son of a bitch!" He felt violated. There was no feeling of fear, only anger and frustration. He had never wanted to kill any man so badly in his life as he did this savage. He did not grieve over the loss of Sam Running Fox, he didn't know the man that well. But it was a damn dirty shame to see a man killed purely for pleasure. Stone Hand could have killed them both but he obviously wasn't through playing with Jason. Adding emphasis to the devil's brazen contempt, Jason just then noticed that Sam's horse was gone, no doubt stolen by the renegade.

CHAPTER 7

Every muscle in her body ached. At times during the past two days she thought she could not stand any more. Her feet tied by a rope that went under the horse's belly, her hands tied to the Indian saddle, she held on for all she was worth. She did not doubt that if she was bounced from the saddle and slid under the horse's belly she would be trampled to death. She could not scream out for help because of the rawhide thong that bound her mouth. There was no one to hear her if she did. And the savage had set a torrid pace, leading her horse through mesquite and brush, up streambeds and over rocks and ridges, all at a furious pace that ate up the miles and wreaked havoc on her body. She was not accustomed to riding great distances and certainly not on a crude Indian saddle.

For the moment she was alone with her despair. He was gone, leaving her bound to a tree, her arms behind her and her feet pulled up beside her. She could move only a little but she tried to shift her position to keep her limbs from getting numb. She had time now to think about her dreadful situation and pray that she would be saved from the fate she knew was promised her. She knew that her abductor could only be none other than the infamous Stone Hand, and from what she had heard from her father and Jason, she knew that it was just a matter of time before he decided she was no longer useful alive.

When she first regained consciousness, after he had suddenly swept up behind her and attacked, she was angry. When he tied her up, she tried to strike out at him. Without saying a word, he struck her hard across the face, over and over until she collapsed, whimpering to the ground. As they rode that first day, she became more and more frightened of the silent savage on the horse before her. He stopped several times to drink and water the horses at the tiny streams they crossed. But she was not allowed to drink until they camped that night. After he had eaten some dried meat he carried, he amused himself by beating her. It was obvious that he intended to humiliate her as well as administer some pain, for the beating was given with a large switch upon her bare bottom.

When he had come to stand over her and then reached down and pulled her riding skirt up above her waist, she thought he was intent on raping her. He laughed when he detected the terror in her eyes. But when he ripped her undergarments away, exposing her buttocks, he picked up a large willow switch and flailed her backside until she could no longer stand it and fainted. Then she was left alone for the night. The next day she was forced to ride on her raw and bloodstained buttocks.

Alone now, she felt the tears well up in her eyes and trickle down her cheeks. Her voice cracked when she started to sob and she fought to restrain it for it tore painfully at her parched throat. "Please come," she pleaded aloud, "please come!" John must be feeling the agony she felt and would surely be on his way to save her. Her father and Jason Coles were probably leading a patrol after her already. But in her heart she feared she would be long dead by the time anyone came to rescue her.

She heard a faint noise behind her and he was there. Before moving to face her, he administered a hard kick to her back, a pleasure he seemed to enjoy frequently. His evil leer sent shivers down her spine. He shouted angry words into her face. She could not understand any of them but she did not fail to grasp his meaning when he threw a rifle down in the dust before her. She realized that it was not his. He was telling her that he had killed the owner of the weapon. And she was afraid she knew who it belonged to. In the confusion of the Cheyenne tongue that he screamed at her, the name *Coles* was spat out several times. What did it mean? Was it Jason's rifle? She feared that Jason Coles was dead by this savage's hand. The thought of it was unbearable. She could not help herself. She began to cry again. This seemed to infuriate the Indian. He slapped her hard across the face and uttered more strange words of anger and contempt.

Sarah was as good as dead. Of that there seemed to be no doubt. It was just a matter of time. The abuse at the hands of her captor was terrifying and she spent the first two days of her captivity in constant fear for her life. As the hours wore on, she became tired of being afraid, of dreading every second to come. She even became somewhat oblivious to the frequent kicks and slaps. Stone Hand was openly contemptuous of her weak and fearful cowering and she became tired of that. Anger began to replace some of the fear in her mind. If that rifle really belonged to Jason Coles, then he was dead. There seemed to be little hope that her father's soldiers could find them. So she quit praying for rescue and resolved to meet her fate, whatever it was to be, with a defiant face. The only thing she prayed for now was the opportunity to cause her captor some measure of pain before he killed her.

Her transformation must have been evident in her face because Stone Hand was studying her curiously. He uttered a few words in Cheyenne and drew back his hand to slap her. When she did not cringe but glared at him defiantly, he did not deliver the blow. Instead, an evil smirk creased his face and he uttered a few more words before turning away. She could not know that he was pleased to see her find some fight. It meant it would take her longer to die when he decided to slowly kill her.

Jason bent down and studied the prints closely. The Indian was trying to cover his trail now, no longer leaving him a plain trail to follow. To Jason it meant that Stone Hand had established a base camp, he had holed up and this was where he would play out the end of the game. He would have to move very carefully, searching every rock and blade of grass for sign. It took a while but he finally found another toe print leading toward a low butte that led to a rocky draw. The tracking was painfully slow.

On foot, Jason led his horse along another narrow valley floor that ran down to a small shallow pool of water on the far side. While he moved as quietly as he could, the narrow walls of the draw closed in closer and closer. Any second, he thought. What is he waiting for? He constantly scanned the steep walls above him, his eyes darting from side to side, rock to rock—never concentrating on any one rock for more than a split second. There were a hundred spots for the savage to lie in wait. This is suicide, Jason's common sense screamed at him.

Another few yards, still no report of rifle fire— twenty or thirty yards to reach the end of the passage and the clearing beyond. He almost wished for a shot to ring out. At least he would be free of the apprehension. But the quiet of the canyon only deepened. Yard by torturous yard, he pushed on until at last he was in the clear and able to draw a breath in relief.

His sharp eyes picked up the faint print of a moccasined foot beside the pool. He stopped to examine it. Stone Hand had been careless to leave the print. Jason guessed that his foot had slipped off the rock beside the print. As he studied the print, he was suddenly startled when he felt the blood spatter on his face. At almost the same instant, he heard the impact of the bullet on Henry's shoulder, followed immediately by the report of the rifle. Henry's front legs buckled and Jason stood frozen for only a fraction of a second before hurling himself sideways to avoid being pinned under his horse.

There was no time for conscious thought. He acted on reflex, his reactions swift and decisive. He automatically drew his rifle from the saddle, even as his horse was falling, and almost in the same motion he rolled over and over behind a gnarled tree trunk for cover. His eyes searched frantically for the source of the gunshot. There was no second shot. At first he counted himself fortunate that Stone Hand had missed and had hit his horse instead of him. But after a few moments' thought he realized it wasn't luck at all. He had been an easy target. The Cheyenne shot his horse purposely, he was sure of this. It fit with Stone Hand's devious mind. It was just another part of the deadly game the renegade wanted to play. Now the hunter became the hunted . . . and the hunted was on foot. Stone Hand demonstrated his affinity for cruel mental games in the way he had staged the ambush. Instead of simply shooting Jason's horse while he was riding through the narrow draw, Stone Hand had amused himself by letting his prey sweat it out. Then when he thought he was safely through the likely ambush, he shot Henry. Stone Hand enjoyed a war of nerves as well as actual combat.

He lay behind the tree for a long time, weighing his options. They were few. He knew he had to find better cover than the tree he was behind. Glancing around him, he decided his best route of escape was to make a dash for the stream and follow it up through the rocks. That route offered the best cover from Stone Hand's rifle. He looked back at his horse and the heavy feeling of his loss settled on him. Henry was trembling and several times made attempts to get up. But it was obvious to Jason that his horse was mortally wounded. He hesitated, not wanting to do it, before he finally pulled the trigger and ended Henry's suffering.

He still had no clue where Stone Hand's shot had come from. He tried to scan the surrounding hills and ridges, foot by foot, rock by rock. Somewhere, he figured, on the hill to the north of his position, the renegade had to be watching. He would almost have to be there to have shot Henry in the right shoulder. There was little choice, he decided—run for the rocks that cradled the tiny stream or stay pinned down where he was. He pressed his back against the tree trunk and eased himself up to a standing position. With one last glance at his dead horse, he suddenly pushed away from the tree and at a dead run dashed across the open area between the tree and the stream. He saw the sand kick up in front of him moments before he heard the shots. In a moment's time there were bullets kicking up dirt all around him and he ran for all he was worth. The open space was maybe twenty yards across, and by the time he reached safety behind a large boulder in the center of the streambed, the air around him was alive with the whine and spitting of rifle bullets. Breathless, he sank down on one knee in the shallow stream and gasped for air.

The son of a bitch, he thought between gasps. He wasn't trying to hit me. He doesn't want his fun to end too soon. There was no doubt the Indian was still playing with him. The thing that irritated him most was that he had no choice but to participate in the game. Now the hunt was on. At least it might occupy the Indian's mind and possibly save Sarah from some abuse.

He did not linger behind the boulder. As quickly as he could, he made his way up into the rocks, following the course of the stream. As he made his way over the rough terrain, he took inventory of his situation. He was on foot but at least he had his rifle. He cursed himself for not having taken his ammunition belt from the saddle before he ran for the tree. He had six cartridges left. Stone Hand was sure to come down to the dead horse as soon as Jason ran up into the rocks. He wouldn't pass up the opportunity for ammunition and supplies. He would have to cross the same open area that Jason had just fled from. So Jason decided to position himself to cover the open ground. Selecting a good-sized rock that afforded him protection from two sides, he settled in to wait for the Cheyenne's move.

An hour passed. There was no sound beyond that of an occasional insect buzzing by his head. He changed his position several times as the unyielding boulder pressed hard against his bones. "The bastard," he swore, "he's got all the time in the world." The time passed.

Along toward evening, a breeze kicked up and he noticed storm clouds forming over the hills. Moving this way, he thought. Soon the breeze increased until the wind gained force enough to blow the sand around and the sky began to darken. He had to squint in an effort to keep watch on the open ground below him. Just as darkness fell, the storm hit with full force. Lightning flashed, the crash of thunder came almost at the same instant, and then large raindrops began a steady tattoo on the rocks around him. Suddenly the bottom seemed to drop out of the heavy clouds overhead. In a moment he was soaked.

It soon became too dark to see, except during the brilliant flashes of lightning. He decided to work his way farther down the hillside to a crevice in the rocks where an overhang offered some protection from the rain. It was difficult to see where he was stepping between lightning flashes but he made the best time he could. On the positive side, it was just as difficult for the Cheyenne to stalk him in this downpour.

Under the overhang of the crevice and out of the direct deluge of water, he considered his options once again. They were few, but he knew that if he was to stand a chance of rescuing Sarah, he would need more than the six cartridges he had. He needed to retrieve his canteen as well as his cartridge belt. As he shifted his position to avoid a torrent of water gushing through the crevice from the hill above him, it seemed ridiculous to worry about his canteen but he knew that when the rain stopped it might be a month before another one came and he didn't care much for the prospect of being without water. He weighed the possibility of getting to his horse and back safely. It was risky but he didn't see that he had any other choice. "Best go now," he murmured, "before it slacks up." His chances of getting to his horse and back without being seen were definitely better in this downpour.

A thought flashed through his mind of the girl and he wondered how she was faring on this stormy night. He tried not to let his mind form pictures of what might be happening to her. At least he knew Stone Hand was occupied now with dealing with him. Maybe it would buy some time for Sarah.

After some consideration, he decided to leave his rifle under the rock ledge, where it would be dry. He could move more easily and a good deal faster if both hands were free. His pistol would serve just as well at close range, and he knew that if he had to use a weapon it would be at close range because of the poor vision afforded by the stormy night.

Placing each foot carefully, he descended the steep slope, following the stream that had by this time been transformed into a torrent, until he neared the clearing. The night was as dark as a cave, with only occasional flashes of lightning that illuminated the rocks for seconds before blanketing him once more in darkness. The rain continued to beat down, plastering his shirt to him like a second skin. Near the bottom of the ravine he stopped and waited for the next flash of lightning. When it came, he could plainly see Henry's carcass. The split-second image afforded by the lightning provoked an uncontrollable wave of melancholy for the loss of his horse. Henry would be hard to replace. Moving quickly now, he made straight for the dead animal. When he reached the body, he dropped down on his stomach, his pistol out, and paused to listen. There was no sound other than that of the storm.

His cartridge belt was gone! He swore softly. "Too late." The ammunition, along with his saddle pack and canteen were all missing. Stone Hand had probably taken them right away while I was getting my tail up in the rocks, he thought. He had no choice now but to get himself back up out of sight. He would have to make do with the few bullets he had left.

In the darkness, the rain pouring from the brim of his hat, he waited for the next lightning flash, planning to move back to the cover of the rocks. When it came, the crash of thunder came at almost the same instant as the flash that vividly illuminated the small clearing so that every rock and twisted tree stood out in sharp detail. And standing not twenty yards from him was the savage who hunted him, Stone Hand!

Jason had never seen the man face-to-face but he recognized him at once. In the frozen moment of brilliant lightning, the man appeared to be more spirit than mortal. And though it was for no more than an instant, the image of the infamous killer was seared into Jason's brain. Dressed only in buckskin leggings and breechclout, a necklace of claws that hung almost to his belt, and hide armbands just above his biceps, he imparted an eerie, almost ghostlike countenance. And like the flash of lightning that had brought this image, he was gone.

Jason reacted immediately, although it seemed he was frozen for a few moments. He rolled over behind the carcass of his horse, his pistol ready, and prepared to shoot when the next bolt of lightning flashed. When it did, he could see no sign of Stone Hand. The man had disappeared. Like a spirit, he could not help but think. He questioned his mind for a moment, wondering if he had really been there or if it had been a vision. It was him, he told himself. Vision or reality, spirit or man, it didn't matter. Jason was ready to deal with whatever Stone Hand was. One thing was certain, he had to leave that location right away. Stone Hand would be moving to position himself behind him and he was going to make sure that didn't happen.

He decided to make a dash for the stream and the rocks on each side of it. Without hesitating to give it further thought, he got up and ran for cover, his boots splashing in the rain soaked sand. There was no concern to disguise his tracks. The Indian knew where he was and where he was heading. Now it was a footrace for the rocks and Jason did not want to be cut off from his rifle. The last thing he remembered, before everything went black, was the sound of the rushing water as he started to jump the stream.

When he awoke, his head throbbed with a stabbing pain that seemed to engulf his entire skull. It took a few moments to clear his vision and to allow his brain to right itself. When the world stopped spinning and he came to his senses, his first lucid image was that of the savage Cheyenne raider standing over him, watching his victim impassively. The rain had stopped, the thunderstorm having long since departed. How long had he been out? He could only guess. It must have been for a considerable length of time because the sun was beginning to lift itself over the distant hills.

"Hard head." The Cheyenne grunted. Jason knew enough Cheyenne to understand. He tried to raise his hand to examine the back of his head but discovered that his hands were tied behind his back. Then in a rush his wits returned and he looked around him in a frantic search for Sarah. She was there, off to one side of a small campfire, trussed hand and foot. Unable to speak, for there was a band of rawhide tied across her mouth, she attempted to motion to him. He felt completely impotent.

"You all right?" he called out to her. Before she could answer, he received a hard backhanded slap across his face from their captor.

"No talk!" Stone Hand hissed.

Sarah tried to nod to Jason but he could not see her response. Stone Hand stood over him, glaring down defiantly at his conquered enemy, his feet widespread, fists on his hips, his bearing that of complete dominance. The physical bearing of the infamous Cheyenne renegade seemed to convey a promise of violence. Jason could well imagine the

fear Stone Hand's fellow tribesmen held for this de-
monlike warrior. There was no evidence that compassion had ever cracked the rocklike face that
stared down at his captive. He stood there a long
while then he suddenly turned and went over to
the campfire. There he squatted on his haunches
before the fire and proceeded to eat a breakfast of
the dried jerky taken from Jason's saddle pack.
There was no indication that he was planning to
feed his captives. Jason surmised that the savage
had no long-term plans for them so feeding them
would be a waste of food.

While their captor took his meal, Jason looked toward Sarah. Their eyes met and he was at once horrified by the glazed expression of despair he saw
there. He did not want to think about the circumstances that had created her look of hopelessness.
He could only imagine the cruelty suffered at the
hands of an animal like Stone Hand. Her eyes told
him that the last remaining shred of hope she had
been clinging to had vanished with his capture. He
could not know that until that moment she had resolved to stand up to her captor with courage. Now
she gave up all hope.

In an attempt to help her keep her hopes alive, he
tried to encourage her with a nod of his head and a
slight smile. She did not respond. Instead, she
averted her eyes as if ashamed for him to see her
torn riding skirt and her disheveled appearance.
He wished he could tell her how sorry he was to

have let her down. But as long as he still drew breath there was hope. The bastard had better not make a mistake! Jason had never been a practitioner of the doctrine of despair. He would bide his time and wait for the opportunity he had to assume would come. He was counting on the knowledge that Stone Hand enjoyed his dominance over him too much to end it abruptly. It wouldn't be quick. No, Stone Hand would want to watch him suffer first. He didn't have long to wait before the savage proved his theory.

His hunger satisfied, Stone Hand stood up and stretched. His body, broad and sinewy, was not typical of the average Cheyenne warrior, whose muscles were smooth and supple. Stone Hand's, by contrast, were like steel straps, wrapped tightly around his limbs, never seeming to relax, displaying a power that lay coiled like an angry rattlesnake. He stood before them now, cold in his appraisal as he looked at Jason and then Sarah and back to Jason. There was no disguising the look of intense satisfaction behind the cold, measuring eyes as he contemplated the cruelty he was about to impart. This was not going to be pleasant, Jason told himself and steeled himself for whatever was to come.

It started simply enough. Stone Hand walked over and stood over Jason for a long moment, glaring down at him, a decided look of disgust for the man who had the insolence to think he could trail

Stone Hand. Jason saw the kick coming and tried to roll with the blow to minimize the effect. The heel of Stone Hand's foot caught him beside the head, knocking him facedown in the dust. Before he could struggle to right himself, Stone Hand's toe landed solidly in his rib cage, forcing the wind from his lungs. Jason rolled over on his back, helpless to defend himself. Stone Hand glared down at him with the years of contempt he had built up for all white men. Jason regained enough breath to speak.

"I have heard that Stone Hand is a mighty warrior," he started slowly, drawing on his knowledge of the Cheyenne tongue. "His medicine is big. He has taken many scalps." Stone Hand stared down at him impassively. "This man I see now must be someone else, stealing Stone Hand's name. A warrior as mighty as Stone Hand would not attack a man who cannot fight back. There is no honor here. Maybe Stone Hand's scalps are all women's." Stone Hand's expression did not change. "Cut my hands loose and we will see whose medicine is strongest."

Stone Hand sneered. "The white coyote thinks to make a fool of me. I do not fight with coyotes." He drew his scalp knife from his belt and held it up before him, a hint of a smile creased the steel-like countenance. "I skin them."

It wasn't going to work. Jason would have to hope for another opportunity. Stone Hand was too clever to let his ego throw away his advantage.

However, the savage was not above amusing himself by taunting his victims.

"So, the white face has come to kill Stone Hand and save the soldier chief's daughter." He waited for Jason's reply. When there was none, he chided, "I was told that you are a great tracker. Why did it take you so long to find me?" Jason remained silent. "Maybe this white bitch is your woman. Is that why you came? I saw her mate with the soldier medicine man. Maybe she is not your woman." His lips parted in a cruel smile. "But you are the one who comes for her."

"Maybe I came after you to see if there really was a mighty warrior called Stone Hand . . . a mighty warrior with big medicine. But all I have found is a cowardly dog who is brave as long as I am tied up."

Stone Hand smiled. He seemed genuinely pleased with Jason's attempts to goad him. But he would not be baited. "Stone Hand does battle with the grizzly and the mountain lion. He does not waste time fighting with prairie dogs. When I am ready, I will slit your throat." The smile broadened. "Maybe I will send the soldier chief one of your eyebrows so he will know what happened to his great tracker. The wolves and coyotes will have the rest of you."

Jason was not getting every word because the Indian was talking rapidly, but his Cheyenne was sufficient to permit him to understand what his fate was to be. He glanced quickly in Sarah's direction, wondering what Stone Hand's plans for her might be. He hoped, for her sake, that he planned to keep her as a wife or trade her. But he had learned enough about this fierce savage to know that the man preferred to ride alone with no ties. His inclination might be to kill her as soon as he had done with her.

Stone Hand did not miss Jason's quick glance toward the girl and he was quick to pounce on it. "You want her for your woman?" Jason shook his head no. Stone Hand insisted. "I think you want her. Now she is Stone Hand's woman. Before I kill you, I will let you watch me take her." His sneer indicated the pleasure the thought brought him. "If she pleases me, I may let her live a few more days until I have my fill of her."

He had been holding the scalp knife during his taunting of the helpless man, turning it in his fingers, testing the cutting edge with his thumb. Suddenly the smile froze on his face, transforming it into a mask of undiluted fury, and he grabbed a handful of Jason's hair. Jerking his head back, he pressed the blade against his neck. Jason braced himself but the fatal slash did not come. Instead, Stone Hand pressed just hard enough to bring blood. "It will not be that quick for you, white man," he said with a hiss. He released the handful of hair and shoved Jason over backward. Then Stone Hand turned his attention to Sarah, who had gasped in horror when the savage had threatened to slash Jason's throat. He took the dozen or so steps over to the terrified woman, swaggering triumphantly, pleased with his dominance over the two captives and gratified by the woman's terror.

Stone Hand did not ordinarily rape his victims. There were only occasional reports of his having sexually assaulted women before killing them. The thing that drove him was his passion for slaughtering the white invaders of his lands. That passion was so great that he felt little interest in the fulfillment of sexual desires. For the most part, he had no sexual desires. Killing was his passion and the thought of mating with a member of a race of people he hated so fiercely was repugnant to him. His desire to torment his captives was so great, however, that he would rape this white woman only because he knew the pain and humiliation it would cause them.

Impassive, he reached down and taking a handful of Sarah's blouse, ripped the garment away, revealing a white undergarment that puzzled him for only a brief moment before he grabbed it and tore it from her bosom. Her exposed breast prompted a curious grunt as he paused to examine the stark whiteness of her skin. Sarah, almost in shock, whimpered softly as the fearsome savage leered down at her, the rawhide gag cutting her mouth as she strained to pull away from her attacker. Her reaction pleased him and he turned to see Jason's re-action.

Jason felt as helpless as he had ever felt in his entire life. He was bound hand and foot. There was nothing he could do to help Sarah. All he could do was encourage her to try to make it as easy on herself as possible. "Sarah," he called out, "don't fight it. It'll just make it worse. Try not to concentrate on it!"

"No talk!" Stone Hand hissed. He looked menacingly at Jason. Then he reached down and pulled Sarah's riding skirt up over her hips and ripped her undergarments away. Before untying her ankles, he paused to marvel at the smooth, pale hips and buttocks, still raw with the welts of the whipping he had administered. After he had satisfied his curiosity, he roughly turned her over and prepared to mount her.

Sarah was crying, almost out of her mind with the awful anticipation of what was to come. Jason strained at his bonds, knowing it was useless. Still, he could not help but try. It was hopeless. The rawhide cut into his wrists as he pulled against his bonds. It was no use. The renegade had not been careless in securing his prisoner. At last he gave up the struggle and lay back. From his position against a gnarled tree trunk he could see Sarah's face. It was a mask of terror. Her eyes, wide with fright, seemed glazed as she stared, unseeing, as the savage groped her from behind. He could do nothing to help her.

Unable to watch the assault, Jason turned his head away. The fury that was burning inside almost drowned by the frustration of his helplessness. Her scream when the savage entered her tore through his brain like a knife.

When it was over, Stone Hand tied the whimpering girl securely to a small tree and swaggered over to gloat before Jason. "She was not very good. Maybe she will be better the next time." He stood leering down at Jason, an evil smile was etched across the brutal features of his face. "How do you like your woman now?"

"You yellow dog, untie me and we'll see how strong your medicine is."

Jason received a kick in the stomach for his retort. Stone Hand laughed when Jason doubled up from the blow. "Jason Coles, big Indian hunter, I was going to kill you now but I think I will let you watch me mount your woman once more before I take your scalp." He placed his foot beside Jason's face and shoved him over on his side. After checking his bonds to make sure they were secure, he left his two captives to hunt for food.

Jason waited until Stone Hand had ridden out of camp before he spoke to Sarah. She was sobbing uncontrollably now that her attacker had left her. Jason was afraid the tragic incident might have destroyed her mind. When he tried to talk to her she seemed not to even hear him.

"Sarah, listen to me. Can you get loose?" She did not answer. "Sarah, I know it was a terrible thing but you're still alive. That's what you have to concentrate on now." Even while he said it, he knew both of them were as good as dead. It was just a question of time before Stone Hand decided to execute them. Still he tried to calm the hysterical girl. "Sarah, don't think on what he did to you. You'll go crazy if you do. We've got to try to save ourselves if we can. He'll be back before long. Can you get loose?"

Gradually her crying subsided and she was quiet for a few minutes. Then she spoke, her voice almost cracking. "I can't get loose. I can't even move."

"All right, all right . . ." He tried to sound calm. At least she was thinking rationally now. "Sarah, listen. I'm sorry I let myself get taken like this but there's nothing I can do about that now. I'm tied up tighter'n hell. And, if I know that buck's way of thinking, he ain't gonna give me a chance to get loose before he takes a knife to my throat." He paused when he saw tears beginning to well up in her eyes again. "Get a-holt of yourself, girl. You've got to get your wits about you if you want to come out of this alive."

"He's going to kill us. What can we do?" Her voice was cracking with fear.

"Sarah, listen to me. I wish I could paint you a

pretty picture but it's time to face the truth of this situation. You're right. He's going to kill us. But you still have a chance if you have the courage to fight for your life."

"What?" She almost screamed it. "What do you mean? I can't fight him!"

Jason remained calm. "I don't know what chance I have. He may decide to cut my throat and be done with it as soon as he gets back. Ain't nothing I can do about it. But you may have a chance. He's gonna come after you again before he kills you." Her eyes opened wide with fright and he heard her gasp. "I'm sorry, Sarah, but there's no time to be afraid. He has to untie your feet again to do it and he'll probably untie your hands again instead of leaving them behind your back like that." It began to appear that he was losing her again. He could see the signs of shock in her eyes. "Sarah, are you all right? You've got to be strong, girl. This is the only chance you've got. You're the only one with a chance to save yourself."

"I can't." She sobbed. "I can't fight that beast!"

"You've got to or you're dead! He ain't gonna take no wife. This is the only chance you'll have." She looked at him as if he were a madman. When he was sure she was calm again, he said, "Sarah, the only chance you have is to get him where he's weakest, where any man is weakest."

It took but a moment before she realized what he meant. "I can't . . ." She didn't finish.

"Yes you can. It's either that or die." Time was running out, there was no point in being subtle. "Sarah, when he comes at you, you've got to hurt him. It's life or death, remember that."

"Jason, I can't . . . I'm afraid . . . I don't think I could even try."

"Well, if you can think of any other way to save yourself, I'd like to hear it. He ain't likely to take you along with him."

Further discussion was interrupted by the sound of hoofbeats and within a few seconds Stone Hand rode into the camp.

The savage dismounted, keeping a wary eye on Jason. He immediately checked the bonds of his two captives. Content that all was as he had left it, he held up a small rabbit he had killed. Throwing it at Sarah's feet, he said, "I will eat now. Prepare this rabbit, woman!"

Sarah could not understand his words. She didn't know what the savage wanted. She was further confused when he reached down and cut her hands free of the thongs that bound them. She looked to Jason for help.

"She don't talk Cheyenne," Jason said. "She don't know how to skin a rabbit anyway."

Stone Hand looked at him in disbelief. "Then what good is she?" He looked back at Sarah and roared, "What good are you?" She tried to shrink back away from his wrath but could not escape the blow he administered to her face. Then he leered at

Jason. "She is useful for only one thing, white man."

Jason was desperate to try anything so he said, "Untie my hands and I'll skin your rabbit for you."

Stone Hand threw back his head and laughed. "Jason Coles, you would be my squaw? You want me to untie your hands? I am not stupid."

So they watched in silence while he cooked his rabbit, squatting in front of the fire opposite them. When it was done to his satisfaction, he ate it. He said nothing while he ate, stopping only once when Sarah reached down to ease the rawhide straps around her ankles. He fixed her with a look that caused her to withdraw her hand from her ankles immediately, like a child who receives a stern look from a parent.

After he had sucked the last bit of meat from the bones of the rabbit, he stood up and emptied his bladder at the edge of the campfire. Sarah turned her head to avoid looking at him, which amused the savage and he stepped closer to her while he finished. She closed her eyes in an effort to shut him out. He reached down and grabbed a handful of her hair, jerking her head back, causing her to scream. He drew his scalping knife from his belt and held it before her eyes, now wide with fright. In one quick thrust, he cut the bonds that held her feet together. "I think your white man wants to see you breed again, coyote bitch." He replaced his knife and pulled her skirt up to her waist. "This time is your last if you don't please me."

Jason called out to her. "Sarah—"

"No talk!" Stone Hand roared, furious at Jason's insolence. He threw the terrified girl aside long enough to walk over to deliver a hard kick into Jason's stomach. When he returned, Sarah tried to back away, her eyes almost glazed with fright. Jason rolled over, trying to see her face and was at once dismayed at the fear he saw in her eyes. He had seen that look in the eyes of a fawn cornered by a mountain lion. It was an expression close to hysteria.

He could see their one chance for survival vanishing. She was too terrified to act. With one last look of contempt for Jason, Stone Hand prepared to attack his victim again.

Then she did it. She suddenly thrust her hands upward between his legs, screaming in defiance.

Stone Hand's reaction was explosive. He bellowed with the pain that stopped him cold. Stunned and angry, he at first tried to back away from the desperate girl's clutches. But she held on, realizing the leverage she now held over her attacker. Almost blinded by the pain, Stone Hand tried to strike her but the sudden increase in pressure she retaliated with brought him to his knees again and he tried to grab her wrists and free himself. She responded by attacking as hard as she could. He collapsed, helpless and humiliated, no longer caring about pride or dignity. Encouraged by the advantage she now realized she held, she continued to punish the savage until he could no longer stand it and lost consciousness.

Now their situation was changed but still desperate. The Cheyenne was evidently helpless for the moment but for how long Jason could only guess. He had never seen a man rendered unconscious in this fashion before. Sarah's first reaction upon seeing the man lose consciousness was to retreat immediately. But knowing he would kill her for sure now, she determined to keep her advantage.

Jason started inching his way toward Sarah by working his bound hands and feet back and forth, dragging himself along the ground. "You did a brave thing, girl. Just don't let go now. I'm coming." He dragged himself up close to her. "Quick, take his knife and cut me loose." For a moment, he wondered if she had nerve enough left to do it. Her eyes were glazed as if she were in a trance. Then she looked at him and nodded, reached for the knife, and began sawing through his bonds. In a matter of seconds he was free.

"He's starting to move!" she whispered. "He's waking up!"

Moving swiftly now, Jason took the knife and cut the rawhide thongs from his ankles. He tied the thongs securely around Stone Hand's wrists and ankles and lashed them tightly behind his back. That done, he took a step backward and said, "He ain't going nowhere now." He looked back at Sarah and she seemed to have fallen back into a trance-like state.

"You did a brave thing, Sarah. Not many women could have done that."

She sat there, her head down, saying nothing. She stared at her right hand as if it did not belong to her. Then, instinctively, she scrubbed it on the hard sand and wiped it on her skirt. It was at that moment that she became aware of her near-nakedness and hurriedly clutched her clothing around her. She felt dirty and even though she had saved herself from further assault she felt as though her life was ended. And then she was sick. Dragging herself away from the fire, she retched repeatedly—her stomach, though empty, trying to expunge the disgust and abhorrence inside her.

Jason watched her closely. He was afraid the incident had driven her out of her mind. She would not be the first woman to go crazy after an assault by a savage. "Sarah," he said her name softly. She did not respond, seeming not to hear. "Sarah," he repeated. "Look at me, Sarah." He reached out and gently turned her chin toward him, forcing the shattered girl to look at him. "Sarah, it's over. You're safe now and what you did was what you had to do. You saved my life and I'm mighty grateful for that. Now you've got to let it go." She continued to stare into his eyes. Gradually he saw her pupils contract and she seemed to acknowledge his words. He breathed a sigh of relief. It appeared she was going to be all right. "Good girl," he said softly. He wet a piece of her torn blouse from the canteen and cleaned her face.

Stone Hand had never known such fury and hatred before. The humiliating defeat he had suffered at the hands of a woman had at first totally confused his mind to the extent that he was not sure exactly what had happened to him. He had never experienced pain so devastating and incapacitating before, so intense that he lost consciousness. When he regained his senses and found himself tied hand and foot, and now the white man's captive, he was almost blind with anger. This monumental insult must be avenged for he could not live with it on his conscience. He would free himself no matter what it took and take restitution on the two hated whites. The woman's death would be slow and painful. He promised himself that.

Jason studied the sullen Cheyenne raider and contemplated his options as far as what action he should take. As he watched the notorious murderer, sitting motionless, staring at the far horizon, he knew what he wanted to do. His inclination was to shoot the mad dog, put a bullet through his twisted brain, and do the world a favor. He glanced at Sarah, who was equally as sullen as the savage, forcing herself to eat the jerky left in Jason's saddle pack. That was all they had to eat since Sarah would not permit Jason to leave her alone with the prisoner while he hunted for game. She had not voiced an opinion but he felt certain she would rather he shot the Indian now. But he knew Colonel Holder wanted Stone Hand to stand trial so the reservation Indians would see him as a criminal and witness his hanging. It was a distasteful choice but he determined he would take him back alive and let the army punish him.

When they were ready, Jason lifted the prisoner up onto his horse. Then he helped Sarah up on the horse that had carried her away from the Cheyenne village. He himself rode Sam Running Fox's paint. They started back to Camp Supply. They had ridden only a half day's ride when they met Colonel Holder and the cavalry patrol.

The reunion between father and daughter was awkward. Colonel Holder, while a caring father, was not a man to show deep feelings. And a lifetime of discipline in not showing emotion added to the stony countenance he displayed upon greeting his daughter. To be sure, he embraced Sarah and expressed concern for the ordeal she had survived. But in Jason's opinion the man did not demonstrate the compassion needed to provide Sarah with the assurance that her soul should not be damaged by the episode with Stone Hand. After a brief fatherly hug, the colonel assigned a party of troopers to escort Sarah back to meet an ambulance that was trailing the column. Sarah, for her part, seemed at a loss. Upon first seeing her father, she sobbed uncontrollably and rushed to receive his consolation. Jason could see the confusion and disappointment in her face when her father briefly patted her and after asking if she was all right, gave her another little squeeze before shuttling her off with the escort. As she was leaving, she glanced quickly at Jason and he tried to smile reassuringly.

"I'll see you back at Supply, Sarah. Everything'll be all right. You just try to get some rest."

She did not reply but stared at him for a moment before nodding her head and following the troopers. He noticed that she avoided looking at the sullen figure of Stone Hand, seated motionless on his horse, his hands still bound behind his back.

Colonel Holder stood watching his daughter ride away until she and her escort had disappeared beyond a hill. Then he turned to Jason. "Well, Coles, I guess I owe you thanks for bringing my daughter back."

"No, sir," Jason replied. "It's the other way around. She's the one who saved my bacon. If it wasn't for that little girl's spunk, I'd be feeding the coyotes right now."

"Was she violated?" He asked in a low voice, not wishing to be overheard by his soldiers.

"Colonel, she was, and I'm right sorry to have to tell you that. But she ain't dead. That's the main thing."

"Damn!" His voice still low, he shook his head and uttered the oath again. "Damn!"

Jason wasn't sure whether the man was genuinely sorry for his daughter or concerned about the stigma he felt might be attached to himself. He felt compelled to chastise the colonel for what he considered a grave lack of compassion for the young lady after what she had just gone through. "Colonel, that's one helluva fine little lady there. She did a helluva thing to save both of us. You should be proud of her."

"I am, I am," he quickly responded, then immediately turned his attention to the captive. "So this is the devil they call Stone Hand." He walked over to the morose savage, staring straight ahead as if seeing beyond the horizon. "You son of a bitch! Your murdering days are over. I personally will hold the rope that hangs you." Stone Hand continued to stare straight ahead. Colonel Holder turned to a young lieutenant and ordered, "Mr. Harris, take charge of the prisoner."

As Stone Hand was led away, he glanced briefly at Jason and snarled. "Do not think it is finished."

"If it was my decision to make, you'd be dead already," Jason replied.

"You will both die, you and the woman." There was no time for more talk before a trooper led his horse away.

CHAPTER 8

For the first time in her life, Sarah Holder was
afraid to be alone at night. When she had arrived
at Camp Supply, her father had her own tent set
up for her and that was the way she preferred it.
Now she seemed to fear every shadow that fell
with evening's gloom. There were only a few other
women in the camp. Of these, Sergeant Major
Kennedy's wife was the first one to step forward
and take Sarah under her wing. Cora Kennedy was
an army wife, as much a veteran as her crusty husband, and she quickly saw the young girl's need
for a female's care. As soon as she got one look at
the devastated girl when she was brought back to
camp in the ambulance, she knew Colonel Holder
would not have the slightest notion about healing
Sarah's wounds. Cora was at once aware of the
deep scars that had been inflicted upon the girl's
mind and she wasted little time in ordering
Sarah's tent struck and moved next to her own.
Sarah was grateful for Cora's support and will-

ingly escaped into the open arms of the sergeant major's wife.

Colonel Holder was somewhat dismayed with his daughter's apparent dependence upon Mrs. Kennedy. He could not understand why Sarah resisted his urging to return East immediately. He would have thought she would be all too eager to escape from the scene of her brutal attack. He felt compassion for his daughter, but at the same time he could not help but feel it an injury to himself that his daughter had been violated by a savage Indian. He would not admit it, even to himself, but he would feel much more comfortable if the reminder of that insult to his person was removed from his sight.

A week had passed since her return to Camp Supply and while she was making some progress in her recovery, there was a stain on her mind that she feared she could never remove. She knew that she had been scarred by the ordeal suffered at the brutal hands of the Cheyenne. Try as she might, she could not escape the feeling that she was soiled beyond cleaning. When she allowed it—lying awake at night, or even during periods of the day when she was alone—her mind would reach out and snatch her back to that terrifying moment. She could still feel the searing penetration of her body and the horror that even now was alive and real. She would soon find herself reduced to a shuddering shell, fighting to free her mind of its burden. She wondered if her mind would ever be free of it.

Everyone in the camp made a special effort to be nice to her but she could still feel their stares whenever they thought she was not looking. Her father seemed unusually cold to her. His one thought seemed to be that she should leave. And she was not ready to leave. She did not feel she was healed inside and she wanted to stay near the only person who understood her feelings, Cora Kennedy. Cora mothered her and talked to her and tried to keep her busy helping her cook and clean and sew. Then, too, there was the matter of Stone Hand. Somehow she felt she would never be free of her feelings of guilt and defilement until the savage was dead. So she could not leave until the monster was executed.

All these things contributed to the state of fear and depression she now dwelt in. But the one thing that injured her most was the coolness of John Welch. He was there to greet her when she had first returned from her ordeal. He had been obviously worried and concerned for her safety and was anxious to offer his assistance as a physician. But the thing she needed was his understanding and a show of affection. For one who had avowed his undying love for her so recently, he was now conspicuously detached. It was not hard to guess that he now saw her as defiled, damaged goods, and certainly less desirable than the fresh young virgin he had sought to woo. It was difficult for her to un-

derstand why he looked at her as if she had somehow betrayed him. She had done nothing wrong.
His visits to her tent were polite and clinical with
no mention of picnics or evening rides. The visits
brought more pain to an already overloaded mind
and she finally told him it was no longer necessary
for him to call. He responded politely and graciously, saying that she could call on him anytime
she needed medical assistance.

There was one whose attitude had not changed
toward her, Jason Coles. If anything, he displayed a
tenderness and thoughtful concern that was quite
unexpected for one of his rough background. There
was an honesty about Jason that she knew was real.
He did not look down on her for having been
raped by the Indian and he constantly concerned
himself with persuading her that she should not be
ashamed of it either. She knew he only remained in
Camp Supply because of her. His work was ended
with Stone Hand in custody. Still he was there to
call on her at least once a day and sometimes more.
She wondered if he would leave after Stone Hand's
hanging, which was scheduled two days hence.
These were the thoughts that occupied her mind on
this bright summer morning as she sat outside
Cora Kennedy's tent, soaking in the sun's healing
rays, watching Jason Coles approach on horseback.

"Morning, Sarah." He stepped down from the
saddle and threw the reins loosely over the tent
rope.

"Morning, Jason," she replied.

"Right pretty morning, ain't it? How are you feeling?"

"Fine," she said, her tone not convincing. "Would you like some coffee? Mrs. Kennedy might have a biscuit left from breakfast if you're hungry."

She was at least making an effort to make light conversation, he thought. But the hurt was still in her eyes. "Why, yes, ma'am, I wouldn't turn one of Cora's biscuits down," he said, still looking deep into her eyes. He hated seeing her this way and he could not help but blame himself for much of her sorrow. It had been a mistake on his part, telling Colonel Holder that Sarah had been violated by Stone Hand. But dammit, he was her father. He hadn't expected the colonel to respond the way he did. If Jason had suspected that the colonel would inform John Welch about his daughter's tragic encounter, he would have lied about it. Still, he supposed the colonel thought he should seek medical advice—thought he was doing the right thing. The young doctor's reaction didn't help Jason's opinion of his integrity.

Cora, hearing the exchange from inside, came out with a cup of coffee and a plate with several biscuits on it. "I ain't never known you, Jason Coles, when you wasn't hungry." She offered him the plate then looked at Sarah. "You want some coffee, honey?" Sarah shook her head no.

"It's just that you make the best biscuits this side of the Canadian, Cora. Otherwise I'da said no."

Cora looked at him in mock disgust. "Jason, you're a bigger liar than Maxwell Kennedy." She placed the plate in front of him. "I ain't got time to chitchat with the likes of you. I've got chores to get done." She left the two alone to talk.

They sat in silence for a few minutes while Jason sipped the hot liquid. Sarah felt no pressure to generate polite conversation. Jason was as comfortable with silence as anyone she had ever met. When he had finished the biscuit he was working on, he threw out the dregs of his coffee cup and sat down facing her.

"I reckon you'll be thinking about going back to Baltimore before long."

"You, too?" she replied. Then realizing that he had meant no more by it than to ask an honest question, she quickly apologized. "I'm sorry, Jason. It's just that Daddy keeps pushing me to leave. I think he'll just be a lot more comfortable when I'm gone."

"Oh, I don't think that, Sarah. Your daddy's just awful busy, that's all. And he's worried about you."

She smiled at his efforts to reassure her. "Perhaps," she said. "But I think he'll be a lot happier to have me gone."

"Baltimore is a long way away from here," he said. "It's like another world. Folks back there don't even know there's a place like Camp Supply in the world."

She smiled again. His attempt to influence her attitude was so obvious that she could not resist teasing him. "You're not trying to work on my mind again, are you, Mr. Coles?"

He flushed. "Why no, ma'am, no such a thing."

"How about you? What are your plans? I guess you're going to wait around to see the hanging."

"I don't know. It depends, I reckon. I might go north. I've got me a little valley staked out up in Colorado territory that would make a fine place to raise horses. It might be time to quit chasing around after Indians and settle down. It's a mighty pretty little valley with good water and pastureland."

"It sounds like a peaceful place. Are you sure you're ready to settle down? It might be a lonely life."

"Well, yes, ma'am. It might be. I reckon it'd be a lot less lonely if I knew someone who wanted to go with me, raise a family maybe. It'd be a good life."

"Is there someone?" she asked.

He quickly responded. "No, ma'am. I reckon I'm still looking for the right kind of woman."

She smiled and looked directly into his eyes. "I hope you find her, Jason. You're a fine man and any girl would be lucky to have you as a husband." His eyes brightened for an instant, encouraged by her comment. Then she added, "She will have to be a woman of better stock than I. I don't think I could ever live in a wilderness like your valley."

No, I guess you couldn't, he thought. To her he said, "Well, I think I'll ride out for a little scout around the camp. Maybe I'll run across a deer or something. I'm getting downright tired of salt pork." He climbed up on his horse and turned to leave. As an afterthought he checked his horse and asked. "Are you going to stay on for a while?"

"I've been thinking about that and I've decided that maybe Daddy's right. There's no reason for me to stay here any longer. So I think I may as well go on back to Baltimore as soon as a patrol is heading back to Fort Cobb."

"Oh," was all he could reply for a moment. "Well, I'll see you later." He spurred his horse and rode away through the willows by the stream and out across the hills beyond.

He scolded himself for a fool as he rode away, blabbering on about his ranch in Colorado. When he took an honest look at the conversation he had just had, he realized that it must have seemed to her that he was hinting that she might go with him to his ranch. "Damn fool," he muttered. "I bet she got a good laugh outta that." Admittedly he had given it some thought, but it was more or less idle fantasy. He encouraged the little mare to pick up the pace, anxious to get far from the camp. "She like as not wouldn't make much of a wife out here. She's too used to city life. Hell . . ." He tried to dismiss it from his thoughts and decided a two-or-three-day hunting trip might help his mind right then.

Stone Hand stood motionless before the tiny window in the rough log guard house. He peered out through the iron bars for hours on end, looking toward the far hills. He drew his medicine from the hills. The spirits of the rocks and earth spoke to him. They told him that his medicine was strong, stronger than that of the soldier chiefs.

He ate very little of the food that was brought to him twice a day by the sentries, taking only a few bites now and then. He ignored the guard outside the window as well as the one by the door. At times he appeared to be in a trance, his eyes staring but seeming not to focus. It was during these times that he sought to communicate with the spirits and ask for their help to enable him to conquer his enemies.

He had very few visitors, since he had been a loner even among his own people. But there were occasional visits by one or two of the young men of the tribe. They would come from the reservation and stand outside the window and stare at the man who had taken so many white scalps, hoping to absorb some of his powerful medicine. Only occasionally would they speak to Stone Hand and he never responded beyond a grunt. It was a curious ceremony for the guards to observe. It was almost as though the Indians regarded the renegade as a spirit and they hoped to gain some measure of strength by simply being in his presence.

Because of the wall of silence between the reservation Indians and this most notorious of outlaws, the guard was quite surprised when a young Cheyenne of seventeen or eighteen brought the prisoner a corn cake wrapped in a cloth and asked if he could give it to Stone Hand. The guard permitted it but only after he had inspected the bundle and broken the bread into small pieces to make sure nothing was inside. Then he stepped back and motioned to the young boy to give it to the prisoner. He failed to notice the knife that was deftly slipped into the cloth as the boy pushed the bundle through the bars.

For the first time since Sarah had come to Camp Supply, John Welch declined an invitation to dine with the colonel and his daughter. The doctor was apologetic when he respectfully sent his regrets to his commanding officer, saying that he would not be able to return from the clinic at the reservation until late. Sarah was not surprised. John had avoided her since she had acquired the stigma of having been raped by an Indian. While she tried to convince herself that she would no longer have serious thoughts about the handsome young surgeon, still the rejection hurt her deeply. There was no way she could convince herself that her feelings for John were of a casual nature. She had fallen hard for him and it was not an easy thing to cast him from her mind. At times she almost convinced herself that she hated him when she thought about those terrified nights she had spent in captivity. She had prayed that John would find her, come to her rescue, and take her to safety in his arms.

She had always gotten more than the average amount of attention from the opposite sex, even when she was no more than a child. Now, to suddenly find herself undesirable and even to be avoided was enough to send her into a fit of depression. If her father shared her assessment of Captain Welch's attitude, he made no mention of it. He took John's excuse as legitimate and unavoidable. And since Jason Coles was out of the camp on a hunting trip, their only dinner guest was the colonel's adjutant, Captain Horace Sykes. Sykes was not much in the way of a dinner companion. He was a man of middle age and so boringly obtuse that the three of them ate in virtual silence for the most part of the meal. They had just finished eating and the men were lighting cigars when an enlisted man rushed in with the shocking report that chilled the blood in her veins.

"The Injun got away!" he blurted to the stunned diners.

"Stone Hand?" Colonel Holder gasped.

"Yessir," the excited trooper returned. "He killed both guards at the guard house, slit their throats and took off!"

There was a long moment of stunned silence before anyone spoke. Then the colonel. commanded, "Captain Sykes, mount a detachment right away. We can't let that devil get away!"

"Sir," Sykes responded, "you mean right now? I doubt if we'd have much luck trailing him in the dark."

Colonel Holder hesitated. "No, of course not, I mean have a detachment ready to move out at first light. Where's Jason Coles"

"He's not in camp, sir. I think he's on a hunting trip somewhere."

"Where? Did he say where he was heading?" Colonel Holder did not like vague answers when he needed action.

"I don't know, sir. You know Coles rarely tells anyone where he's going."

"Send somebody out to find him. Send one of the scouts. Tell him to get back here. I need him!"

Sarah, a terrified witness to the last few minutes, was aware only of the crashing beat of her heart against her breastbone. *He was out!* The beast had escaped, just as he had threatened when he promised to come back and kill her and Jason. Her brain was numb with fear as she sat silently at the table. The trembling in her hands went unnoticed in the urgency of the moment. Her father's excited orders to his adjutant and Captain Sykes's responses were but a distant echo in the far regions of her conscious mind, heard but not recorded.

There was only one image that dominated her mind and seared an imprint on her brain . . . *Stone Hand!* His evil face filled her mind's eye. He would come back! He would kill her!

The word spread quickly through the camp. When a sentry came to get the sergeant major, Cora Kennedy listened while she silently helped her husband on with his boots. As soon as he had left, her first thoughts were for Sarah Holder. She hurriedly picked up a shawl for her shoulders and went directly to the colonel's tent. Not pausing to announce her presence, she raised the flap and entered to find what she feared she might find. Sarah Holder was still seated at the table, her supper only half finished, her eyes staring but unseeing.

"Oh, dear God," Cora said. "You poor child." She went to the frightened girl and putting her arms around her, pulled her close to her bosom. "You poor child."

Sarah seemed to be in a trance. She did not respond beyond allowing herself to be cradled close to the older woman's heart. Cora recognized the signs she saw in the glazed eyes of the young girl. She had seen it before in the faces of children after an Indian massacre. The wide-eyed, nonseeing look of a stunned animal told her that Sarah was in deep shock. She helped her to her feet and with her arm around her shoulders she walked Sarah back to her tent and helped her down on her cot. Sarah, still trancelike, did as she was directed without resisting. "You just rest there a bit, honey," Cora said. "I'll be right back with the doctor."

Colonel Holder, occupied with his anger at having the notorious renegade escape, killing two of his men in the process, was unaware of his daughter's condition until he saw Captain Welch and Cora Kennedy coming out of Sarah's tent. He stopped abruptly as they approached him. "What is it?" he asked. "Is Sarah all right?"

Cora didn't wait for the doctor to respond. "No she isn't. Your daughter is bad off and she's going to need some attention."

Colonel Holder said nothing but glanced at John Welch, who spoke to confirm Cora's diagnosis. "I'm afraid this latest thing has caused Sarah to go into shock. She seems to have lost touch with reality for the moment."

The colonel was obviously taken aback. "What? Will she be all right?"

"I don't know. There's no way to tell on something like this. Usually, if it's not too serious, a person will come out of it in a matter of a few minutes to a few hours. We just have to wait and see."

"Can't you do something for her, give her something?" The colonel was impatient.

John shrugged his shoulders. "There's nothing I can give her. We just have to wait and see. She needs rest now. That's all I can suggest. Her body has to recover from the strain her brain is undergoing."

"Damn!" was all Colonel Holder could muster.

"I'll stay with her," Cora volunteered.

Holder was relieved. "Thank you, Cora. I really appreciate that. That devil is probably hightailing it as far away from here as he can run but I'm not taking any chances with that maniac. I'll have a guard detail stationed by her tent." He immediately turned his attention to the sergeant major, who was approaching from the command tent. "Somebody find Jason Coles!"

"I'm sending two scouts in opposite directions to find him. As soon as they get enough light to see, they'll be on their way."

CHAPTER 9

Jason stood for a few minutes, watching the lone rider in the distance until he was certain the man was definitely coming his way. Though the rider was still little more than a black speck pulling a small dust cloud, Jason felt it prudent to back his horse down below the crest of the hill. It was best to keep out of sight until the traveler was identified. There seemed to be little doubt the man was following the river and he appeared to be in a hurry. Jason dismounted and situated himself in the tall buffalo grass just below the crest of the hill. He checked his rifle and laid it down on the ground beside him and watched the horseman approach. Below him, beneath the crest of the hill, Birdie snorted, now aware of the approaching horse. Jason gazed at his horse for an extended moment. Birdie was a dependable mount but she was no match for Henry. Jason sorely missed Henry. He felt his loss more than for that of any horse he had ever owned. The little mare was a willing replacement though and Jason resolved not to become so attached to her as he had to Henry. Max Kennedy jokingly referred to Jason's horses as the ugliest collection of uncurried flesh on the prairie, but Jason knew his Indian ponies were head and shoulders above the army's sleek mounts when it came to taking care of a man in the open.

He glanced back in the direction of the approaching rider. He could make out the man's features now as he neared the bend in the river below the hill Jason was crouched upon. It appeared to be Long Foot, one of the colonel's scouts. He was easy to recognize by the way he rode slouched over in the saddle, giving the impression that he was sleeping as he rode. Jason stood up and took the few steps to the top of the hill.

"Long Foot!" he yelled, waving his arms above his head.

The scout pulled up short at the sound, and wheeled his pony around toward the source. Upon seeing Jason, he immediately urged his pony up the hill.

"What you in such an all-fired hurry for?"

The scout dismounted even before his horse stopped, running the last few steps to keep from falling. "Colonel say you come, damn right."

"What for?" Jason asked. It was plain to see there was urgency in the command. What, he wondered, was so important that Long Foot was sent in search of him. Before Long Foot could answer, he asked, "How'd you know where to find me?"

The Indian smiled. "Long Foot damn good tracker."

"Horse piss." Jason grunted. "If I hadn't hollered, you'd still be riding down the river."

Long Foot shook his head. "No. Long Foot find you. Damn right." The smile faded from his face when he remembered the urgency of his mission. "Colonel say you come," he said. "Damn quick," he added.

"What's up?" Jason was already tying up his saddle pack, preparing to ride.

"Stone Hand."

"Stone Hand? What about Stone Hand?" The name commanded immediate concern.

"Him fly. No hold spirit. Damn right!"

Jason was impatient. "Spirit my ass. Whaddaya mean, 'Him fly'? You mean he broke out? He's loose again?"

Long Foot grinned as he shook his head up and down with exaggerated vigor. It obviously brought some degree of amusement to the Indian. Even though in the pay of the U.S. Army, Long Foot, like many of the other Osage scouts, found it amusing that this one Cheyenne renegade gave the soldiers fits. There was no need to encourage Jason to hurry. His thoughts were already concentrated upon Sarah and what terror might be going through her mind, for good reason, too. That savage was sure to want to take his revenge for the shame she had inflicted upon him.

There were still a couple of hours before dark so they set out for Camp Supply. A couple of hours were all they figured they could push Long Foot's horse anyway. The pony had been ridden hard all day to find Jason and probably couldn't have gone much farther. They made camp by a muddy creek to rest the horses and pushed on early the next morning.

Sergeant Major Maxwell Kennedy stood outside the headquarters tent and watched the two riders cross the stream by the willows. He knew who it was even though the fading light of day cast long shadows across the shallow stream. When they pulled up in front of the tent, he greeted them.

"Well, I see Long Foot found you."

"More like I found him," Jason responded as he stepped down from the mare. "What the hell happened, Max?"

Kennedy filled him in on the details of the renegade's escape. Jason listened, his face a mask of serious concern. When Max finished talking, Jason asked, "How is Sarah taking it?"

Kennedy paused and shook his head slowly. "I swear, Jason, I ain't sure that girl's gonna keep her sanity. Cora's taking care of her. Sarah won't hardly let her out of her sight." He pursed his lips tightly and shook his head again. "It's sad. I swear, it's sad." He paused again, as if thinking about what he had just said. Then he looked up directly into Jason's eyes. "Colonel Holder started yelling for you as soon as he found out Stone Hand had escaped. I reckon he figures, next to Sarah you're the one that bastard wants the most and maybe you'll get him before he gets you."

Jason did not respond right away, his mind occupied with a picture of a distraught Sarah Holder. Kennedy's words brought no fear for his own safety. In spite of what the reservation Indians thought, Stone Hand was a man and Jason feared no man. "Where is the colonel?"

"He's out with a patrol. He's taken to going along on patrols the past few days."

Jason nodded his understanding. "Max, you've got a whole bunch of scouts in camp, some of 'em damn good." He glanced at Long Foot, still sitting his pony as evidence. "You telling me can't none of 'em pick up that devil's trail?"

Kennedy followed Jason's glance at Long Foot then locked his gaze on Jason's eyes again. "Jason, don't none of 'em want to pick up his trail. They're all spooked by that bastard. He's got 'em all convinced he's some kind of spirit or something. Won't all of 'em admit it, but they all think it."

"Shit!" Jason responded in disgust, knowing that by now there was no trail to follow. "Any notion where Stone Hand might be?"

"None."

"Where are the patrols looking?"

Kennedy shrugged. "Anywhere . . . everywhere. They're just covering section after section. Hell, he could be anywhere."

"That's a fact. Well, he'll probably show his hand again now. Somehow he always seems to know when I'm in camp." He glanced accusingly at Long Foot, who returned his gaze with an expression of innocence. "I'm going to take care of my horse. Then I reckon I'll look in on Sarah."

Kennedy nodded then said, "Cora's in there with her now. She spends most of the time with her."

Jason was shocked when he saw Sarah Holder. She was pale and obviously distraught. The flame of youthful enthusiasm and almost constant cheerfulness had given way to a hollow-eyed wariness that left her with a haunted spirit. It seemed a strain to fashion the faint smile she managed for Jason.

"Jason Coles," she quietly announced as he stepped inside the tent flap after nodding a brief greeting to the sentry stationed outside.

"Sarah."

Evidently his concern was written plainly on his face upon first seeing her, for she was quick to comment. "I must look a real sight." She reached a hand up in a halfhearted gesture to smooth her hair. "I haven't been feeling really well lately."

"Sarah, I don't like the way you're looking right now."

She interrupted before he could finish his statement. "Oh? I'm sorry you don't find me attractive." Her attempt at humor was obvious and rather feeble, her smile forced and unconvincing.

"You know what I mean," he retorted, ignoring her coy remark. "You've let this thing get to you. You've got to snap out of it and get hold of yourself. You can't sit around in this tent, hanging on Cora's apron strings." Her expression told him that he was just talking to hear himself make noise because she wasn't buying it. "I won't try to lie to you. You're in danger as long as that devil is loose. But you've got to go on living. Even that madman isn't crazy enough to show his face here. He ain't likely to take on a whole cavalry regiment just to get to you."

She simply stared at him for a long while before finally speaking, her voice barely above a whisper. "The Indians say he's a spirit."

He was exasperated. "Do you believe that?"

"I don't know . . . no. It's just that he does seem to be able to go anywhere he wants."

He reached down and tilted her head up toward him, forcing her to look into his eyes. "He's mean and he's slick. But he ain't no spirit. Your daddy, the U.S. Army, and Jason Coles are all determined he ain't gonna cause you any more trouble. He'll slip up somewhere and, when he does, I'll be right there to nail him." He took both her hands in his and smiled. "Now I want to see the old Sarah back again. Don't let that devil get into your mind."

She made an effort to return his smile. "I'll try," she said. "I guess you're right. I shouldn't let him take over my mind."

He gave her hands a little extra squeeze before releasing them. "Good girl. I'll talk to you later." He got up to leave. "You need to get out of this tent for a while and get some fresh air. Do you good. You're looking too pale to suit me."

She smiled. "Yes, I know. You've already told me you didn't like the way I look."

CHAPTER 10

John Welch glanced up to see the tall scout approaching the field clinic. He couldn't help but think the man looked as much like a savage as those he hunted. John did not deny the need for Indian scouts but he had little use for white men who turned savage, as Jason Coles obviously had. If a man's profession was to fight the Indian, then he should be wearing a uniform. There were plenty of real Indians to do the scouting. Deep down he harbored a real dislike for Jason Coles. Maybe it was because he was so cocksure of himself. Maybe it was his air of independence. John wasn't sure. He just didn't care for the man.

"Coles," he acknowledged as the scout pushed the tent flap back and entered.

"Captain," Jason returned.

"What can I do for you?"

"I wanted to talk to you about Miss Holder."

"Oh?" John raised an eyebrow, wondering what concern it was of Jason's.

"Yeah," Jason continued, failing to notice the raised eyebrow. "I'm real concerned about her. I mean the way she's taking this thing, moping around that tent all day. I'm afraid she's going to get funny in the head about it if she doesn't let it go."

"How did you think she would react, being raped by a savage? I'd be surprised if she behaved any other way."

Jason was impatient. "I know, I know, but ain't there anything you can give her to ease her mind or something? Maybe you could spend some time with her . . . something."

"I've already seen her. There's nothing physically wrong with her. She'll probably get over it in time and I'm pretty busy in the clinic right now."

Jason looked around at the cots, which were empty except for one trooper in the corner. "Yeah, I can see that." He wasn't sure why he had bothered to come see the surgeon. He didn't like the man and he liked him even less for his attitude toward Sarah since her return from captivity. He wished it wasn't so but a big part of Sarah's problem was the fact that Welch had avoided her like the plague since her tragedy. "You sure as hell had a lot more time for her before she got raped. I don't reckon that had anything to do with it, did it?"

John recoiled from the comment. "What . . . ?" he stammered. "I don't think I like your impudence, Mr. Coles. My personal business is none of your concern. Now you can get the hell out of my clinic!"

Jason did not reply for a moment. He stared straight into John's eyes, his contempt undisguised. "You sorry son of a bitch. I reckon she ain't good enough for you now, is she?"

"Get out!" John shouted. When Jason did not move, he called for the orderly at the front of the tent. "Walters! Escort this man out of the clinic!"

Walters responded when ordered to but he didn't exhibit a great deal of enthusiasm. He nervously measured the considerable bulk of Jason Coles with his eyes before glancing back at the mortified captain. Jason turned toward him.

"Don't get excited, boy, I'm leaving." He had no quarrel with the orderly but he was sort of hoping the doctor would try to physically remove him from the tent. He wondered how satisfying it would be to plant his fist in the middle of that pretty face.

Walters was visibly relieved as he stood aside and watched Jason exit the tent. Outside, Jason pulled his hat brim down against the glare of the afternoon sun and stood there a moment thinking about the confrontation with John Welch. He didn't feel good about it. It bothered him to have angered the surgeon. He *was* a sorry son of a bitch as far as Jason was concerned and needed to be told so. No, he was angry that Sarah cared for the man and that his attention was really what she needed at that moment. And he was disgusted with the shallow young officer for turning his back on Sarah when she was in such desperate need of understanding from everyone who cared anything about her.

Across the hard-baked clay of the makeshift parade ground, Cora Kennedy paused to watch the figure just emerged from the clinic tent. She had heard the shouted order to "Get out!" and had stopped to see who had been ordered from the doctor's tent. Seeing who it was, she somehow sensed what had caused the young surgeon's ire to rise. She, too, was aware of the coolness that had followed John Welch's call on Sarah when Jason brought her back into camp. For a man who was so passionately courting the young lady, he sure came up short when it really mattered. He had not been back to see Sarah since her tent had been moved next to Cora's. It was not the child's fault that she had been violated. It was not right to condemn her for it. Her opinion of John Welch had plummeted after that. She put aside her sewing and went to see how the girl was doing.

Long Foot squatted low on his haunches and studied the faint hoofprint only partially visible on the grassy bank of the trickle of water that etched a line down the length of the ravine. He said nothing for a long time, continuing to stare at the print as if trying to read into it. Finally he stood up and called out to Jason, who was further down the stream searching the bank for sign. "Here."

Jason came back to him immediately. "Where?"

"Here," Long Foot repeated, pointing to the faint markings in the grass.

As Long Foot had done, Jason squatted to examine the print. After a moment, he said simply, "Stone Hand."

"Damn right," Long Foot replied. "Long Foot damn good scout."

He was a good scout all right. Jason couldn't deny that because that one faint print seemed almost impossible to find. Long Foot was damn good . . . or lucky. Either way they had something to go on when it seemed they were going to have to give up on a trail they had followed for half a day. It had not been an easy trail, Stone Hand's trail never was. Jason suspected the renegade had not given any thought to the notion that he was being trailed. Still his trail was hard to follow because of his natural instinct to be evasive in all his comings and goings. For that reason one could never assume a destination simply because the tracks were leading in a certain direction. With Stone Hand, they were sure to change directions several times before finally leading to an end. There was no guarantee it was Stone Hand they were trailing but the attack on the stagecoach looked to be his work. There had been no survivors among the three passengers, the driver, and the guard. And the guard, his body mutilated, was missing his left eyebrow. If it wasn't Stone Hand, someone was using his signature.

"My guess is he's heading for that Commanche camp to trade whatever he got off the stage." He glanced at Long Foot for confirmation and received an affirmative nod of the head. "According to them Pawnee scouts of Colonel Holder's, that bunch of Commanches moved north to the fork of the Washita after the colonel raided their camp."

"Damn right, maybe," Long Foot solemnly agreed.

They mounted and rode off in the direction indicated by the print even though it led away from the fork of the Washita. After another change in direction back to the north, the trail petered out and once again the illusive Stone Hand seemed to have vanished.

"Shit!" Jason exclaimed in disgust after searching the grassy hillside for some sign. "This ain't getting us nowhere." He jerked Birdie's head around to the north. "The bastard is more'n likely heading to the Commanche camp. We're just wasting time here." Long Foot followed as he galloped off toward the fork of the Washita.

They found the camp right where the Pawnee scouts had said it would be. The colonel's raid had reduced the number of tipis to about twelve, still too many for Jason and Long Foot to ride into. So they hid their horses and crawled up to a place behind a couple of fallen trees and watched the camp for some sign of Stone Hand.

After a few hours, night began to descend upon the camp. Still there was no sign of the Cheyenne renegade. Finally, after the cookfires were dying out, Jason gave up the vigilance. He had guessed wrong, he figured. There was nothing left to them but to return to Camp Supply and wait for another lead.

It was the middle of the afternoon when Jason and Long Foot crossed the creek and skirted the willows where Sarah and John Welch had spread out their picnic blanket. Jason only glanced at the spot as he let Birdie pause for a drink before riding into the camp. Long Foot split off and made straight for his tent while Jason went to report to the colonel.

"Hello, Jason."

"Max." Jason returned the sergeant major's greeting. "Is the colonel here?"

"Nope. He's over at the agency. Any luck tracking that renegade?"

Jason slowly shook his head. "Hell no. I thought we were on to his trail, followed it all the way to the fork of the Washita. Nothing. He just seems to vanish. I wish to hell I could tell you I knew where to look for him but I ain't got the slightest notion. Nothing to do but wait till he strikes again, slaughters some other poor farmer or stage driver."

"At least he's operating further away from here. Maybe he's not as bold as he used to be. Might be that he's decided it's healthier to stay away from Supply."

"I doubt it, Max. I think he's just biding his time. He ain't about to quit until he's had his revenge."

The sergeant major shook his head, his face reflecting the concern he felt inside. "Yeah, I reckon. Damn, I wish he'd stay away from here. Sarah's been getting better every day. At least she's getting outside the tent a little bit now. And she don't hang on Cora's apron strings like she was."

The thought of Sarah beginning to show signs of pulling out of the melancholy that had all but consumed her was good news to Jason. "I reckon I'll drop in to see how she's getting along."

"She'll be glad to see you. I believe she thinks a lot of you. At least she talks about you a helluva lot."

Jason didn't visibly react to Kennedy's comment but inside he could feel his heart skip a beat at the mere suggestion that she gave him more than a passing thought. He forced himself to linger awhile longer talking to Max before taking his leave and making his way toward Sarah's tent. If he had chanced to look back at the sergeant major when he walked away, he might have been embarrassed to see the broad smile on Kennedy's weathered face.

He tapped gently on the tent pole and waited. After a few moments, Sarah was in the doorway.

She smiled when she saw the tall scout standing there. "Well, Mr. Coles," she greeted him, her voice cheerful, with no trace of the melancholy that had burdened her the last time they had talked.

Jason was pleasantly surprised. "Well now," he started. "Ain't you as pretty as a prairie flower this afternoon."

"Thank you, sir." She smiled sweetly for his benefit. "I missed you."

"Well, I'm mighty glad to see you've perked up some. When I left I wondered if you were ever going to be yourself again."

"I decided what's done is done. I can't live the rest of my life being afraid to come out of this tent."

"Good for you." He reached out and patted her hand.

"Daddy said there was no reason to believe that monster is anywhere within fifty miles of here. It's been almost a month and none of the scouts have heard any word of him. I think he's not fool enough to remain this close to the regiment anyway, don't you?"

"Probably not," he said. He didn't want to tell her that he and Long Foot were pretty sure they had been on the renegade's trail only two days' ride from the camp. There was no need to put any fearful thoughts in her head. The colonel could be right and the Indian could be headed out of the territory. But Jason wouldn't bet on it.

"So I've decided to leave for Fort Cobb in three

weeks' time to arrange for transportation back home," she said.

"I reckon that is the best thing for you, to go on back East to where your friends are and where you don't have to sleep in a tent." He turned to leave but took only a couple of steps before turning around to face her again. "I'm going to be gone for about a week, I reckon. I should be back before you leave."

She stood up and offered her hand. "Take care of yourself, Jason Coles."

CHAPTER 11

Jason bent low to examine the mutilated body of a man, middle-aged perhaps, it was hard to tell for the body had been burned badly. The crude cabin was still smoldering. The killing was still fresh for the body smelled of charred meat. It would be a few hours before the stench of rotting flesh set in. Whoever had committed this atrocity was not long gone. The sign was too fresh. He glanced up when Long Foot signaled with his hand.

"Here."

Jason got up and went to the rear of the cabin, where Long Foot knelt beside another body, that of a woman. At first glance, the body appeared to be that of a man. Half buried under some charred timbers, her form was partially hidden. Her scalp had been completely lifted in an attempt to take all of the hair.

"Damn," Jason muttered softly.

Long Foot nodded solemnly. He turned the woman's head around so Jason could see the face.

The left eyebrow had been slashed from her face. "Stone Hand, damn right."

Jason nodded his agreement and continued to stare at the horribly mutilated corpse. "She must have had a beautiful head of hair for that devil to butcher her like that."

"Not long gone," Long Foot announced.

"Not long gone," Jason agreed. "Look around. Find a shovel or something and let's get these people into the ground. I reckon we can do that much for 'em."

"We need be quick. Damn right. Stone Hand not long gone."

They worked quickly, placing the two bodies into one shallow grave. They had never been this close behind the man they hunted and Jason knew they were spending precious time but he didn't feel right about leaving the bodies for the buzzards. As soon as the man and his wife were in the ground, he and Long Foot mounted and rode off to the north, following a trail that was unusually careless for the phantom he had tracked for so long.

It wasn't far before Stone Hand's natural bent for caution took over and the trail vanished at a shallow creek that was little more than a trickle. Jason and Long Foot scouted around until one tiny dislodged pebble and a partial print provided the clue they needed to determine the renegade's trail. Jason studied the print for a few moments and then stood up and looked in the direction the trail indicated. It pointed toward a low line of mountains. "That son of a bitch has a camp somewhere. Could be in those hills."

Long Foot shook his head no. "Them hills sacred. No Cheyenne go there, damn right."

"Why? Burial ground?"

"No, no burial ground. Sacred. Big Medicine. Spirit of rocks and trees live there. No Cheyenne go there."

"Maybe," Jason said, "but this ain't no ordinary Cheyenne." No one had ever known where Stone Hand's permanent camp was. Maybe that was the reason. Maybe Stone Hand wasn't afraid of the spirits. What better place to have a camp. "Come on. I don't want him to gain any more ground on us. We'll stay hard on his trail but I'm betting he heads up into those sacred mountains of yours."

"No Cheyenne go there, damn right," Long Foot mumbled as he followed Jason's lead.

It was a hard trail to follow. Jason expected no less after many weeks of trying to track the elusive Indian. They lost it time and again but they were dogged in their determination not to lose him. Jason could feel it this time. He felt the nearness of the renegade. They were close. The Cheyenne was clever but Jason would not be denied. The trail was fresh, they both felt they had closed the distance between them and the renegade. And then it ended . . . in the middle of nowhere . . . leaving them staring stupidly at a sheer rock wall at the end of a box canyon.

"Damn!" Jason swore and pulled Birdie up short. He quickly wheeled his horse around and dismounted. "He gave us the slip. We missed it somewhere, dammit. He damn sure didn't ride up that cliff."

Long Foot looked about him furtively. "Some people say he's a spirit."

"Don't start that shit. He's about as much a spirit as my horse."

"Damn right," Long Foot said, nervously searching the canyon walls with his eyes.

It was easy to see why they had missed it the first time. A gnarled old tree that appeared to be growing right out of the middle of a huge boulder hid the gulley directly behind it. The gulley cut through the rocks and led up into the hills. It was pure luck that led Jason to the crude trail when he decided to dismount and relieve himself under the scant shade of the twisted old tree.

"Well, I'll be damned," he muttered, then called Long Foot, who was still scouting the trail behind them. When Long Foot joined him, he said, "We could have scouted this place all day and not found this trail."

Long Foot bent low to examine the faint impression in the dirt. "Hoofprint, damn right." He rose to his feet and stepped back to gaze up into the forbidding hills. "This bad place, damn right."

Jason studied the Indian's face for a moment. He knew what he was thinking without asking. Long Foot had no stomach for climbing up into these "sacred hills" and the fact that Stone Hand had ascended this trail probably more than convinced him that the renegade was some kind of evil spirit. He climbed up on Birdie, still watching Long Foot. "Come on. He's getting a lead on us."

Long Foot did not budge. "Can't go there. Spirit of rocks and earth live there." He looked at Jason apologetically then added, "Damn right."

"Ah, horseshit! If any spirits lived up in them hills, they sure as hell wouldn't tolerate a no-good son of a bitch like Stone Hand. This is just another pile of rocks and dirt like all the other hills around here. Only this one must have Stone Hand's camp hid up there somewhere."

"This place bad, damn right," was all Long Foot would offer. It was obvious the Indian had no intention of risking his soul by defying the spirits.

"Well, I'm going after him. You scout around the north end of this hill, see if you can find a way around to the other side. There might be a trail coming out." He nudged Birdie and started up the narrow trail into the boulders.

The going was hard for the first hundred yards. After a steep climb through huge boulders that appeared to have been strewn over the hills by some giant hand, the trail widened by a good six feet. Still it wound through the giant maze, climbing at a more gradual rate now. The place had an eerie quality about it. It seemed of another world. Little wonder the Indians thought it a supernatural place, inhabited by spirits. Jason could not help but feel the foreboding atmosphere that seemed to permeate the rocks and sand. There seemed to be no living thing here.

The trail was plain to see at this point. There was no effort to hide it. It would have been pointless at any rate because the narrow passage through the boulders was the only access Jason could see. Because of that, he constantly watched the rocks above him. The trail was made for ambush and by this time Jason had a feeling that Stone Hand knew he was being trailed. Long Foot would tell him he was foolish to continue up the narrow cut in the rocks. Death could be waiting around any of the many turns in the trail. Knowing this, his nerve endings seemed to be tingling, so strong was the presence of Stone Hand.

He dismounted and looped Birdie's reins around a scrubby bush that was growing between the rocks. He was close to the savage. He could sense it. He drew his rifle up close in front of his chest and started walking toward the next bend in the narrow passage. Suddenly a small bird fluttered off her nest, scolding loudly as she passed directly over his head, and it occurred to him that there had been no sound of any kind before that. He stopped stone still. Maybe he had scared the bird but his in-

stincts told him different. He took it as a warning
and dropped to his hands and knees, watching the
jagged column of rock that hid the trail beyond the
turn ahead. His nerve endings were alive. This was
it, his instincts told him. He knew Stone Hand was
waiting on the other side of the jagged column.
Slowly he inched up to the rock, glancing overhead
every few seconds, expecting an attack at any instant. Everything was quiet again, as quiet as
death, as he advanced inch by inch toward the
edge of the rock. He knew that hell itself would be
waiting beyond that rugged monument. Still he
pushed ahead until he reached the very edge of the
boulder. He stopped and listened. The silence was
stifling. Very carefully, he rose to one knee and listened. After a few moments that seemed more like
an hour, he decided it was time to fish or cut bait.
He knew he had to move fast if he was going to
catch Stone Hand by surprise. He took a couple of
deep breaths and prepared to leave the safety of the
boulder. Once he committed, it would be a question of who caught who by surprise. He hesitated a
moment more. "What the hell," he mumbled and
launched himself, rolling across the narrow trail.

He came to rest on his belly, his rifle raised and
ready to fire at whatever he came face-to-face with
on the narrow path. There was no one there. The
path was empty. Jason quickly scanned the trail
from side to side, his rifle aiming and in sync with
the movement of his eyes. He lay still for a mo-

ment, his breathing the only sound he heard. He had been sure Stone Hand was waiting for him on the other side of the boulder. Lying there, pressed against the rock wall of the trail, he looked further up the trail. Up ahead the path widened again. And beyond that he could see a small open area of grass and a few scraggly trees.

He rose to his feet. So, he thought, the renegade did have his secret camp up here. No sooner had he thought it when he was spun around by the impact of the lead slug into his shoulder, knocking him to the ground once more. The crack of the rifle reverberated through the narrow stone walls as he rolled over on his back, fumbling desperately to bring his own rifle to bear. Stupid! he thought, for having presented the Indian with a stationary target. The narrow canyons exploded with the eerie scream of a Cheyenne war cry as Stone Hand leaped from the rocks above, his war ax poised to finish the wounded scout.

In the time it took for Stone Hand to close the distance between them, which was barely seconds, Jason calmly raised his rifle and took dead aim. He fired twice, cutting the Indian down not ten feet from him. By then the pain in Jason's shoulder had increased until it felt like a fire was burning in his flesh and his arm became numb and useless. He raised the rifle with one hand and held it on the crumpled body before him. For a few seconds,

Stone Hand did not move. Then he slowly began to struggle to pull himself up to his knees.

Jason strained to raise the rifle to bear on the man in front of him. Stone Hand pushed himself up on his feet, his right hand holding his side in an effort to stem the flow of blood that covered his fingers. Dazed and confused by the stinging fire in his midsection, he glanced at his rifle, lying some ten feet away in the sand. Jason could see that the savage was thinking of attacking again but the sight of the rifle pointing at his stomach caused him to reconsider. He seemed puzzled that the white scout did not shoot him again. Instead, Jason continued to hold the rifle on him. Stone Hand could not know that the hand that held the rifle had gone completely numb and was incapable of squeezing the trigger.

With obvious effort, Stone Hand backed slowly up the trail, watching Jason intently.

Jason did not move, he couldn't. He simply sat there, his rifle aimed at the renegade, who appeared to be dragging himself off to die like a wounded coyote. At that point Jason was content to let him go. He couldn't get far before he was bound to collapse. Jason was sure of this, just as he knew from having been shot before that the numbness would soon leave his shoulder to be replaced by intense pain.

He sat there until Stone Hand was out of sight around a bend in the narrow passage. As he had anticipated, he slowly regained the use of his arm, although the pain was like a hot knife. Slowly, and with great effort, he pushed himself up, using the stone wall of the passage for support. On his feet at last, he waited for a few moments until he was sure he was steady. He ejected the spent shell from his rifle and cautiously inched his way up the trail after Stone Hand. He was aware now of the pounding in his chest. His heart was hammering against his ribs as he focused his eyes on the bend in the passage, ready for what might be lying in wait for him. Still he advanced slowly toward the turn, step by step. He was certain he had gotten the best of the brief encounter. The Indian had been hit twice, hurt too badly to fight. Jason knew a kill shot when he saw one and it was his guess that he had dragged himself off to sing his death song. Still he would exercise extreme caution, just as he would with a rattlesnake until he was sure it was dead. He was even with the stone corner of the bend now and once more he steeled himself for the sudden exposure he must make. As before, he made his move quickly with rifle raised and ready to fire. But there was no one there. He stood there for a few moments, his heartbeat pounding in his ears. He heard his rifle clatter on the rocks at his feet and realized he had dropped it. His arm had gone numb again. He pulled his pistol out of his belt with his left hand and moved again up the trail.

At first Jason thought the renegade had disappeared into thin air again. A second look told him he was wrong for there was a trail of blood leading to an opening in the rock wall of the passage. Jason quickly moved to the opening and slipped inside, dropping to one knee as soon as he was out of the sunlight and engulfed in the cool darkness of the opening. It was a foolish move, he told himself, going into a cave after a wounded animal. But it was too late by then. He had committed himself. Hugging the side of the cave, he blinked rapidly, trying to see where he had landed. After a few moments with no bullet ripping into his flesh, he assumed he was not going to die after all, at least not at that moment. Gradually his eyes adjusted to the darkness and he could see that he was indeed inside a small cave in the rocks. There was a passageway leading off to the rear of the cave. Obviously this was where the wounded man had dragged himself. Jason followed. He knew the man was dying, otherwise the savage would not be on the run. He would have tried to set an ambush.

His eyes were totally adjusted to the darkened passage now and he could see that he was in a stone chamber that had once been a waterway, probably centuries before, maybe before man ever set foot on the land. The walls were smooth and worn, the floor solid rock, covered now by a thin layer of dust. In the twilight of the tunnel numerous streaks of fresh blood glistened in the wayward rays of sunlight that managed to filter through the cracks in the ceiling. Jason continued slowly, his body close against the wall of the tunnel, wary of the ambush he might be advancing toward. Still he pushed on. He wanted to confirm his kill.

And then the tunnel ended, closed off by a solid wall of rock. Jason stopped cold and immediately dropped to one knee, searching both sides of the cave, overhead, behind him. Where did the trail go? He could feel his heart pounding again as he braced himself for the attack he feared was coming. Where was the bastard? He was beginning to think the Indians' tales about Stone Hand were true. Maybe he was a spirit. He damn sure vanished within this stone tomb. There was no possible explanation for it. The light was not good in the passage but he could definitely pick up the trail of blood leading to the stone wall at the end of the tunnel. There was a dark area directly before the wall, darker than the rest of the floor that led up to it. Jason inched forward to inspect it when he realized that it was a hole in the floor of the cave. His heart was racing again. This was where the savage had disappeared to.

Exercising extreme caution, he peered over the edge of the hole into empty black space. He backed away for a moment to consider the apparent probability. There was no doubt that the Indian had taken this way out. The hole was just wide enough to permit a man to drop into it. There was no telling how deep it was or what lay at the bottom of it. He looked around until he found a sizable rock, then he dropped it into the hole and listened. He counted to eight before he heard the rock contact what sounded to be water. "That's a helluva drop," he muttered.

Jason backed away from the hole and sat down with his back against the wall of the cave. By now his wound was burning with a numbing pain and he knew that he had to take care of it pretty soon. But first he had to think over the events of the previous minutes. The Indian had been wounded pretty seriously when he dragged himself in here to die. It did not surprise Jason that Stone Hand would fling himself into the dark pit rather than have his body mutilated or taken back to the reservation for display. Jason didn't blame him but it wasn't the way Jason wanted to end it. Now the reservation Indians would be convinced Stone Hand was indeed a spirit with no body to exhibit as proof of his destruction. The colonel would be disappointed but there was nothing he could do about it.

He sat there for a long while before deciding the incident was a closed one. Weak from the pain of his wound, his body suddenly weary, he struggled to his feet and retraced his steps back out into the bright sunlight. Tired as he was, he seemed to appreciate the warmth of the sun in a new way. It felt good on his back. He looked up at the sky and noticed for the first time that day how blue it was.

"It's a whole lot better world with that son of a bitch at the bottom of that hole," he said.

Long Foot was waiting beside the crevice at the base of the mountain. He had positioned himself with his back against a huge boulder, facing the start of the hidden trail, his rifle lying ready across his lap. When he heard the sound of approaching hoofs, he slowly raised his rifle and aimed at the opening behind the gnarled old tree. Great was his relief when he recognized Birdie's white face. Still he kept the rifle trained on the figure on Birdie's back until he was clear of the branches of the tree and he could see that it was Jason. The relief was apparent in his face. "Damn," he muttered.

Jason could not help but be amused by the somber Indian's expression. "What's the matter with you? You look like you didn't expect me to come back."

Long Foot got to his feet. "Maybe, maybe not, damn right." He climbed on his horse and rode to meet Jason. "I hear gunshots. Stone Hand get away?" Then he noticed Jason's arm hanging limply at his side and the blood streaking his buckskin shirt. "Damn. You shot!"

"Me shot all right," Jason returned, mocking the scout's broken English, "and I need to get it bandaged up pretty quick."

"I find water on other side of mountain. Follow me and I fix up wound, damn right."

Long Foot did a first-rate job of cleaning out his

wound and applying a bandage made from a sleeve of Jason's one clean shirt. While he was being doctored by the scout, Jason recounted the events that had taken place in the narrow walls of the trail up the mountain. Long Foot was visibly upset that Jason had not brought Stone Hand's body back, or even a scalp, as evidence of the renegade's death. He was relieved somewhat when Jason assured him that he had damn near cut him in two with two rifle slugs in his midsection before the Indian had plunged to his death. But he was not relieved to the point where he could rid his mind of the notion that Stone Hand might possibly be a spirit. Jason, exasperated with the scout, told him that he could crawl down that deep shaft in the floor of the cave and get Stone Hand's scalp if he wanted to take the chance on not being able to get back out.

"Not me. Damn right!"

Long Foot sat back on his heels and evaluated the work he had done on Jason's shoulder. He seemed satisfied it would do until they got back to Camp Supply. There, he suggested, it might be wise to let his sister-in-law take a look at it. She had the gift of healing.

"I'll be all right," Jason said. "You done a good enough job on it."

The ride back to Supply was long and uncomfortable for Jason. His arm hurt and the longer he rode, the more inflamed the wound became. By the time the tents of the army camp came into view,

Jason was feverish and slumping in the saddle. Long Foot had been watching him closely for the past several hours, even suggesting once that it might be wise to stop and rest. Jason insisted on continuing. He felt it important to let the colonel, and certainly Sarah, know that there was no longer any threat from Stone Hand.

Sick with fever, Jason was irritated by the feeling of growing helplessness that caused his brain to spin and he strained just to remain upright in the saddle. A few more miles, if he could just hold on, and he could rest. Long Foot was going to have to get the bullet out of his shoulder. That was a fact, for it had surely festered. The willows—he remembered seeing the willows by the stream that ran along the outside perimeter of the camp, the willows where Sarah and John Welch had picnicked— and then everything went black.

When he opened his eyes, he at first wondered if he was dead. The face looking down at him was surely that of an angel. Her dark eyes peered deep into his, searching, and when he blinked to make sure he was not seeing a vision, she smiled. Then he was certain she was an angel.

"You sleep a long time," the angel said, her voice soft as a summer breeze. He tried to sit up but she gently held him back. "Not yet. You are still too weak." He relaxed.

"Who are you?"

"I am called Magpie. I am Raven's sister." When

he still looked puzzled, she added, "Long Foot's wife."

"Oh, Long Foot's wife."

She laughed and he could not help but notice that the sound of her laughter reminded him of the music made by a busy mountain stream. "I am not Long Foot's wife. Raven is Long Foot's wife. I am Raven's sister."

For a reason he could not explain, he was glad she was not Long Foot's wife. He studied her face intently. Magpie? he thought. The name somehow didn't seem to fit the face he found so striking. It seemed more fitting that her name should be something more melodious, like Lark or Wren. So, he thought, my angel turns out to be Osage.

He turned his head to examine his shoulder. It was wrapped in a clean cloth and no longer throbbed, and he realized his dizziness was gone. "You take care of this?" She nodded yes. "Cut the bullet out?" She reached behind her and held up a lead ball. He grinned. "Then I reckon I owe you my thanks."

"I am happy that you are feeling well again. I worried about you. You were very sick."

"How long have I been sleeping?"

"Two days."

"Two days!" He bolted upright again. "Where am I, anyway?"

"Lie still," she cautioned, her voice calm and soft. "You'll start the bleeding again. You are here in Long Foot's tent at the soldier camp."

"I need to see the colonel," he protested.

She smiled and gently pushed him back down. "The soldier chief has already been here to see you. Long Foot has told him about Stone Hand. You must rest now."

He lay back and after a few minutes fell asleep again. His sleep was filled with dreams of Stone Hand and Long Foot, of Sarah and Magpie. Several times, in a state of almost waking, he was aware of a cool hand on his forehead. When next he opened his eyes, it was to behold the same angelic face that had been there before. It brought an instant feeling of contentment. In addition, there were two more sensations that he was acutely aware of—he felt like getting up, and he was starving.

While Magpie busied herself getting him something to eat, he was visited by Long Foot and his wife, Raven. Long Foot, especially, looked relieved to see his friend bouncing back to health. "I think you dead for sure, damn right," he announced.

Jason smiled. "I reckon this ol' hide's too tough to kill. I sure can't figure why I got so sick over a shoulder wound though."

"Stone Hand, his bullets make big medicine."

"I reckon," Jason agreed. "And I thank you folks for looking after me."

"Magpie took care of you. She wouldn't let anyone else near you." He looked at Raven for confirmation. She nodded in agreement.

CHAPTER 12

Colonel Holder frowned as he listened to Jason's accounting of the business of dealing with Stone Hand. He welcomed the news of the renegade's demise but he would have preferred to have a body to display for the reservation Indians. When Jason finished, he thanked him and expressed concern for Jason's wound. Jason assured him that it was not significant.

"You ought to have Captain Welch take a look at it," Holder advised.

Jason shrugged. "I reckon not. Long Foot's sister-in-law did a pretty good job on it." He didn't explain that he would damn near see his arm fall off before he would let John Welch look at it.

"Suit yourself." The colonel rose from his desk to shake Jason's hand. "Thanks, Coles, I appreciate your help on this thing. I know you just hired on to track that renegade down, but if you want to stay on awhile I can keep you on the payroll."

"'Preciate it, Colonel, but I reckon I'll take a ride

up to Colorado Territory. I want to get a cabin started before winter hits."

Holder smiled broadly. "I hear you saying the words but I just can't believe Jason Coles is ready to settle down in one spot."

Jason grinned. "Well, I don't guarantee I'll stay there but I'm ready to give it a try. I've been thinking about maybe taking a little trip over toward the Bitterroots to do a little trading with the Nez Percés. They've got a fine stock of horses that I'd like to breed."

"Appaloosa?"

"Yessir."

"You better watch your scalp, Coles."

There was scant need to warn Jason to be careful. His little valley was well hidden and he had never crossed trails with any of the mountain tribes, those that still roamed free of the reservation. But there were still a lot of free bands between his valley and the Bitterroots. The Shoshone and the Crow were usually friendly but he tried to avoid the Northern Utes and Blackfeet. There was never any thought in Jason's mind about foregoing the trip because of the potential danger. There was always danger. The simple fact was that the breed stock he wanted was in Nez Percé territory, so that's where he would go to get it.

He said his good-byes to Colonel Holder and went outside to find a stern-faced Maxwell Kennedy waiting for him. The sergeant major took him by the elbow and led him away from the head-quarters tent before he spoke. The look on his face told Jason that he wanted to talk about something awfully important. "Damn, Max, you look like you bit into something rotten."

The sergeant major ignored Jason's remark. The stern expression deepened. "So, you'll be leaving us?"

"I reckon." There was a moment's silence. "What's on your mind, Max?"

Kennedy looked quickly from side to side to make sure no one else was in earshot. "Sarah," he whispered.

"What about Sarah? I was just on my way to visit her. Is she all right?"

"The colonel is planning to send her back East, back to Baltimore."

This was not news to Jason. "The last time I talked to her she said that was what she wanted."

"I know, I know," Max returned. "But things have changed since you went out after Stone Hand."

"What things?" Jason prodded. He was beginning to become impatient with the sergeant major's hesitancy to spit it out.

Max hesitated, reluctant to say the words. "Well, for one thing . . . Sarah's going to have a baby."

The words hit him with much the same impact with which Stone Hand's bullet had smashed into his shoulder. A baby! His mind reeled for a moment. In considering all the trauma that had cascaded upon her as a result of the terrible ordeal with the savage . . . the assault, the violation . . . no one had even considered the possibility that she might have been left carrying the child of that murdering savage.

"My God, Max . . ." was all he could mutter for a few moments while his brain staggered back to an even keel.

"The colonel doesn't know. Cora made me swear not to tell him. She's afraid he might do something terrible if he knew. You know how damn proud he is."

"My God," he repeated softly under his breath. "That poor girl." He looked up quickly. "How's she taking it?"

"Hard. Cora's been afraid she's going to do something drastic." Max watched Jason closely, measuring the scout's reaction to the shocking news. He knew that Jason was more than a little fond of the colonel's daughter and he wanted to make sure the news of her condition didn't repel him. When he could see that Jason had nothing other than compassion for the girl, he said, "I thought you ought to know before you went to see her."

"Don't tell me. Let me guess. You don't like the way I look again." She said it with a hint of sarcasm but it was not vicious sarcasm. Had her expression not been so somber, it would have passed for a joke.

He had spoken not a word after his polite greeting upon entering the sergeant major's tent, where Sarah was sitting with Cora Kennedy. They were peeling potatoes when he tapped on the tent pole. It was obvious to her that the tall scout was having difficulty arranging his words for what he wanted to say. His expression told her that he had already been told of her condition. Cora filled the void.

"Well, for goodness sakes, look what drifted in from the hills." She got up, handing her pan to Sarah, and moved to the cookfire. "Come on in, Jason, there may be some coffee left in the pot. We heard you were mighty sick for a spell. I was thinking you should have seen the doctor but Max said your Indian friends were taking care of you."

"Much obliged," he mumbled when Cora handed him the cup. He moved over to a corner of the tent and sat down. "Yeah, they done a good job all right."

Sarah lowered her gaze back to the potato she was working on. "Sergeant Kennedy told you?"

He nodded. "What are you going to do?"

She glanced up, perplexed. "What do you think I'm going to do? I'm going to have a baby." Her gaze dropped back down to the pan of potatoes. "What choice do I have?"

"I mean, are you going back East?"

Sarah looked up again, her face a mask of anger

now. "I can't go back to Baltimore. Wouldn't that be wonderful? To show up at Mrs. Abigail Worth's School for Girls with my little half-breed bastard."

Jason felt almost scorched by the intensity of her eyes. He took a moment to answer, glancing at Cora Kennedy, who was standing motionless, the coffeepot still clutched in her hand. It was obvious that the topic had been discussed at length between the two of them without a satisfactory solution to the young girl's dilemma. "You'll stay here then?" he asked.

She was impatient with his apparent lack of understanding. "I can't stay here. I can't let Daddy know I'm going to have a baby. It would kill him."

"What are you gonna do then? Looks like you're either gonna have to let the colonel find out about the baby or let whatever you said her name was at the school know. What are you gonna do?"

"I don't know. It seems I don't have any other choices and neither of those two will do."

There was a long silence while Jason made up his mind to make his next statement. He got up from the camp stool and walked to the tent flap and tossed the dregs of his coffee cup outside. Then he handed the empty cup to Cora and turned to face Sarah. "There is one more choice if it wouldn't be too rude for you. You could come with me to Colorado. We could take Long Foot and his wife to help you with the baby. He's been talking about leaving Camp Supply anyway. Nobody here would have to know anything about it."

There was a silence longer than the one before. Neither woman spoke at first. Both stared open-mouthed at the scout, who was now flushing visibly after having blurted out his invitation. Cora looked at Sarah, her face brightened considerably, searching for the young girl's reaction to Jason's proposal. Sarah hesitated a moment longer before responding.

"That's sweet of you, Jason, but I don't think of you in that way. I'm fond of you but not in that way."

Jason was quick to explain. "Oh, no, ma'am. I didn't mean nothing like that." He had to admit that at one time he had considered the possibility but now he was not so sure. Sarah would always have a special place in his heart but she could never be the woman he could see in his future. He hastened to reassure her. "I meant that it would be a place to have your baby without anyone knowing. Long Foot's wife would more'n likely take the baby and raise it as her own. Indians are like that, especially Osage. They don't ever mind a few extra younguns in the tipi."

Cora looked from Jason to Sarah, then back to Jason, where she allowed her gaze to rest. She was thinking what a wonderful solution it would be if there were more to Jason's offer than just being a good Samaritan. Sarah could do a great deal worse than Jason Coles. As she studied Jason's eyes, she concluded there was no longing there. Pity, she thought, waste of a good man. She spoke up. "Seems like a mighty good solution to your problem, honey. Jason might have a pretty good idea there."

"Daddy would never stand for it . . . running off to the wilderness with Jason Coles. Why, he'd probably kill both of us."

"He doesn't have to know," Cora quickly replied. "He plans to send you back to Fort Cobb anyway. When you get there, instead of going on to the railroad, Jason can be there to take you with him. As far as your father will know, you'll be on your way to Baltimore."

Sarah gave the notion serious thought then she spoke. "You'd do that, Jason?"

"I would."

It was late summer when they left Camp Supply and started out toward the Colorado Territory. Sarah, with a military escort, traveled in the same ambulance that had delivered her to Camp Supply some months earlier. The only difference was the absence of Captain John Welch on this return trip. Jason, accompanied by the scout, Long Foot, Long Foot's wife, Raven, and Raven's sister, Magpie, set out in generally the same direction but on a different trail. Max and Cora stood with Colonel Holder and watched the departing parties until they had cleared the willows by the stream and plunged into the rolling prairie.

"Damn . . . excuse me, Cora . . . but I'm relieved to see that girl on her way back East." Colonel Holder exhaled. "She had no business coming out here in the first place. Folks back East just can't realize how savage these people out here are."

"That young lady has too much spunk to spend her life teaching little girls how to hold their teacups," Max said. "Yessir, that's quite a little lady you got there, sir."

The colonel ignored the remark, shifting his gaze toward the small party of four disappearing over a gentle slope in the prairie. "What do you suppose makes a man like Jason Coles want to go up into the mountains to settle down? I offered him a steady job here but he said he wants to raise horses."

"Hard to say, sir. Coles is a hard one to figure out." He stole a quick glance at his wife. She met his gaze with the hint of a smile.

"Took one of my best Osage scouts with him, too. Oh, well, I give him two months at the most. He'll be back." With that he turned and went inside to his desk.

Colonel Holder had expressed his relief at having his daughter on her way back East. He loved his daughter in his own way, certainly. After all, it was customary for a father to love his daughter. It was the right thing and Lucien Holder was always one to do the proper thing. But he had never been home long enough to become attached to Sarah. The periods between their seeing each other were so long that she seemed a stranger each time he returned home. He felt compassion for her and the tragedy she had suffered that summer but he could not overcome the feeling that he had personally been insulted by the brutal attack on his daughter. He wished that Sarah had not come to see him at all. Now, happily, she was on her way East and he could get back to the business of commanding his regiment.

CHAPTER 13

Sarah studied the broad back of Jason Coles as he rode easily in the saddle, moving with each rolling motion of his horse as if he were simply an extension of the little Indian pony. As for her, she was mounted on a roan only slightly smaller than his, one that he had picked for her because of its gentle nature and easy gait. Behind her, the somber Long Foot rode, slumped on his horse as if half asleep. Behind him, Raven and Magpie brought up the rear, leading three packhorses. It was a silent train for the most part, broken only by an occasional snort from one of the horses or a soft command from Long Foot to one of the women. The country they crossed was wild and empty of living things as far as Sarah could see. How, she wondered, could Jason possibly know where he was going. In all directions the landscape was the same. If he was uncertain at all, he gave no indication of it. She decided at first that he was using the position of the sun as a guide, but on the third day out from Fort Cobb, it turned cloudy and then completely overcast. It seemed to make no difference to the tall scout. He rode on, looking back occasionally to give her a reassuring smile. When they reached the mountains, he led them straight through the passes, never once hesitating or backtracking. Sarah was amazed at the man's sense of direction.

The riding was hard and boring. She had never spent so many long hours in the saddle and she was stiff and sore after the first day's travel. At least it was not as brutal and terrifying as the forced ride as Stone Hand's captive. As she followed along behind Jason, her mind wandered, daydreaming part of the time, wondering sometimes if she was making the mistake of her life—and always trying to avoid thinking about John Welch. Other times, she found it almost amusing to be in her situation. What would her friends back in Baltimore think if they could see her now, riding silently between Jason and Long Foot?

Then her mind settled on the two Indian women riding along behind. The one called Raven was a pleasant enough woman. At least she seemed to be to Sarah. They never communicated, because Raven could not speak English. But she always went promptly to work each time they made camp, never seeming to complain even though Sarah never shared the camp chores with her. Magpie was a different sort. Jason said she was Raven's younger sister but she did not favor Raven in the slightest. Where Raven was short of stature and well rounded in figure, Magpie was thin and taller with finely etched features that gave her a striking beauty. An odd choice of names, Sarah thought. Magpie, it didn't fit for one so blessed with her looks. Her beauty went unnoticed at first, simply because the girl seemed to have her head bowed all the time. After a few days on the trail, Sarah noticed a pattern of behavior developing with the young Osage maiden. Any time there was a stop to rest or eat, Magpie was quick to see if Jason needed anything. At first, it was under the guise of checking his wound but her attention to the tall scout continued after the wound really required no more attention. It amused Sarah because Jason didn't appear to notice, although he always had a smile for the young girl. Although Magpie and Raven never talked to Sarah, Raven always smiled warmly whenever their eyes met. Sarah decided she would be a good friend whenever they got to know each other a little better.

Long Foot was confused. Jason took this woman with him but they slept in separate blankets. He said nothing for the first two nights but his curiosity was eating him up and would not permit him to remain silent any longer. After the women had set up their camp on the third night, Long Foot came up to Jason as he hobbled the horses for the night.

"Women set up good camp. Damn right," he offered as a casual comment to start the conversation.

"Yeah," Jason agreed, "you got a right smart little wife there."

"You take colonel's daughter as wife?"

Jason, not bothering to look up, continued tying off the hobbles on Birdie. "Nope, I don't take the colonel's daughter as wife."

This served to further puzzle Long Foot. "Why not? She fine-looking woman."

Jason smiled up at his friend. "I'm just helping her, that's all." He winked. "And she is a fine-looking woman at that."

His answer did nothing to lessen Long Foot's puzzlement. "Then, why she come with us?" Long Foot had agreed to go with Jason to his valley and help him start his ranch. He had assumed Sarah had come with them for the obvious reason any woman rides off with a man.

Jason stood up. He looked at the Osage scout for a moment before deciding. There was no reason not to tell him that Sarah was going with him so she could have her baby. It wouldn't be a secret for much longer anyway. So he explained Sarah's reluctance to let her father know she was pregnant and, likewise, her reluctance to go back to her friends in the East and have her baby. Long Foot nodded solemnly, listening attentively, and appeared to understand the girl's feelings.

"You make baby?"

"No. I didn't make baby." Jason was willing to let it go at that but Long Foot was curious.

"Doctor make baby, damn right." Like most of the people in the military attachment at Camp Supply, Long Foot knew that John Welch had courted Sarah strongly before her misfortune. So it was natural to assume that the doctor may have fathered the child.

"No, dammit, it's not the doctor's," Jason's retort was sharp. "It ain't nobody's baby but hers."

Long Foot couldn't figure that one out. He puzzled over Jason's response for a long moment. Then enlightenment lit up his face gradually, like the rising of the sun in the morning, as he started to add it all up. His wide eyes and openmouthed expression told Jason that he understood. Jason cut him off as he was about to speak.

"That's right. It's his."

"Stone Hand!" he whispered. Then, as an afterthought, "Damn right."

Long Foot seemed very much in awe of Sarah after that, an attitude that disgusted Jason somewhat. It was as if she was like the Virgin Mary, carrying the seed of that evil spirit. Jason wondered if he was going to have to go back to the Oklahoma Territory and dig up Stone Hand's carcass just to show Long Foot he was a man, no more, no less.

It took over a week of hard riding to reach Jason's valley. At first Sarah dutifully kept track of the days and nights on the journey. Then one night she realized that she had lost count and could not recall what day of the week it was. She fretted over it for a while. It seemed important to know what day of the week it was. It wasn't long before the boredom of the trail caused her to lose interest so that she no longer cared what day it was or even what month it was. One day was like the next and the one before it. Because of this, it was a welcome sight when, after winding through a steep rocky pass and topping a fir-covered ridge, Jason halted the little party and said, "There it is."

At first sight she understood why Jason loved the little valley. It was just as he had described it back at Camp Supply, only the beauty of the green valley far surpassed Jason's words to describe it. The floor of the valley was green with lush grass, dotted with summer wildflowers. The gentle breeze that swept down from the northern end caused the grass to sway first one way and then another, causing the valley to churn like a gentle sea. She could see why Jason had picked it to settle in. The tall ridges on each side framed it with a protective rampart of aspen and pine. Above the ridges, stretching upward toward the clouds, the mountain peaks stood like silent sentinels. There was a feeling of safety about this place that told her she would be all right here.

Jason had told them that he had started a cabin the last time he came to the valley but had been able to complete no more than the main walls halfway up. But, as he explained, it was a good start and he should be able to complete the cabin in plenty of time before the nights began to chill in the fall. In the meantime, he had packed in a couple of tents that he had managed to confiscate from the quartermaster at Supply. They could live in those until the cabin was built. He was very contrite when he explained that he planned one of the tents for Long Foot and his women and the other he planned to share with Sarah. He was quick to assure her that he would arrange some blankets to insure her privacy. It was simply that tents were bulky items and he thought it best to pack one less if it wasn't absolutely needed. Sarah laughed at his concern for her modesty and informed him that if she didn't trust him to be a complete gentleman she wouldn't have come with him in the first place.

Raven was not content to live in an army tent indefinitely. She and Long Foot had lived in one for a short time in Camp Supply but in her mind it was no fit place for a family to live. She extracted a promise from Long Foot to go back to the prairie to hunt buffalo as soon as the cabin was finished. With such a rich source for lodgepoles provided by the valley, it would be ridiculous not to build a warm tipi. Jason promised her that he and Long Foot would go on a hunting expedition before the summer was ended. First, work had to be done on the cabin. She was content with the promise. In the meantime she and Magpie, with Sarah's help, went about the business of setting up their temporary home.

The days that followed were filled with hard work and no wasted time. Jason set in to the building of the cabin with a vengeance, determined that Sarah's baby would enter the world with a roof over its head. Raven and Magpie helped. Long Foot was not inclined to perform manual labor but Jason didn't care. The women were hard workers and Long Foot would more than likely have been in the way. Besides, it was necessary to have someone free to hunt for food and Long Foot was well suited to that task.

As the weeks passed, the little valley began to take on a more settled look. When Jason finished the cabin, he and Sarah moved inside. Long Foot and the two Indian women preferred to remain in the tent. The Osage scout said the little cabin was too much like living inside a tree. They took the tent that Jason and Sarah had shared and set it up in tandem with theirs, giving them a long, roomy abode, almost luxurious. Raven even backed off a little on her nagging for Long Foot to hunt buffalo for her tipi.

The weeks piled on top of each other until months had passed and the end of summer approached and was gone. The nights began to cool and the days shortened. Jason built a table and chairs and a platform for Sarah's mat so she wouldn't have to sleep on the earthen floor of the cabin. He offered to make one for Magpie and Raven, too, but they declined, preferring to sleep on their mats of buffalo hides and blankets. Jason had never fancied himself as much of a carpenter but he had to congratulate himself on the work he had done. It was a right tidy little cabin, snug and tight against the weather. Sarah was pleased and that's what mattered most.

With the passing of the summer, Sarah began to show, causing the other two women to constantly fuss over her. The time spent with Raven and Magpie seemed to be good for her. She began to teach them English and, reciprocating, they tutored her in their dialect. Once, when Long Foot returned from the hunt with a handsome mule deer, Raven dried and softened the hide and made Sarah her first buckskin dress. Sarah was delighted with the gift and found it to be much more comfortable in her changing physical state.

The relationship between Jason and Sarah was an equitable coexistence. They shared the cabin but Jason partitioned off a bedroom for Sarah and he slept on his pallet by the front door. For Sarah's part, she had found the tall scout fascinating in a wild sort of way from the first time she laid eyes on him. On considering his qualities, and she often did while watching him working to build their home, she admitted there was much to be admired in the man. Aside from his concern for her comfort and his willingness to take care of her while she carried the child of a savage renegade, he had become a trusted friend. She was grateful to the extent that she almost wished she loved him. But she knew that that would never happen. Sometimes she hated herself for it, but she still found her mind wandering back to that picnic by the willows and she knew John Welch would be forever in her heart.

The winter was mild for those parts and the little band made it through with few discomforts. There was snow, of course, there was always snow in the mountains, and the streams froze over for months. But they had stored plenty of meat and firewood and Jason had packed in ample supplies of baking soda and salt, coffee, and dried beans. So it was not a hard time by any stretch of the imagination. Still, it was joyous news to Sarah when Jason came in one morning after checking his traps to tell her that the ice in the stream was melting. The coming of the spring was so gradual that she wasn't really aware of it until, suddenly, one morning it arrived, seemingly overnight.

Spring! The word itself brought a shiver of anticipation to her spine. She looked down at her swollen belly, grotesque on her slender frame, and marveled that she did not explode. She was huge. She no longer walked, but waddled like a duck as she went about her daily routine. Magpie was especially fascinated with her condition and insisted on patting Sarah's rounded stomach every day . . . like patting a melon, Sarah thought, to see when it might be ripe. In her own mind Sarah hoped the birth would not be a difficult one. Her stomach was so huge and she remembered how violently ill she had been in the first three months. She constantly feared this offspring of

Stone Hand was going to prove to be from the same violent savagery that had spawned the father. Raven assured her that everything appeared normal and that she would take care of her. In the privacy of their tent, however, she would confide to Magpie that she had never seen an expectant mother swell so outrageously and she worried that something might be wrong with the child. The two women could not discount the possibility that an evil seed may have been planted. None of these thoughts were shared with Jason of course since it was obvious to them that the man set no store in talk of such things as evil spirits. They decided that it was no fault of Sarah's at any rate and they would help her have her baby, whatever it was. Long Foot, when apprised of their fears, held a more pragmatic opinion of the problem. "Wait till baby comes. If good baby . . . good. If coyote, kill it . . . damn right."

The snow melted in the mountain passes and still Sarah continued to swell. She became confined to the cabin due to a difficulty in walking. Jason began to worry that something was wrong and Sarah might be in danger if she didn't give birth soon. It got to the point where she could no longer stand without experiencing severe back pain, and lying on her pallet provided very little relief. Jason worried that it may not have been a good decision to bring her up into the mountains to have her baby. He even considered loading her up on a travois and taking her to see a doctor . . . and the only doctor he knew the whereabouts of was John Welch. When he broached the subject with Sarah, she told him in no uncertain terms that she would die first, rather than go back to Camp Supply with her belly the size of a small buffalo. So he had little choice but to watch her suffering and fret over his inability to do anything for her.

There were other things on Jason's mind that caused him to be anxious. Spring was developing into full bloom and he was eager to make the journey to the Bitterroots to trade for the horses that would be the foundation for his breeding. But he felt he could not leave before Sarah had the baby and the trip would take several weeks, weeks during which the women would be left alone. He needed Long Foot with him to help with talking to the Nez Percés. Jason knew Cheyenne well and he could converse a little in Commanche and Crow, but he had little knowledge of Nez Percé. Long Foot claimed to know the talk, damn right. There being nothing he could do to speed up the birth, he was forced to content himself with fretting and waiting.

One afternoon the clear blue sky over the valley became crowded with puffy white clouds, which were rapidly pushed aside by boiling gray clouds that rolled over the mountains and filled the little valley with darkness even though it was still early afternoon. Long Foot approached Jason, who was smoothing out the frame of a crib he had been working on.

He pointed to the darkened sky. "Raven say baby come, damn right."

Jason was startled. "Now? She's having it now?" He dropped what he was doing and started toward the cabin.

Long Foot grabbed his arm. "No, not yet." He pointed up at the dark clouds again. "Soon, baby come, damn right."

Jason sat down to his work again. "Damn! You got me all worked up over nothing. I'll tell you what's coming soon, a thunderstorm, that's what's coming."

"Damn right," Long Foot agreed and turned to leave Jason to his work. "Baby come, too," he muttered to himself.

It was a boy and it fought its birth with the ferocity of a mountain lion. It came during the peak of the storm, amidst the crashing of thunderbolts and jagged flashes of lightning that tore the very fabric of the sky and threatened to drown the tiny valley. The birth was as difficult as the women had feared it would be and Sarah's screams of pain could be heard above the thundering storm. Raven and Magpie were terrified, convinced they were standing in the face of some sinister spirit of Stone Hand revisiting earth in the form of his son. In spite of their fear, however, they stood fast and helped Sarah deliver. All souls survived the storm and when it was over Sarah fainted with exhaustion, leaving Raven and Magpie to clean and care for a robust little infant who seemed reluctant to be thrust out into the world. His cries of defiance rang out across the little valley, causing the two Indian women to stare at each other in amazement and not without a small measure of apprehension.

In the weeks that followed that stormy night, the eerie circumstances of the baby's birth were gradually forgotten and soon it was a matter of three women with one baby to care for. Sarah, at first reluctant to take the baby close to her, soon overcame her abhorrence of the infant, her natural motherly instincts eventually outweighing the shame and contempt she had felt while carrying it. In the beginning, however, she had to be talked into nursing her baby. Only the obvious fact that the baby would starve otherwise finally persuaded her. Neither Raven nor Magpie could provide milk for the infant and Sarah's breasts were plainly swollen to the point of pain, a fact that embarrassed Sarah greatly. She had felt all along that she had no choice but to have the renegade's offspring but she had given little thought toward caring for it after it was born. She would have been hard-pressed to know what to do with it had it not been for the two Indian women.

Jason sat by the fire and cleaned his Winchester. The nights were still a bit brisk but it was nice sitting by the fire. He was thinking about the plans he had for developing a breed of horses with the Appaloosas as the starting seed. Magpie came out of the cabin, carrying the baby. Sarah had just fed the infant and Magpie took the child so that Sarah could rest. Jason paused in his cleaning of the rifle and watched the slight Osage girl as she settled herself on the other side of the fire. He couldn't help but wonder if a baby brought out the natural beauty in all women, and not just the mother of the child.

"You look real natural, holding that baby. How come you're not married and having babies of your own?" As soon as he said it, he felt awkward.

She blushed and lowered her head when she replied. "I have not been spoken for," she said simply.

"I find that hard to believe . . . as pretty as you are." He knew that he often found himself admiring her lately.

"I have not been spoken for by the man who has my heart," she replied, her voice barely above a whisper.

The awkwardness again . . . he did not understand why the girl made him nervous whenever they were alone together. It didn't make sense. She was no more than Long Foot's sister-in-law but somehow he seemed to sometimes get tongue-tied when he tried to make simple conversation with her. She probably thinks I'm some kind of fumble-footed fool, he decided.

When the baby was a month old, Jason decided it was time to make the trip to the Bitterroots. He was reluctant to leave the women alone but he was anxious to get started and he figured they would be safe enough if they stayed close to the cabin. He and Long Foot gave them a quick lesson in how to aim and fire a rifle. Sarah was quick to inform Jason that she had fired a rifle before and knew how to use it. When she demonstrated by clipping a limb off a tree that stood some fifty yards from the cabin. Long Foot was impressed enough to utter, "Damn right."

It would be a long trip to the country of the Nez Percés. Long Foot questioned the wisdom of starting such a journey. He pointed out that it would be necessary to cross through many mountain passes and travel through several different territories, those of the Utes, the Shoshones, and the Bannocks, to name a few. Jason knew what he wanted, however, and when Long Foot suggested that Jason trade for horses with the Bannocks, he explained why it was out of the question.

"Three years ago at Bent's Fort, I met a fellow named Wiley Haverstrom. Wiley trapped the Bitterroot Mountains for a couple of years before he got wilderness fever and came out to civilization. He had a horse he said he traded from the Nez Percés, said they breeded 'em. Well, I ain't never seen another one like it. It was one spunky animal . . . and handsome, too. I've had it in the back of my mind that if I was gonna breed horses, that's the breed I want." He cinched up Birdie, waited for her to blow, then pulled up on the girth again. Then he looked at Long

Foot and said, "I'm pulling out. If you feel queer about leaving your womenfolk alone, I'll understand and no hard feelings." He stepped up in the saddle. "I can sure use your help if you decide to go."

Long Foot shrugged. "I'm going, damn right."

Jason wheeled Birdie around. Sarah was standing in the doorway of the cabin, watching. When Jason caught her eye, she smiled. He walked Birdie over to her and reached down and patted her gently on the shoulder. "I'll be back as soon as I can. I might be gone a month though. You should be all right."

She took his hand and squeezed it. "Don't worry about me. I'll be all right. Just get back as soon as you can. We don't want to be left alone here any longer than we have to."

"I will." He gave her a big smile. When he turned back around, it was to find Magpie staring at him. He would almost call it a longing gaze. He smiled at her and said, "Look after things, Magpie." He didn't know why he said it. He wondered why everything he said to her sounded stupid.

She smiled up at him and replied, "I will."

"I'll be back with breed stock that'll put us in the horse business sure 'nough." He pulled Birdie's head around and nudged her in the belly. "Come on, Long Foot. We're burning daylight."

CHAPTER 14

Sarah had no plans to become attached to the baby. She tried to tell herself that it was like a tumor that needed to be removed from her body. Once removed, she wanted to have done with it and she planned to give the baby to Raven to raise as her own. Jason had told her that Raven would take the baby to begin with, and judging by her behavior with the infant, it appeared she was more than willing to take it. In fact, both sisters competed for the baby's attention and Sarah was sure Magpie would take her baby if Raven decided not to. But Sarah's resolve to give her baby away was weakening and she wondered if she really could do it. The baby was almost three months old now and was a robust little renegade. She found it impossible to be unaffected by his charm and discovered that now she was competing along with Magpie and Raven for his affection. It was obvious to her that she was soon going to have to make a decision that would be crucial to her future.

Jason and Long Foot had been gone for more than a month and the women watched the ridges above the valley daily, hoping to sight the two of them returning. For that reason, Sarah's heart skipped a beat when she caught sight of the riders on the south ridge. She was playing with the baby in the sunshine of the cool summer morning when a slight movement in the corner of her eye caused her to look toward the mountains.

Her first thought was one of instant joy. Jason was back! But as she stared at the riders she realized there were three of them and they led no horses behind them. As she gazed at them, the three slowly walked their horses to a point no more than four or five hundred yards from the cabin. There they stopped and looked down on the valley. She could see now that they were Indians and she felt the heartbeat quicken within her breast. Glancing back at the cabin, she saw Raven standing by the door. She had seen their visitors, too, and was staring in their direction.

Moving deliberately so as not to display alarm, Sarah gathered up the baby and slowly moved back to the cabin. Magpie came out of the tent and stood by her sister. When Sarah came up to them, she spoke softly.

"Can you tell who they are?"

Raven glanced at Magpie for confirmation, then answered. "They look to be Utes." This was all she could offer, then she added, "We're in their country."

"Why do they just sit there? What do you think they want?"

Raven shrugged her shoulders. "I don't know. I think they are not sure what to do. They are looking to see where our men are, I think."

Sarah stood silent for a few moments longer. "Magpie, go into the cabin and bring one of the rifles out here. We'll let them know we're not unprotected." The girl did as she was told. While she waited for the rifle, Sarah had another, somewhat disturbing, thought; she hoped it would send the proper message to their visitors and not have the opposite effect and entice the Utes to attack them to get the rifle.

When Magpie returned, Sarah handed her the baby and took the rifle. She made a show of cocking the lever and standing with the weapon at the ready. There was no indication from the Indians that her demonstration had moved them. They sat silently watching the three women for several long minutes. Then the leader turned his horse and slowly made his way along the ridge. His two companions followed. Their pace was leisurely as their ponies picked their way around the rocks and trees, keeping the little valley in sight all the time. At the north end of the valley, they turned and rode off to the east, still at the same leisurely pace until they disappeared from sight.

The incident was unnerving to Sarah. Their little valley had been discovered. Now what could they expect? Would they soon be visited by a full war party? "Damn," she uttered. Where was Jason? He should have been back by now. Their valley was no longer safe. They would have to start taking turns as sentries and keep the rifles loaded and ready for instant use. The two Indian women were as concerned as she and for the next three nights they stood watches all night long. But the Utes did not return. When several days had passed, Sarah had to conclude that the Indians had no interest in the three women. They were merely passing by and not knowing where the men of the camp were, they thought it best to leave them in peace. With the passing of a week, the fright of the incident had dulled until it was no longer in her mind and the three women went back to their daily routine.

Another two weeks passed before Jason returned. Sarah was feeding the baby one evening when Magpie came running from the creek, shouting the news that Long Foot and Jason were coming down the north ridge, driving a string of ponies. Sarah put the baby in his cradle and went out to watch them come in across the valley. There was a definite sensation of excitement when she first sighted Jason, riding easy in the saddle as he guided the horses in front of him. Maybe it was purely relief after having been alone with Raven and Magpie for so long. Maybe it went deeper than that. She didn't bother to analyze it. She was just glad to see him.

"Magpie, run open the corral," she called out and quickly looked back toward the approaching horses. If she hadn't known for certain that it was Jason, she might not have recognized him. He had obviously not bothered to take his razor with him and his face was almost hidden by a full growth of whiskers. And his hair had grown to shoulder length. What a sight, she thought, and ran to the corral as the horses thundered by her, heads tossing, hooves pounding. They were wild but they were handsome in their wildness. Muscular animals, they looked to be more sturdy than the typical Indian ponies she had seen. She counted fourteen as they raced by her. Jason must have done some shrewd trading. She had expected him to return with possibly two or three.

"Sarah!" Jason called out to her. He pulled Birdie up short at the entrance to the corral and stepped down from the saddle.

She came to meet him. "Welcome back . . . stranger," she added, laughing. "That is you behind all those whiskers, isn't it?"

He laughed, embarrassed. "It's me all right. I reckon I did go a little wild but I didn't think it was worth the effort just to look pretty for Long Foot."

She laughed with him and gave him a hug. "We're glad to see you back."

"We're right glad to be back. There's some rough

country between here and the Bitterroots, rough if you're driving horses." He looked toward the cabin. "Where's Magpie?" Sarah pointed toward the corral gate. "Oh . . . Everything all right? Any problems? The baby okay?"

"Everything's fine," she replied. "We had some visitors a couple of weeks ago but they didn't stop to chat."

"Visitors? Who . . . what visitors?" He was immediately concerned.

"Nothing really. There were three Indians. Raven thinks they were Utes. They showed up one day over there on that ridge"—she pointed to the southern end of the valley—"rode along the ridge there and stopped and watched for a while. Then they left. That's all there was to it."

Jason frowned as he thought about that. "You ain't seen 'em since?"

"No, nobody else."

He shrugged. "I guess there's no harm in it." He suddenly smiled and nodded toward the corral. "We might have had some trouble if they had seen these Appaloosas, though." He took a few steps over to the corral and propped one foot on the bottom rail, his arms rested on the top. "Aren't they a handsome lot?"

"Yes, they are a handsome lot. They sure have strange markings. What did you call them? Appaloosas?"

"Yeah, Appaloosa. I think that's what the first

trappers in that country called them. I don't know where they came up with that name, probably 'cause the Nez Percés used to camp along the Palouse River. 'Course the Indians don't call 'em that. They just call 'em horses." He laughed. "I got six fine-looking mares, one of 'em I'm thinking about breaking for you. Three more"—he pointed them out—"that one, that one, and that one there, are all right but not as good-looking as the other six. See that big boy over there? With the rump almost all black? He's the king stud. The rest of 'em were just thrown in for trading." He turned to her for her approval. "I reckon I made a pretty good start."

She smiled her approval.

The next few weeks were busy weeks for Jason. He found that he had more work than he had planned. His original thinking was that he would be lucky to return from the Bitterroot country with two or three good horses. With fourteen, plus their original string, they had a sizable herd. His first priority was to repair and expand the little corral he had built. Then there were things to be built for the cabin. And, too, Long Foot was getting impatient to go down to the plains to hunt buffalo. Raven was again pressuring him to get her the necessary hides to build her tipi. Finally Jason told him to go on and go, he wasn't much help when it came to ranch work anyway. So at sunup one morning

Long Foot, Raven, and Magpie packed up the essentials and set out over the mountains. Long Foot planned to join a band of Cheyennes who had left the reservation and were supposed to be living in the mountains south of Jason's little valley. He figured they would be down from the mountains to hunt buffalo and, if he could find them, his own hunt would no doubt be more productive. Long Foot was confident that he would return with hides and meat enough to see them all through the next winter. Jason let him take his good buffalo gun and extra horses to pack the meat.

The days that followed were pleasant days for Jason. He worked on his tiny ranch. Sarah took care of her baby, now confident to tend to the infant without the help of Raven and Magpie. The days were warm and sunny and the nights were cool and clear. Jason could understand how a man could be content to live out the rest of his life in this manner if it were not for the constant threat of Indian trouble. He wondered if there would ever come a time when it wasn't necessary to keep a rifle handy. Even so, it was a sight better than living in a settlement.

Sarah looked to be thriving in this way of life. He wondered if she still thought about John Welch. It could get mighty lonesome out here in the mountains . . . for a woman or a man. She seemed to have bloomed into full womanhood with the arrival of

the baby, and in Jason's mind she was more beautiful than she had ever been. Motherhood seemed to
have softened her features. Her smile was warmer
and she appeared to have lost the bitterness she
had displayed before the birth of her son. Jason
was thankful for this. He had feared she would remain bitter to the point where she might go crazy
with the shame she had felt. It was good that she
had obviously decided to go on with her life.

He bent down to rinse the last traces of soap
from his razor. Then, laying it aside on a flat rock,
he reached down into the clear, cool stream, his
hands cupped, and splashed the water on his face.
It made him shiver involuntarily but he repeated it
several times more until he was satisfied his face
was clean. He picked up his kit and headed back to
the cabin. From habit, he glanced over at the corral
to double-check himself, noting that the gate was
closed properly and the horses were secure for the
night. Sarah would be getting his supper ready
pretty soon if she was through feeding the baby. He
always tried to stay out of the cabin before supper
to give her privacy while she nursed the little one.

He walked quietly, a manner that came natural to
him after years of scouting. She did not hear him
when he approached the cabin and was not aware
of him until he stood in the doorway. Jason did not
intend to surprise Sarah. It just happened that he
was a minute or two early. The sight of her stopped
him in his tracks. He was unable to react beyond

gazing at the picture before him. She held the baby in her arms, nestled to her bare breast, her rough buckskin dress untied and opened from her waist up. He could not help himself and he stared unabashed at the fullness of her bosom. The soft white curves of her breast imprisoned his gaze and left him speechless, unable to mumble an apology and helpless to turn on his heel and leave.

Surprised, she almost gasped at first, but seeing the obvious paralyzing effect it had on him, she said nothing and made no move to cover herself. She looked into his eyes and there was no mistaking the longing and hunger there. She realized at that moment how devastating the scene must be to his mind and how lonely his life must be. He was too shy to ever show his need but she knew the need was there. She also recognized the instant heating of her own blood as the room seemed charged with the energy of his desire. She did not try to fool herself with the notion that she was in love with him. But she could feel his hunger and his need and she knew the man was too decent to take advantage of her. So she stopped him when at last he appeared to take control of his emotions again and started to retreat from the cabin.

"Jason," she whispered softly, "it's all right. Don't go."

He stopped again, confused and embarrassed. "I'm real sorry, Sarah, I . . ."

She did not let him finish but extended her hand to him. "It's all right. Come . . ."

He went to her and took her hand. She pulled him closer to her and placed his hand on her breast. His brain was reeling, unable to do anything but stare at his rough hand against the creamy smooth skin of her breast. When he looked up again, it was to meet her steady gaze and she smiled when their eyes met. Her lips parted, inviting his kiss. He could not help himself. He was lost in his desire for her and he leaned closer to her until finally their lips met. He was lost. Nothing in the world mattered to him at that moment beyond his desire for this woman. She was surprised by the tenderness in his embrace.

"Wait," she whispered, "let me put the baby to bed." He backed away a step, thinking the moment was over. She read the look in his eyes and quickly reassured him. "I'll just be a moment."

He started to stammer something but could not think of anything proper to say. So he remained frozen there, hardly believing what was happening to him. When the baby was settled in his cradle, she came back to him and immediately slid into his arms. Placing both arms around his neck, she pulled his lips down to hers. He responded with a passion that could only be spawned by years of lonely life. She understood his need and met it with equal desire.

Her passion was a searing flame within her

bosom when she led him to her pallet. Even at that moment, she did not try to pretend she was in love with Jason. She knew she was not. But what had started as a charitable act to answer his obvious needs had now progressed to the fulfillment of her own desperate desires.

He was almost boyish in his fumbling attempts to remove her buckskin dress and she realized that his experience in the act of making love was not a great deal more than her own. "Here, let me do it," she said and deftly slipped out of her skirt and undergarments. The sight of her naked body was almost too much for him as he hurriedly fumbled with his own clothing. She marveled that this great bear of a man, this Indian fighter of such reputation, was now a boy in her arms, a boy in absolute awe of her body. She led him tenderly until they were joined as one and the rage of his passion took them both away.

When it was over, she held him in her arms for a long time, letting him absorb the love that was so obviously missing in his life. For that moment she knew he was totally happy and she felt a twinge of sadness that she could not tell him that it would be forever. She almost wished it would be, that she could feel that way for this decent man. But in her heart she knew that she could not lie to herself. She felt he understood and was grateful for the moments of passion. But he, like she, did not speak of love. As much as it pained her to acknowledge it, she knew she could never rid her mind of John Welch. He was not worthy of her love, she admitted that. But common sense did not often enter in when it came to choosing the person one loves.

She realized her mind was drifting when she heard the baby start to whimper, causing Jason to stir. He had been close to going to sleep on her shoulder. When the baby whimpered again, he rolled over to let her up.

"Sorry," she said and hurriedly began to dress. "Let me see what's wrong with him and then I guess I'd better feed you some supper."

"Sarah," he said, holding her arm for a moment, "I reckon you know I'm not in love with you. I thought I was once."

She paused before answering. "Yes, I know." She took his hand and gave it an affectionate squeeze. Then she went to the baby.

"I'm sorry," he said. "I shouldn't have said that."

"No, don't be. It's all right, I understand." She smiled and added, "We both had a need and it was very special for me." There was nothing else to say. They both felt the awkwardness that filled the moment now that it was over.

"I think I'll check on the horses before we eat," he said and excused himself. He needed some time alone. She watched him walk out the door then turned back to the baby.

* * *

There was a coolness between them after that night, not at all unfriendly, but one brought about by some degree of embarrassment on the part of both parties. It was as if a barrier had been crossed that would have been better left uncrossed. Sarah tended to spend more time looking after the baby and Jason made sure he did not walk in on her while she might be nursing the infant. An air of extreme politeness developed and after several days of this, Jason began to question whether it had all been a dream that had never really happened at all. Things were back to normal by the time Long Foot and Raven and Magpie returned.

CHAPTER 15

"What are you going to do about your father?"

Sarah glanced up from the deerhide shirt she was sewing for the baby. Magpie had helped her soften the hide and she and Raven had shown great interest in teaching her how to fashion the softened hide into a comfortable garment. She paused for a moment before she answered Jason's question. "I don't know," she stated simply.

"You know you've been gone a year now and he hasn't heard a word from you. Surely he knows by now that you didn't go back East." Jason was concerned that the colonel would have already sent out patrols in search of his daughter, convinced that she had never reached Fort Cobb. Sarah had been confident that he would not pursue the matter once she had gone. She reasoned that they had rarely corresponded before, when she was in school in Baltimore. So she didn't expect her father to worry about her at all. Jason knew that Sarah's mother had been dead for more than four years, and since her death Colonel Holder had turned to the army for solace. His daughter had been left to his sister to educate and provide the family a young girl required. Maybe Sarah was right, he concluded. Maybe her aunt in Baltimore was content to believe her niece was still in Oklahoma Territory while her father thought she was back East.

"Maybe I'll go back to Baltimore before winter sets in. I guess I can still teach at the school." She paused as if to reconsider. "They probably think I died," she said, smiling at the irony of it. "If they could see me sitting here, sewing a deerhide shirt, they'd think I had lost my mind."

"I reckon you'll leave the baby with Raven when you go back."

"I don't know," she quickly answered. "Maybe, maybe not."

This surprised him. "You thinking about taking him with you? Back to Baltimore?"

"I don't know," she repeated curtly.

He could see that the decision had evidently been weighing heavily on her mind. He turned to look at the baby, sleeping now. "I reckon he'd be a big hit with your proper friends back in Baltimore." As soon as he said it, he realized how it must have sounded to her. "I'm sorry," he stammered. "I didn't mean it to sound like that."

At once her face flushed with anger and then after a moment her features relaxed into the calm facade she most often presented. "It's all right.

You're right, though. My little bastard wouldn't fit in very well where I'm going. I guess I'll leave him with Raven. I don't know. I haven't made up my mind about what I'll do." She gazed at Jason for a long moment as if deciding whether or not she was going to say more. "Jason, I owe you a lot. I'm very grateful for your thoughtfulness and the help you gave me." She paused when she saw his puzzled expression. "I guess I'm just trying to tell you that I know I've been difficult to live with some of the time. But you never got mad or even complained."

He shrugged. "I think you're being a tad hard on yourself. I know this life is mighty hard on someone of your upbringing."

"I just want you to know how much I appreciate your help."

He laughed. "You're talking like you're getting ready to go somewhere."

She smiled and nodded her head. "I think I'm ready to go back home if I can call on you one more time to help me." She sighed. "I'm gonna miss that baby. I still might change my mind about leaving him. God, I never thought it would be such a hard decision."

"When do you want to go?"

"Not for two or three more weeks, while I'm still feeding the baby."

So, he thought on his way out to tend to his horses, she's going back East after all. It would seem kind of empty around here without her, but the baby would still be here to keep things lively. In the long run, back East was where Sarah ought to be. Then he wondered if Magpie and Raven and Long Foot would stay on. Whatever suits 'em, he decided.

Summer was nearing an end. Raven and Magpie were busy drying meat for the winter now that the tipi was completed. Sarah waited now for Jason and Long Foot to return from a hunting trip in the mountains. Jason had agreed to take her to Denver to arrange for her trip back East before the snows came. She was ready to go. Life on the frontier no longer appealed to her and she yearned to see civilization again, and not just trading post civilization, real civilization with dances and teas and Sunday socials . . . real houses with tables and chairs . . .and beds with clean sheets. She wanted to wear dresses with slips and ruffles and dance with men in waistcoats and ties. And she was sick of venison and elk. Oh how she wished Jason would hurry so she could leave his valley.

A shadow fell across the baby blanket she was working on, causing her to turn toward the open doorway. At last, Jason had returned, she thought. But the figure that blocked the afternoon sunlight was not as tall as Jason. Long Foot? she thought, her eyes squinting from the sunlight that all but blinded her as it created a glaring aura that outlined the figure standing in the door. As her eyes adjusted to the glare, she could see that it was an Indian but it was not Long Foot. Then, in one horrifying second, she recognized him. Stone Hand!

Frozen with fear upon encountering a demon returned from the grave, Sarah gasped. She was unable to make any other sound. The terror that filled her entire being was threatening to strangle her and she suddenly felt dizzy. The room started to spin around her, and she feared she was about to faint. She closed her eyes and opened them again, desperately hoping the specter was an illusion. It was not. Now she wished she could faint but she could not.

The Indian grunted something in Cheyenne and reached down behind him and dragged an object through the open doorway. When her eyes were able to focus again, she realized the object was Raven. She was bleeding from her mouth. The blood covered the front of her deerskin bodice. One of her front teeth was missing. Another dangled, broken, barely attached by a root. The sight made Sarah suddenly nauseated. She would never forget the look in Raven's eyes as she gazed vacantly into space. Stone Hand growled something to the helpless woman and punctuated it with a slap across her face.

"Baby," Raven forced through her broken mouth. "He come for baby." She turned her gaze to stare at Sarah, who was still approaching a state of shock. "His son."

Raven's head slumped forward but Stone Hand reached down and roughly jerked her chin back up. He shouted something at her, at the same time gesturing in Sarah's direction. Raven dutifully, though painfully, repeated his words in English.

"You baby's mother. You go with him, take care of baby. His son." Raven was silent for a moment then added in a low voice, "You must feed baby. When baby quit nursing he kill you."

Sarah realized this last was a warning and not a translation of Stone Hand's words. She was gripped by a numbing fear that seemed to paralyze her. Stone Hand watched her face closely to see if she understood. Then he placed his foot between Raven's shoulder blades and forced her facedown on the earthen floor. Without hesitating, he reached down with one hand and grabbed a handful of her hair, forcing her head back. With the other he drew a long knife from his belt and in one quick move reached down and cut her throat. There was but a rasping gurgle, like a person makes clearing his throat, and Raven was gone.

Sarah did not know she was screaming until the renegade slapped her hard across her face, again and again, until she was quiet. Then he grabbed her by the arm and threw her across the room toward the baby's cradle. She whirled around to face him, defiant for a brief moment. He stood before her. With one hand, he grabbed his crotch and gestured, taunting, as if inviting her to try it again.

Then he slapped her with the back of his hand and pointed to the baby. Gesturing, he made her understand he was ordering her to pick up the baby and go with him. She did as she was told, no longer defiant, for she remembered Raven's warning and realized the same fate awaited her if she did not prove herself useful. When they started through the door, Stone Hand paused to look down at the still warm body that had been Long Foot's wife. He stood for a moment as if evaluating a piece of work he had just completed. Satisfied, he bent down and with the knife that had taken her life he sliced off her left eyebrow. Sarah quickly turned her head, sick with terror.

CHAPTER 16

Jason guided his horse down through a grassy meadow which was strewn with white boulders and occasional dead logs left by the countless storms that rumbled through the mountain passes. Birdie picked her way carefully around the larger boulders and through the screen of evergreens. A packhorse laden with fresh meat followed behind him. Long Foot brought up the rear, leading a second packhorse. Within a few minutes, they emerged from the trees and topped the ridge along the eastern side of the valley. They were almost home.

Suddenly Jason threw up his hand and halted the horses. He motioned for silence and listened. There was a sound on the wind. It drifted up from the valley below, at first faint, then gaining in intensity until Long Foot recognized it as a chant. Almost at the same second, they both realized it was a song of mourning they were hearing, a death song, and it was coming from their valley. Jason hesitated no longer. He gave Birdie a firm kick and started off down the ridge at a gallop. Long Foot was close behind.

They found Magpie sitting before Raven's tipi. Her dress was open above her waist and her lap was filled with the blood that flowed from the slashes across her breast. She continued to sing her song of mourning as she stared at the two men approaching her. Jason was the first to reach her, dismounting on the run even before Birdie came to a full halt. But she looked past him to Long Foot, sobbing as she told him of the murder of his wife.

"Stone Hand!" Jason roared in disbelief. "How can that be? I cut him in two. I saw him go down!"

Long Foot's grief could not be contained. The scout moaned with a pain that tore at the very core of his soul. He went inside the tipi, where Magpie had carried Raven's body, and prostrated himself before his dead wife, sobbing in agony. Outside, Jason listened, horrified, while Magpie described the abduction of Sarah and the baby.

Magpie was alive only because she was up on the north ridge, picking wild berries. She heard screams and hurried back as fast as she could but she was too far from the cabin to be of any help to her sister. When she reached the fork of the stream that divides the base of the valley, it was in time to see the end of the assault. It was Stone Hand, come back from the dead. She hid in the stream while she watched him take the three best horses in the corral. He forced Sarah, with the baby, onto one of the horses while he mounted another. Before leaving, he turned the rest of the horses loose. Then he led Sarah and the spare horse out across the valley toward the south. When he was out of sight, Magpie left her hiding place and ran to the cabin where she found her sister lying in a wide pool of blood, her body still warm.

It was as if a huge boulder had been dropped upon his chest. Jason was stunned by the young girl's accounting of the assault. When his senses returned to normal, the shock was replaced by a feeling of urgency approaching panic. He had to find her! He felt sick inside when he let his mind speculate on the torment she might be enduring at the hand of that devil. Stone Hand had somehow survived that fall down the dark shaft inside the cave. Was there a ledge halfway down? And a secret passageway to the outside? Thinking back to that day, it didn't seem possible. Maybe the bastard was supernatural. After all, Jason had seen many a man die with less serious wounds than those inflicted upon the renegade. He could barely contain his anxiety to start out after Stone Hand, but he knew he must wait until Long Foot and Magpie prepared Raven's body for burial.

Long Foot's grief was without measure. He cried openly as he and Magpie worked feverishly to fashion a burial platform for his wife. At the same time, a fury was building inside him to avenge her murder. Demon or not, Stone Hand must pay for this deed, the senseless slaughter of an innocent woman. He must pay, and pay dearly. In truth, while Long Foot was fond of Sarah, he was really concerned less with rescuing her than seeking his revenge upon Stone Hand. So he and his sister-in-law worked quickly to prepare Raven for her journey. When it was done, Jason stood ready with the horses and supplies.

While the burial preparations were proceeding, Jason rode down the valley, hoping to round up the rest of his horses. All the while, as he rounded up the horses, he labored under a heavy cloak of guilt. He would not have blamed Long Foot for feeling Raven's death was his fault. But Jason had been certain the renegade could not have survived. Long Foot harbored no such notions, however. He did not doubt that Jason had killed Stone Hand. He was convinced that Stone Hand had returned from the spirit world to claim his son.

They had not scattered far. He found them grazing in the lush grass of the valley. They would need fresh horses, so he turned the two packhorses loose and caught up two to replace them. He rounded up three others and along with the packhorses he drove them back to the cabin. He allowed a fleeting moment of regret for having to leave the rest of his horses behind but he could see no other choice. There was no one to care for them. There was Magpie of course, but he could not leave the young girl there alone. There was no telling when, or even if, they would return to his little valley.

He had no choice but to dump the fresh meat they had brought back. There was no time to dry it. He packed as much of their dried meat as he thought necessary on the two packhorses. The fresh meat would have to feed the wolves or spoil. Even though the sun was sinking toward the western ridge, they set out after the renegade, not wishing to waste any more time. At the south end of the valley, Jason pulled up before topping the rise that would put the valley behind them. He took one brief look at the little cabin and his empty corral. Two of his Appaloosas had followed them toward the mountain pass but stopped at the stream. Maybe they would stay in the lush valley and not scatter into the hills. His dreams of a horse ranch seemed destroyed at that moment. A few moments was all he spent gazing at what might have been, and then he turned his horse and continued on toward the south pass.

The trail was not hard to follow through the first three passes. There was really only one way through the mountains that loomed straight up above them on each side. It would be more difficult when they left the last of the high mountains and traversed the lower slopes. Then they would have to rely upon their skills as trackers, for Jason knew from experience that Stone Hand could be impossi-

ble to track at times. He was more confident this
time, however, because of the presence of Sarah
and the baby. It would not be as easy for the
Cheyenne to cover his tracks. Too, he hoped Stone
Hand would not think he was being trailed this
soon and might not push as hard to travel fast.

They camped after dark the first night on an outcropping of boulders by a busy stream. Magpie
scurried about, making the camp and preparing
some food. Long Foot, after seeing to his horses, sat
off by himself, chanting a song of mourning. He sat
there, moaning low, almost in a whisper, for more
than an hour before coming back to the fire and
eating some of the meat Magpie offered him.

Jason watched in silence. His heart was sad for
his friend's loss but there was nothing he could
offer to ease his pain. He thought about the man
they were tracking. Where would he take his
hostages? He was traveling south now but he had
little choice. Where would he go when they were
clear of the high mountains? Oklahoma Territory?
Commanche territory? He seemed to have allied
himself with the Commanches. He might go back
there. Then his thoughts lingered on Sarah and her
baby. From what he knew about the man, Jason did
not have to guess why Stone Hand came for the
baby. He could not abide the thought of his son
being raised by whites. He had killed Raven. Why
her and not Sarah? He could only conclude that the
reason might be that Sarah had milk and Raven did

not. That thought triggered another alarming question. How long would Sarah live after her milk dried up? He had wondered at first how Stone Hand had found his valley. Then he remembered Sarah telling him of the three Ute warriors who had passed by while he and Long Foot were in the Bitterroot country. They must have told Stone Hand of the three women and a baby.

Magpie looked at Jason, her eyes searching his, silently asking if he wanted more to eat. He shook his head no, and she started to turn away. With a hand laid gently on her shoulder, he stopped her. Since her heavy song of mourning on the day of Raven's death, she had remained silent in her grief. As she gazed up at him now, he could read the hurt in her eyes. His gaze shifted down to her antelope skin bodice, which was stained with her own blood from the slashes she had administered in her grieving. His heart reached out to her at that moment and he longed to tell her everything would be all right. Her eyes, unblinking, never left his gaze. After a moment, she came to him, seeking the comforting she so desperately needed. He held her close, his arms around her, her head on his shoulder, and he could feel her body relax in the haven of his embrace. For a few brief moments he felt a peace that he had never experienced before.

They were up and away at first light, holding to the eastern slope of the pass, riding in the shadows of the steep walls that formed the narrow corridor. The shrill cry of a hawk went unnoticed as the two men kept their eyes glued to the trail, their senses keen for sounds out of the ordinary. Long Foot led. Jason knew he could not hold the Osage scout back anyway, his passion to avenge his wife driving him like a forest fire. Jason's only fear was that his friend's rage might blind him to the point of blundering. Long Foot, however, did not miss a sign, even when the trail they followed veered across a rocky crest and turned to the east.

"He turn toward sun," Long Foot said. "Maybe he go to Shoshone."

Jason pulled up beside him. "Maybe, but I doubt it. It's just his nature to change direction. He'll turn back south."

Long Foot nodded slowly, thinking it over, then agreed. "He go Commanche. We catch him." He spoke softly as if to reassure his dead wife. "Damn right," he added, barely above a whisper.

Jason's prediction proved to be correct, for after several miles the trail turned south again and followed a narrow pass through the last of the mountains and into the hills. By noontime they came upon Stone Hand's campsite from the night before. Jason swore when they found it. He had hoped to find it earlier in the day. Now he knew they were still a half day behind them. They had not closed the distance any from the day before. Stone Hand was making as good a time as they were, even with

Sarah and the baby. Jason could imagine how hard it was on Sarah, but he tried to put it out of his mind and concentrate on the business of tracking.

The trail was demanding. Long, wearisome day followed upon the day before. Still they seemed to make no progress in closing the distance between them and the devil they chased. Magpie did not complain even though the trail proved hard on the young Osage maiden. Though she still grieved inside for her sister, she gave no outward sign of her mourning. Death was a familiar partner to all Osage girls and Magpie did not attempt to question the sense of it. Raven was gone and in time Magpie would release her sister to the great beyond and go on with her life. In truth, she did not expect her own life to span many more days for she was convinced the devil they pursued was in fact a spirit form and would undoubtedly destroy them all. The urgency of their journey placed a strain upon all three of them so that each day seemed to be a grim passage of time from dawn to dark with almost no conversation passing between them beyond essential communications.

She leaned forward as the spotted pony she rode hesitated briefly before scaling a rocky mound on the riverbank. She could feel the powerful muscles of the animal between her thighs and the impact of its hooves upon the hard earth of the rise. Up ahead, Jason glanced back to see that she was all right. It was no more than a brief glance. Then, satisfied that she had negotiated the climb with no trouble, he quickly looked away, concerned once again with the trail before him. She had met his glance without expression but inside she was pleased that he showed concern for her. For several months now she had been aware of the strong feelings developing in her heart for the tall white scout. She had assumed in the beginning of their journey to Jason's valley that he longed for Sarah and this was sad because she could also see that Sarah did not have these feelings for Jason. She knew now that there was affection between Sarah and Jason and that he had compassion for her but there had been no indication of a deeper feeling. She was grateful for this because she had feared he would naturally be charmed by the beautiful white woman. Jason was a good man and he deserved a good wife. In her deepest heart she wished she could make him see her. If he could see inside her heart, he would know that she would be a good wife for him.

CHAPTER 17

Colonel Lucien Holder stood staring at the message received from Fort Cobb that morning. It puzzled him. According to the commanding officer, Sarah had indeed arrived at the fort with an escort from Camp Supply but had elected to continue on to the railhead with a civilian guide. This was the part that puzzled the colonel. Why would Sarah engage a civilian guide when she could have been escorted by the next army patrol headed that way?

He had been prompted to inquire about his daughter when he received a rare letter from his sister in Baltimore. It was a rambling letter about her family and acquaintances of his that she had bumped into—nothing really newsworthy enough to interest the colonel. It was the closing of the letter that had startled him. "Give my best to Sarah. Tell her we miss her desperately." Sarah was not in Baltimore! It had been a year. If she was not in Baltimore, then where was she?

The thought that something sinister had befallen

his daughter brought a distraught Colonel Holder to Cora Kennedy's tent in hopes her closeness to Sarah might be able to offer some clue to her whereabouts. Cora knew about the message from the commander at Fort Cobb of course, because Max had told her about it. Her heart went out to the worried father but she dared not tell him where Sarah was. She and Max had argued several times on the subject after the colonel had received the letter from his sister. Max felt they should possibly ease the colonel's mind about the safety of his daughter. But Cora disagreed. It would destroy Sarah, she said. Sarah had made it plain that she didn't want anyone to know about the baby, especially her father. Max gave in to his wife and held his tongue, but it was increasingly difficult to play dumb when the colonel started sending out patrols to search the territory for Jason Coles. It was a difficult time for Lucien Holder.

Barely more than three days' hard ride from Camp Supply, Sarah Holder sat, her back against a gnarled tree trunk that had somehow defiantly forced its existence within a tiny crevice in the solid stone shelf beside the stream. Her baby nursed at her breast. Although there were no physical bonds of any kind to hold her, still she was bound as securely as if hands and feet were shackled, held prisoner by the menacing form standing before her. Stone Hand watched silently as she fed his son. If she had any notion of escape during the day while her hands were free to tend the infant, they were long ago dispelled. Her first and only attempt to escape was dealt with harshly and her face was still swollen and bruised from the beating administered.

She did not even glance up at the dark figure standing over her, staring unblinking at the suckling baby. She no longer made any effort to cover her breast when she nursed the baby. The hopelessness of her plight had dulled her mind to the point of unconcern for privacy. The brute showed no interest in her beyond that of a brood mare for his son. Even her basic bodily functions of elimination were allowed no privacy from the ever-watchful eye of her captor. At first reluctant to relieve herself under his constant gaze, she suffered for almost a full day before she was forced to seek relief. She soon became numb to him and it became as impersonal as relieving herself before the gaze of a horse or a dog.

Soon after her abduction she realized that her role was that of a nursemaid and her life expectancy stretched no further than the supply of her milk. She worried that her breast might dry up soon. But that was during the first two days of her captivity, before the first of many beatings. Now she no longer cared. Her mind and body were too tired to worry about it. If her milk stopped and he killed her, it would be preferable to the suffering she now endured. Were it not for the baby, she would have pushed the issue, forcing him to end her ordeal in a fit of rage. As it was, she waited for the inevitable to happen. Whether it was today or tomorrow, it no longer mattered.

"Come," he said with a grunt and prodded her with his foot. When she looked up, he motioned toward the horses with his head. She had not taken the baby from her breast yet but he was not to be fooled by her efforts to gain more time to rest by pretending the baby was still feeding.

Had her mind not been dulled by her ordeal, she might have noticed that Stone Hand was not pushing as hard as before. She had lost track of the days so she was not aware that it had been seven days since her abduction. Stone Hand felt confident that if there had been any pursuit he was sure to have outdistanced it by this time. It had been a disappointment to find that the white scout, Jason Coles, was not in the valley when he came for his son. His hatred for the army scout was like a glowing coal in the pit of his stomach where the jagged scars from Jason's rifle still ached. The severity of the wounds had almost ended his life but his burning desire for revenge had served to feed his recovery. Coles had been lucky that time and lucky again that he was not in the cabin when Stone Hand came for the baby. But he would not escape Stone Hand's vengeance for long. More important in the renegade's mind now was to take his son to the

Commanche camp of Lame Dog, where he could be cared for by an Indian woman. Then he would return for Coles.

Three more days found them approaching a modest gathering of tipis on the northern side of a shallow ribbon of water guarded by a small group of cottonwoods. This was the camp of Lame Dog. The sight of the lodges caused a quiver in Sarah's heartbeat as she immediately realized her days might soon be at an end. She glanced down quickly at her baby then back at Stone Hand. The Indian met her glance. He seemed to read her thoughts, for his evil face twisted into a crooked smile, chilling her to the bone.

Upon their arrival in the Commanche camp, they were met with several cries of recognition. Had Sarah not been stricken with a sudden concern for her safety, she may have noticed that it was a strange welcome that greeted Stone Hand. Obviously the Cheyenne warrior felt welcome in this village but the greetings were not warm, friendly salutations one would expect upon seeing a friend arrive. Rather, there were sober grunts and nods of recognition. There was a sense of respect shown the renegade—not respect spawned by admiration, but respect such as that shown a rattlesnake. Stone Hand was unmoved by the reception, not caring what the Commanches thought of him. He went where it pleased him to go.

Sarah was terrified. Only hours before she had

languished in a state of dull shock, not caring if she lived or died. Now, with a crowd of angry faces gathering around her and her baby, she realized that she did not want to die. In fact she wanted desperately to live. Some of the women of the village pushed through the crowd of children and warriors to get a better look at the white woman. First one and then another began to poke her calves and thighs as if examining a side of beef. Suddenly one of the more brazen of the curious reached up and pulled Sarah from her horse. Almost in the same motion, another woman snatched the baby from her arms. She landed on the ground and instinctively covered her head with her arms, trying to shield herself from the blows that almost immediately showered her.

Stone Hand was in no hurry to react to the rude greeting afforded his captive. He watched for a few minutes, satisfied that Sarah deserved another beating, before he quietly ordered the women to cease. They did so immediately, not waiting to be told a second time. He threw a leg over his horse's neck and slid down to the ground. The gathering, men and women alike, parted at once, leaving a clear circle around him and his captive.

Sarah, scarcely believing she was still alive, painfully rose to her feet, her face and head throbbing from the multitude of blows she had endured. She looked around her until she found the woman who had taken the baby. The woman stared at her in stoic contempt but she did not resist when Sarah reached out and took the baby from her.

Stone Hand was talking to an old woman. They exchanged several words then looked at Sarah and the baby. A few more words were exchanged and then the old woman gestured to another younger woman. The younger woman nodded then made her way through the small crowd. Upon approaching Sarah, she reached out for the baby. Sarah drew back, refusing to release her son. Stone Hand responded at once with an angry shout and a hard slap that almost knocked Sarah off her feet. She released the baby. The young Indian woman walked away and disappeared among the gathering of tipis. More words were spoken and Sarah suddenly felt her arms pinned behind her back and her wrists being tied. She could only conclude that her execution was near.

Stone Hand, if totally without conscience, was not impractical. He had looked forward to the pleasure the slow death of Sarah Holder would provide but he decided to wait until he was satisfied that he would have no further use for the woman. There was a woman in the village who had recently given birth and she had agreed to nurse his son along with her own. Stone Hand delayed Sarah's death until he was sure the Indian woman was able to care for his son. Meanwhile he entertained several offers from some of the warriors to trade for the white woman. None were as attractive as the prospect of the enjoyment he would derive from killing her.

Two days passed. She remained bound, hands and feet, inside an otherwise empty tipi. She was untied briefly twice a day to eat. She reasoned that she was being fed and was still alive only because of the baby. Alone in the tipi, she cried, afraid for her life, sore from the beatings she had suffered, her breasts sore and swollen with milk, her insides aching from almost constantly having to hold her bladder until mealtime when she was released for a few minutes. Thoughts of Jason Coles and Long Foot, of Raven and Magpie, of her father, and—yes, of John Welch—darted through her conscious mind like fireflies. Brief flashes of memory, they seemed to be fictitious characters in her mind with no connection to her misery. Her only driven, constant thought was to survive. On the third day the baby was returned to her. It was plain to see from the sullen expression on the old woman's face that the young Commanche woman had been unable to feed both infants.

On the morning Sarah's baby was returned to her, Jason knelt behind the low shrub that offered the only protection from sight on the long ridge. Before and below him, in the dusty stand of cottonwoods, lay the Commanche village.

"Thirty-one, two, three," he said softly. "I count

thirty-three tipis. Looks like Lame Dog has picked up some more people."

"Ugh," Long Foot grunted in response, "Lame Dog, damn right." Growing more and more impatient as each second passed, he pressed Jason for action. "We go now, kill Stone Hand."

Jason studied his friend's face for a brief moment before calmly replying, "We go in that village now and we'll be the ones who get killed." He wondered if it was necessary to remind his friend that it was a Commanche camp he was looking at. There was no disguising the pain Long Foot felt as well as his thirst for revenge, but it would be foolhardy to brazenly ride into the hostile camp looking for Stone Hand. "We'll have to wait till dark. Then we can take a closer look and find out where he's got Sarah . . . if she's still alive." He could see his statement was not well received by Long Foot, and Jason began to be concerned that the Osage scout's blood might be too agitated to allow him to function coolly. He sought to remind him of the danger in the task they had come to perform. "We're outnumbered pretty bad and I ain't never known Commanches to be a very gentle folk as it is. So we'd best wait and see what's what before we make our move."

Jason had to take Long Foot by the arm and lead him away from the brow of the hill, reassuring him that Stone Hand would not escape this time. Magpie waited at the foot of the rise, where she held the horses. She studied the faces of the two men when they returned. While Jason's was expressionless, she could read the anxiety that etched deep furrows in the face of her brother-in- law. They mounted and Jason led them back trail for a mile or so until he found a suitable place to wait out the daylight.

Magpie knelt beside Jason where he rested against a young sapling. "Are you hungry?" she asked. "I can boil some of the corn I brought."

"No," he replied, "I'm not hungry." He watched the young girl as she rose and returned to the small fire she had built between two small boulders. He was not concerned about the fire. The smoke would hardly be noticeable. Magpie, he thought, what an inappropriate name for a girl of such obvious beauty. He let his mind muse over the thought. It was a white man's connotation that made the name seem harsh and awkward. Magpie was an Osage girl and, to the Osage, the name was no different from Lark or Sparrow. Possibly her father saw a magpie on the day she was born and named her accordingly. Her older sister, Long Foot's wife, was named Raven. Her parents must have been partial to birds, he thought. I guess she's lucky they didn't sight a buzzard when she was born.

He realized his mind was wandering unfettered into the world of the ridiculous so he gathered his thoughts back to consider the night that lay before them. At this point, he had no real plan. It was difficult to say what the situation might be when they scouted the Commanche camp after nightfall. He hoped he would be able to pinpoint the tipi Sarah was being held in and simply slip into the camp and carry her away. He preferred to see to her safety before coming back to deal with Stone Hand. His concern was for Long Foot. Would he be able to hold him back long enough to get the women somewhere safe?

There being nothing to do until the time came, he decided to get some sleep. While he arranged his large frame in an effort to get comfortable on the hard-packed ground, he looked over at Long Foot. The Osage had not stopped pacing since they made their temporary camp.

"Better get some rest, Long Foot. If things go the way we want, chances are we'll be doing some hard riding all night." To himself he thought, At least that's the way I hope it will go. He knew that Long Foot was here primarily to settle the score with Stone Hand and his passion to kill the renegade might complicate the rescue mission. I'll deal with it when the time comes, he thought.

Long Foot seemed in a trance. "No rest till Stone Hand dead," he mumbled. And then he added, "Damn right."

"Suit yourself. I'm gonna try to get some rest." He glanced at Magpie. His tone softened as he looked into the deep brown eyes that returned his gaze. "You better try to rest, too." She nodded and, spreading her blanket beside him, cuddled up close against him.

"What? What is it?" He had been asleep and now he was aware that someone was shaking him violently. The sleep that fogged his brain quickly dissipated and he sat up to find Magpie kneeling beside him.

"Long Foot!" she cried, her voice filled with anxiety and she continued to shake Jason.

He placed his hand on hers to calm her. "Long Foot? What about Long Foot?" He glanced quickly around him. The Osage was nowhere in sight.

"He's gone!" Her eyes wide with fear, she told Jason that she, too, had gone to sleep. She awakened to discover Long Foot quietly leading his horse out of the camp. He had painted his face for war and upon meeting her gaze had silently ordered her to hold her tongue. Then he rode off toward the Commanche camp.

Jason was afraid this might happen. His friend had been unable to rid his mind of the constant burning he felt inside. Now he had gone to extinguish that fire in the only way that could satisfy him. Damn fool, he thought. He had permitted his lust for vengeance to drown his common sense. Well, he decided, the fat's in the fire now. We ain't got much choice. To her he said, "Come on, we've got to see if we can catch him."

She responded at once and within a few minutes'

time they were off at a gallop. It was a useless effort, for their camp was little more than a mile from the Commanche village and Long Foot would have reached it long before Jason and Magpie. Still Jason deemed it worth the effort to overtake his friend in the hope that Long Foot would take the time to scout the village before riding blindly in. He was to be disappointed, however, for Long Foot's grief had robbed him of any notions of caution.

The cookfires were already burning in front of the tipis in the quiet village as the women began to prepare the evening meal. The sun had fallen behind the rolling hills to the west, spreading soft shadows across the tiny stream toward the open prairie beyond. Darkness was not far away. A man of the village finished hobbling his favorite war pony close by his tipi. As he rose to his feet, his eye caught a movement toward the west. A rider was approaching. Curious, he continued to gaze toward the hills, his vision somewhat impaired by the setting sun behind him. Now a few of the others in the camp caught sight of the rider and paused to watch him as he made his way across the shallow stream and continued toward them. Lame Dog came out of his lodge and stood silently watching.

Long Foot rode straight into the enemy camp, ignoring two Commanche warriors who had leaped upon their ponies and rode out to flank him. He rode into the center of the circle of tipis and pulled up before the lodge of Lame Dog.

Lame Dog stared at the stranger still seated silently on his horse. After a long moment, he spoke. "What business do you have here? It is not a friendly visit, I think. A friend does not come to visit with his face painted for war." He paused before adding, "One warrior makes a small war party."

"I am Long Foot, Osage. There is one among you who is a cowardly camp dog, one who steals babies . . . a killer of women. It is him I seek, a Cheyenne coyote. Where does the coward hide?"

The look of shock that claimed Lame Dog's face was reflected in those of his village who also heard Long Foot's words. Stone Hand was feared as much in this Commanche camp as he was among the Cheyenne and the gathering of people involuntarily backed away a few steps as if afraid the lightning that would surely strike Long Foot might also singe them.

"Where is Stone Hand?" Long Foot demanded.

"I am here, you Osage dog."

An instant hush fell upon the village and all heads turned in the direction from which the ominous voice had come. He emerged from a tipi near the stream and stood, his feet wide apart, defiantly, his face a mask of cool contempt. Long Foot turned his pony to face him. Nothing more was said for a long time while the two men stared at each other. Finally Long Foot broke the silence.

"I have come to kill you."

His simple statement brought a thin smile to Stone Hand's face. "You have come to die," he replied.

Lame Dog spoke then. "Stone Hand is a guest in my village. Have you no honor, that you come and challenge a guest in a peaceful camp? Is this the way of the Osage?"

Long Foot answered the chief although he continued to look straight at Stone Hand. "This dog, this guest of the mighty Commanche, has murdered my wife. While I was away from the lodge, he came in like a sneaking coyote and killed her. Then he stole the white woman and her baby. I say it is my right to challenge him."

Lame Dog listened to his words and considered the seriousness of his charges. He turned to look at the sneering countenance of Stone Hand. He did not doubt that what Long Foot claimed was true. And while Stone Hand was in fact a guest in his camp, he was by no means a welcome guest. On the contrary, many of the men of his village would have turned the renegade away had they not feared the man so much. After some consideration, he decided that the matter should be settled between the two. "If what you say is true, it is your right to challenge Stone Hand."

"You will not interfere?" Long Foot asked.

"My warriors will not interfere."

Everyone in the camp had gathered around them by this time and all eyes turned toward Stone Hand. No one had dared to challenge this fierce Cheyenne warrior before and they were curious to see his reaction to the insults of this foolish Osage. Stone Hand did not disappoint them. He laid his rifle aside and drew his knife, walking slowly toward Long Foot. Long Foot, in response, left his own rifle in the saddle sling and drawing his knife, slid off his horse and stood ready to face his enemy.

Stone Hand's contempt for his accuser was evident in the sneer etched upon his face. "I could have put a bullet between your eyes when you rode in, Osage dog. But there would not have been any pleasure in that. Now I will cut you in little chunks and feed you to the dogs." He began to circle to his left, his eyes unblinking, his evil smile fixed permanently on his face.

The contrast between the two was stark, for Long Foot was slender and smooth-muscled like most men of his tribe. Stone Hand, while not unusually tall, was more massive, his body well muscled and defined, unusual for any Plains Indian. There was no hint of fear in the Osage, however. His grief for his wife was an unbearable weight, for his love for Raven was great. He would have known no fear if he had been facing a grizzly.

The people of Lame Dog's village formed a circle around the two antagonists, a good proportion of them secretly hoping the slender Osage would be able to perform a miracle. Their feelings were of no concern to Stone Hand. He preferred to be feared rather than well received and it was obvious he was enjoying the opportunity to kill the Osage, enjoying it to the extent that he did not want to end it too soon. So he continued to circle, making playful feints with his knife, taunting Long Foot as he circled.

Long Foot became impatient with the sparring and after another of Stone Hand's feints he followed by lunging at his adversary, thrusting with his knife. Stone Hand easily caught his wrist and, with a viselike grip imprisoned Long Foot's hand. With his other hand he ripped across Long Foot's side with his knife, laying open a long gaping gash. Long Foot folded and would have fallen had he not been held up by the renegade's grip on his wrist. He made no outcry but the pain was etched in the lines of his face.

"Your woman put up a stronger fight, Osage dog." Stone Hand hissed in Long Foot's ear. "I will roast your liver over the fire before I feed it to the dogs."

Long Foot strained against the powerful grip of his sneering enemy. It was obvious to all that the Osage was no match for the powerful Cheyenne renegade. They waited for the mortal blow. But Stone Hand was not ready to cut short his enjoyment. With the hand that clutched the wrist, he threw Long Foot backward, causing him to sprawl in the dust of the circle. Long Foot struggled to regain his feet. He held his bleeding side with one hand while he strained to steady himself. Stone Hand began to slowly circle him again, like a wolf circling a crippled calf.

It was at this moment that Jason and Magpie reached the rise above the Commanche camp where he had scouted it that morning. "Oh my God," he whispered when he saw the scene below. Magpie almost cried out when she saw Long Foot staggering and bleeding, encircled by the Commanche camp. "You poor bastard," he murmured to himself, for he knew Long Foot didn't stand a chance against Stone Hand. "Why didn't he just shoot the son of a bitch?" Not understanding his question, Magpie looked at Jason, her eyes wide with terror. He realized the girl was on the verge of panic. "Easy, girl. Just get a hold of yourself. We'll be all right." He reached over and patted her arm. She moved over close to him, pressing close against his side.

There was nothing Jason could do at this point. Long Foot was a dead man already. Jason could tell that by the enormous amount of blood that soaked Long Foot's shirt and ran down his leggings. As they watched, Stone Hand moved in once more and with a powerful thrust sank his knife in Long Foot's ribs. Still the Osage made no sound other than a low grunt. With a violent motion, Stone

Hand snatched the knife back, leaving Long Foot doubled over and fighting to stand up. Stone Hand backed away to watch the doomed man's efforts, amused by the helplessness of his prey.

Jason was almost sick with anger, the frustration almost strangling him. He raised his rifle once, the thought in mind to end his friend's misery. But he could not get a clear shot at either man due to the crowd of spectators. "There's nothing I can do for him," he said quietly, looking at Magpie. She nodded understanding. "I have you and Sarah to think about."

Resigned to the fact that he could do nothing to help Long Foot, he turned his thoughts back to the original purpose of his mission, to rescue Sarah and the baby. Just then it occurred to him that every person in the village was watching Long Foot's execution. If he moved quickly, he might be able to find Sarah before the spectacle ended. At least, he thought, Long Foot's death would not have been for nothing if he could rescue Sarah. The question now was, in which tipi was she captive? He quickly scanned the circle of lodges in an effort to determine which one was the most likely. He decided upon the last one in the circle, closest to the stream. In contrast to the others, it had very little decoration, with no paintings on the sidewalls.

"Come," he whispered to Magpie and, crouching to keep from providing a profile, made his way quickly along the rise until he reached the bottom.

Here he waited for Magpie to catch up. When she joined him, he gave her instructions to hold the horses there at the bend of the stream while he continued on foot.

Making his way along the low creek bank, he crossed behind the last of the lodges before risking another look at his target. What he saw when he cautiously raised his eyes above the sandy creek bank immediately confirmed his guess as to the right tipi. They had been hidden from his view on the rise but now he discovered three horses hobbled next to the tipi. Two of them were Appaloosas—his Appaloosas.

Keeping low to the ground, he pulled himself over the edge of the creek bank. He paused to listen. The noise from the circle in front of Lame Dog's tipi told him that Long Foot's ordeal was not yet finished. He had to remind himself that there was nothing he could do to save Long Foot and to keep his mind on saving Sarah. Wasting no more time, he moved to the rear of the tipi and stopped to listen. There was no sound from within. What if she's not even in there, he thought. Without further hesitation he took his skinning knife and slashed a long tear in the hides. Then very carefully he parted the skins and peered inside. There, on the far side of the tipi, her hands and feet securely tied, lay Sarah, her eyes wide with terror.

"Jason!" she whispered and her face immediately reflected the relief and hope his appearance brought.

Tears of joy brimmed in the eyes that were dark and hollow with despair moments before. It was for a brief moment, however. Then her expression took on a blank, unconscious facade.

He moved quickly, sawing away at her bonds with his knife. "Hurry!" he encouraged while he helped her to her feet. "We don't have much time." He looked around the tipi. "Where's the baby?"

At that moment in answer to his question a Commanche woman entered the tipi, carrying the baby. She stopped short upon seeing Sarah free of her bonds and standing in the center of the tipi. She did not see Jason standing beside the entrance flap of the tipi until she was all the way inside. By then it was too late to give an alarm. He grabbed the startled woman, pinning her arms to her side with one arm while trying to catch the baby with the other. Sarah reacted quickly enough to step forward in time to catch the infant. The woman started to cry out but Jason clapped his hand over her mouth. In a matter of minutes, he had her bound, hands and feet, with a gag over her mouth.

"Quick! Out the back!" He shoved Sarah toward the rip in the tipi. "Go, go . . . hurry!"

Once they had made it safely to the bank of the stream he paused to let Sarah catch her breath while he looked back to make sure they had not been discovered. Sarah's eyes were wide with fright, and although they could ill afford to waste any time he took a moment to calm her. "Sarah, listen to me, you've only got to run about a hundred yards and you'll be safe. Can you do that?"

Eyes still wide, she nodded. Her heart was pounding in her chest but she was willing to do anything to escape the Commanche village. "I can do it," she whispered breathlessly.

"Good." He took her by the shoulders and turned her toward the point where the stream turned around the small stand of scrubby trees where Magpie waited. "Keep as low as you can and follow the creek bank. Magpie's waiting with the horses." He gave her a gentle shove. "Now go."

When she realized that he was not going with her, she hesitated. "Aren't you going?"

"I have to get my horses. Don't worry about me. I'll be along pretty quick. Now go!"

She paused for just a moment then turned and ran toward the trees. After he watched to make sure she was safe, he crawled back over the bank and made his way back to the tipi. He debated for a brief second before deciding to take only his Appaloosas. The thought ran through his mind to take Stone Hand's horse and leave him on foot. But two extra horses might prove to be troublesome to handle. He didn't like the thought of leaving Stone Hand with a horse. He could just cut him loose but then the horse might run toward the gathering of warriors, alerting them of his presence. Finally, he decided to leave the horse. Knowing the savage as well as he did, he knew Stone Hand would simply take any horse he wanted from anyone in the village anyway.

Looking over his shoulder every few seconds in the direction of the crowd of Commanches, he hastily fashioned a bridle from a rope beside the tipi. That done, he paused to take one last look in the direction of the massacre. The noise from the gathering around the combatants relayed a vivid picture of the slaughter as the people reacted to each slash of Stone Hand's knife. He did not have to see what was going on to know that Long Foot was probably dead by this time. The thought triggered a sick feeling in his gut, not from fear or revulsion for the killing, but due to his failure to help his friend. Nothing I could do, he quietly tried to convince himself as he leaped on the back of one of the horses.

Knowing it would be impossible to ride along the shallow creek without being seen from the camp, he struck out straight toward some low hills to the south of the village, keeping the tipis between him and the Commanches. He would gain the cover of the hills before circling around to pick up Sarah and Magpie.

From her vantage point behind the rise, Magpie saw Jason gallop away toward the south. Instantly sizing up the situation, she helped Sarah onto Jason's horse. Scrambling up on hers, she led them out of the bottom and set off in a direction to rendezvous with Jason.

Jason pushed the Appaloosa for all the speed it

would give him. The ground was rough but the horse proved nimble enough to take it at full speed. He doubled back toward the Commanche camp and as he cleared an enormous outcropping of rock, he saw the two women galloping to meet him.

"Good girl," he murmured as they pulled up to him. Magpie was in the lead. She carried the baby. Sarah followed. As soon as they were even with him he wheeled his horse and led them away toward the hills to the east.

They rode hard until Jason knew they had to let up or the horses would falter. His primary thought was to put as much distance between them and the Commanches as possible. There was no communication between the three of them. The women followed doggedly behind him as he led them across flat barren stretches of sagebrush, through shallow streams, by isolated stands of cottonwoods, always pressing toward the distant hills. The only sounds that were heard were the constant drumbeat of the horses' hooves and the rhythmic thumping of their labored breathing. Finally he feared for the horses' lungs and he knew he must rest them. He slowed them to a walk and after another mile he stopped in a small stand of trees next to a trickle of water.

Jason walked back to the top of a grass-covered hill to watch their back trail to make sure no one was following them. That was one of the reasons he walked back. The other was to give Sarah a moment of privacy to nurse her baby. The infant started crying the moment Magpie dismounted and handed him to Sarah. It struck Jason that the baby looked more natural in Magpie's arms than he did in his mother's. Sarah seemed to be in a trance. She took her baby and immediately untied her blouse. It was done without emotion, almost unconsciously. Jason could only wonder at the abuse she must have suffered at the hands of Stone Hand. Her bruised face was evidence enough of her physical torment. The cuts and bruises would soon heal. He feared the scars in her mind would be a lot longer in healing.

When he returned to their hastily made camp, Magpie was holding the baby once more. She was gently rocking the infant and cooing to him in the Osage tongue. Sarah sat beside the small fire Magpie had built, seemingly oblivious to the baby now that she had performed her duty. When Jason approached, she stared up at him for a long time without speaking.

"Are you all right, Sarah?" She did not answer but continued to stare blankly as if seeing through him. He tried to comfort her. "Everything's gonna be all right now. I think we got a good enough head start. It'll be a while before they'll even know which way we went." He waited for her response. Just when he decided she was not going to answer, she spoke.

The words were low and trancelike and she looked straight ahead when she talked. "I haven't got much milk anymore." He started to reassure her that that was all right when she continued. "He'll come after me. He'll keep coming after me till he kills me."

"No . . . no, Sarah." He wanted to convince her that she was safe. "I'm not going to let him kill you."

She laughed. It was a humorless laugh. "You can't stop him. He'll kill you, too." She stared into the fire. "We should have left the baby. He wants the baby."

It pained him to hear her talk like that. Long Foot and Raven had offered to take the baby in the beginning but after it was born Jason thought Sarah might change her mind.

Magpie's English was not very extensive but she seemed to understand the meaning of Sarah's words and she held the baby closer to her bosom, cooing again to quiet his fussing.

Jason stood looking down at Sarah for a moment, not knowing what to say to reassure her in her obvious mental state. Finally, he spoke his mind. "Well, I reckon you're right. He'll be coming after us as soon as he gets on our trail. And I aim to put an end to this thing once and for all. First thing, though, I'm gonna get you and Magpie to a safe place, then I'm going after him. I'm not waiting for him to come to me."

"He'll kill you," she stated without emotion.

"We'll see," he responded. "He might, but I don't plan on it." He noticed the concern in Magpie's face and smiled to reassure her.

CHAPTER 18

It would have to do. Jason was not totally satisfied with the scarcity of trees in the canyon he had picked, but the two women should be safe there. They were only two days from Camp Supply and the army but he was concerned that the renegade might be able to overtake them in a race for the fort. Better to hide out in a well-hidden canyon like the one they were now setting up camp in. He could have made a run for Supply but there were other reasons to lay low for a while. He didn't want to take Sarah back to her father in the state she was now in. At least he wanted to give her physical scars a couple of days to heal. Maybe her mental state might improve also, given a little time.

They were running short of food but he explained to Magpie that he could not take the time to hunt. He figured that if Stone Hand had picked up their trail he would probably be no more than a day behind them. Jason wanted to make sure he intercepted him long before he even had a chance to stumble onto their camp in the canyon. Magpie nodded solemnly. She still had some corn, she explained, and they had plenty of coffee. Food for the baby would soon be a problem, however, for she said that Sarah had very little milk.

It was time to leave but Jason still had some concerns that the women would not be able to defend themselves in the event things didn't turn out the way he planned. There were no trees, save a few scrubby oaks in the tiny canyon he had picked for their camp. But near the point of the canyon there was a broad stand of shrubs that covered the base of the ravine and a portion of the sides. This was the spot where he settled his charges, where he could hide the horses in the bushes. Still not completely satisfied with the camp but resigned to the fact that there was nothing more he could do, he figured it would have to do.

"Well, ladies," he began, "I reckon you can take care of yourselves for a spell." He took his pistol from his belt and handed it to Magpie. "You can keep this just in case. It's loaded and ready to fire." She took it silently, her eyes never leaving his. "If for some reason you have to make a run for it, ride straight through the brush and come out at the foot of the canyon. There's a game trail on the far side of the brush. Follow it till you break clear of the hills then hightail it straight south toward Camp Supply."

Both women watched him with intense attention

though neither spoke. He could sense that they felt they were hearing a farewell speech and in all probability they would never see him again.

"Well, I'm wasting time." With that he turned and walked to his horse.

"Jason!"

He looked back. Magpie ran to him. He turned to face her. "What is it, little Magpie?" His tone was soft, as if comforting a child. Something in the girl's eyes touched his heart and he realized at that moment the depth of his feelings for this innocent Osage maiden.

She put her arms around his waist and hugged him tightly. "Be careful," she whispered. "I fear I will not see you again."

"You will. Don't worry." He was deeply touched by the young girl's concern for his safety. But there was something more. As he took her by her shoulders and held her at arm's length, he looked into her dark eyes and suddenly he was enveloped by a warm blanket of his own emotions. It was as if he had just seen the girl for the first time. The feeling left him with a strange sensation that he had not experienced before. He was held there for a few moments before he forced himself to get back to the business at hand. "I best get going."

He had made a decision to leave the Appaloosas with the women and ride Birdie. He thought it best to ride a horse he was familiar with as well as one that knew him well. He stepped up in the stirrup and threw his leg over. When she felt his weight, Birdie began to prance sideways for a few steps. It seemed that she sensed the importance of their mission and she was eager to begin. With a slight wave of his hand he turned and rode off toward the mouth of the canyon. Birdie picked up a smart pace without any urging. Suddenly she dropped to her knees and tumbled, throwing Jason from the saddle. At about the same instant, he heard the shot.

Jason lay stunned for a moment, the wind knocked out of his lungs. He wasn't quite sure what had happened and he struggled to get to his knees, fighting to get his breath. What seemed to him like minutes were actually mere seconds that he remained on his knees waiting for the heavy pain in his chest to subside. At last he caught a breath and his brain started to work again. Then he realized what had happened. His horse had been shot out from under him! He looked quickly right and left, trying to see where the shot had come from. There was no one. He looked behind him where Birdie lay, already dead, the bullet having gone through her lungs. Able to function now, he started for his rifle in the saddle sling. Two bullets kicked up dust in front of his feet, stopping him in his tracks. The report of the rifle sounded a split second after the dust kicked up. He knew they were not just shots that missed. He would be dead if Stone Hand wanted him dead. He took one more step toward his rifle only to be warned by another bullet in the dust, this time barely missing his boot. Jason stood still then and waited.

In a moment he emerged from behind a high rock formation at the mouth of the canyon. His rifle leveled at Jason, he walked toward him, taking his time as he did, confident in his mastery of the situation.

The son of a bitch, Jason thought, watching the evil grin form on the renegade's face as he approached. As it was with Long Foot, he intends to kill me, but not mercifully with a bullet. Well, that just might be his last big mistake. Come on, you evil bastard!

He was within about thirty feet of Jason now and the grin turned into a sneer when he spoke. "Jason Coles." He spat the words at him, laden with contempt. Then he held his rifle up for Jason to see. Tied to the barrel was a fresh scalp Jason knew it belonged to Long Foot. "Do you like it, Coles? I am going to tie two more with it, yours and the white bitch hiding up there in the brush."

"You're mighty damn confident of yourself, aren't you? My scalp don't come off that easy. You better shoot me while you got a chance. That's the only way you're gonna get this scalp." Jason hoped to goad him into putting his rifle aside.

It was needless goading, for Stone Hand had no intention of denying himself the pleasure of killing Jason. He smiled. "You talk as big as that Osage dog I just cut up. I have waited a long time for you, Coles." He slowly waved the rifle, causing the scalp to swing back and forth, taunting his victim. Then he grasped the lever and rapidly cocked the rifle until all the shells had ejected into the dust. That done, he tossed the rifle aside and drew his knife.

Jason drew his own knife and prepared to defend himself. Bending his knees slightly, he crouched and waited, watching the Indian as he slowly began to circle him. Stone Hand continued to circle, feinting every few seconds but not attacking. Jason sensed that he wanted him to charge so he remained patient, watching and waiting. There seemed to be no sound in the canyon as the two men faced each other, slowly moving in a circle, like two serpents measuring each other. Stone Hand's lust for blood finally overpowered his patience and with a sudden cry of rage he lunged toward Jason like a rabid wolf. As best he could, Jason braced for the collision but the renegade was too strong. He fell on his back, Stone Hand on top of him. They struggled desperately, rolling over and over in the dust, each man straining to free his knife hand while fighting to hold the other man's. Suddenly, Stone Hand broke free and scrambled to his feet. Just as swiftly, Jason was up and on his feet.

Now they circled again, each man having sampled the other's strength. Jason knew now he was in a desperate battle for his life, for his adversary possessed the strength of a mountain lion. After a moment of cautious feinting, Stone Hand charged once again. This time Jason was ready. The two men crashed together, their chests pressing close, their arms above their heads, each man straining to stab with his knife while locking his opponent's wrist with his other hand. Now they were straining against each other like two rams, each trying to overpower the other. But neither man could bend the other back. Finding that his opponent was too strong to overpower, Stone Hand hooked his leg around Jason's knee and Jason, caught off balance, was thrown to the ground. Like a great cat, Stone Hand was on him immediately, his knife blade flashed briefly in the sunlight as he struck. Jason instinctively rolled to avoid the attack but he felt the burn of the blade as it sliced the back of his upper arm. The sight of the blood seemed to incite the savage even more, sensing the prospect of a kill. Jason was too quick for a second thrust, rolling over several times before scrambling to his feet. Stone Hand was immediately after him, crashing into him, searching for an opening to bury his knife. Both men grunted with the exertion necessary to hold off the other's assault. The blood from Jason's wound covered his forearm and hand, making his grip on Stone Hand's knife hand slippery. Stone Hand jerked his hand free and struck at Jason's ribs. Jason managed to slip to the side just enough to escape a mortal wound but the knife found the flesh on the outside of his rib cage. This fresh blood brought a look of triumph to the renegade's face and his lip curled up into a sneer. His overconfidence caused him to loosen his grip slightly and his sneer was frozen by a look of surprise when Jason's knife slashed across his chest, laying open a long gash. Stone Hand backed away and stared down at his chest, amazed. Then the anger raged in him and he charged Jason again.

Back at the foot of the canyon, hidden in the brush, Sarah and Magpie sat, momentarily transfixed by the desperate battle they witnessed. Although it seemed like an eternity it had in actuality been but a few minutes. In that time, Magpie made her decision. She could not sit watching while Jason was fighting for his life. She turned to Sarah, who was huddled, terrified against a scrubby bush. "Here, take the baby." Sarah was almost paralyzed with fear and Magpie had to repeat it several times before the frightened woman reluctantly reached out for her child.

So desperate was the battle that neither man noticed the woman walking toward them, the pistol in her hand. When she was within a distance of twenty or thirty feet, she stopped and raised the pistol. Locked in struggle, the two men lunged and turned, first one way and then another, causing her to hesitate as she tried to get a clear shot. Finally, in desperation, she pulled the trigger, the bullet passed harmlessly beside the renegade's shoulder.

Shocked by the explosion of the pistol so close behind them, both men stepped back. Stone Hand's reflexes were too swift for Magpie as he sprang upon her and wrenched the weapon from her hand before she could get off another shot. Furious at the attempted attack by the Osage girl, he shoved her away from him. Now he had the pistol and having lost his enthusiasm for killing Jason with his knife, he decided to end it with a bullet. Jason, however, was as quick to react as the Cheyenne, and when Stone Hand turned to shoot, Jason was already behind him. When Stone Hand's gun hand swung around, Jason was there to grab his wrist. At the same time, Jason sank his knife up to the hilt in the Indian's belly.

Stone Hand's eyes flashed wide with shock and he stared down at the knife, only the handle visible, in disbelief. Still he struggled against Jason's grip on his wrist. As Stone Hand groped for the knife in his belly with his free hand, Jason jerked it out and sank it a second time. Stone Hand screamed in pain. Then his eyes began to glaze and Jason, looking straight into them, knew he was fading rapidly. His lips almost touching Stone Hand's ear, he spoke, almost in a whisper. "Die, you son of a bitch."

Jason stood over the still body of the infamous Cheyenne renegade. Now that it was over, he felt weak and completely wrung out. It was then that he became aware of his wounds.

"Come. I must clean your wounds." Magpie was now at his side, concerned about the amount of blood he had lost.

"It ain't as bad as it looks," he assured her. "It can wait for a bit." He turned his attention back to the dead renegade.

He and Magpie both stared at the remains of a Cheyenne legend, turned now into a lifeless lump in the canyon's dust. Neither of them noticed the woman walking purposely toward them until she was almost beside them. Jason turned to speak but she brushed past him and stood before the body. There was a wild look in her eyes that worried Jason. She seemed dazed.

"It's all over now, Sarah. He can't hurt you no more."

She seemed not to hear him and continued to stare at Stone Hand. With a cry of anguish, she suddenly picked up Stone Hand's bloody knife and began stabbing the body, again and again, as fast as she could—over and over—the savage's blood spattering on her arms and face until she could not lift her arm anymore. Jason, at first too shocked to stop her, decided it best to let her get it all out. When she lay back in the dust, sobbing, he helped her to her feet.

"You don't need to fear this Injun no more. Spirit or not, he ain't coming back."

From the thicket at the end of the canyon came the thin cry of the baby. He looked down at the once feared Cheyenne butcher and then at the knife still in his hand. He knelt down beside the mutilated body and started to take the scalp. With the point of his knife resting at the front of the savage's scalp lock, he hesitated, seemingly spellbound by the evil presence that lingered near the body. After a moment, he turned and instructed Magpie, in her own tongue. "Take Sarah back to the camp and get her and the baby ready to leave this place." Magpie nodded and took Sarah by the arm, leading her away. Jason returned to his work.

He stared for a moment longer into the face of the devil that had sought to kill them all. Then with a sudden lunge he sank the knife deep into Stone Hand's throat and hacked an incision completely around his neck. He got to his feet to avoid the spreading pool of blood that rushed out into the dust around the body's shoulders. After a final moment's hesitation, he reached down and drew the war ax from the renegade's belt and with one mighty thrust he severed the head from the body.

"Now we'll see if your brothers still think you're some damn spirit. We'll see how many ghost dances are done for you when they see how you're wandering around the spirit world without a damn head." He thought about the last time he had reported that he had killed the man. There would be no doubt this time.

It took but a short while to find Stone Hand's horse hobbled on the far side of the ravine. Leading it behind him, he returned to his camp to find the women waiting for him, ready to ride. If they noticed the bundle securely wrapped in Stone Hand's robe and tied on behind the Indian saddle, they made no mention of it.

"Let's go," Jason ordered. "I wanna be in Supply before dark tomorrow."

Without further comment the women mounted and followed silently along behind. None was reluctant to say good-bye to the little canyon and no one looked back. Behind them, the valley was silent as a tomb. There was no sound of birds or insects, nothing but the heavy silence remained to envelope the headless corpse that would soon be food for the buzzards.

CHAPTER 19

The sun had traveled perhaps three-quarters of its journey across the clear, relentless blue of the sky and the troop, having just stood down from Retreat, was straggling back to the relief of the few shade trees in the camp. Sergeant Major Maxwell Kennedy paused before his tent flap to look at something that had caught his eye out on the prairie to the north. He watched for a few minutes, trying to make out the party approaching.

"Cora," he called, "come out here."

She poked her head through the tent flap and upon following his gaze toward the prairie, she came out and moved to his side. "Who is it, Max?"

He didn't answer for a long time as he continued to stare. As the object moving toward them began to take shape, he began to mumble to himself as if warming up to speak. Finally, he blurted, "Well, I'll be go to hell . . . I thought my eyes was playing tricks on me."

"Lord, Jesus . . ." Cora whispered when she recognized the three approaching the camp. "She's bringing the baby back! I never thought she'd . . ." The words trailed off in her throat as a vision of a mortified Colonel Lucien Holder formed in her mind.

Someone had evidently alerted the colonel, for just then the headquarters tent flap was thrown back and the lean, stern features of Lucien Holder emerged from within. "Sarah," he gasped, barely audible. He stood waiting, his eyes never leaving the small party that was now crossing by the willows. Max and Cora walked over and stood beside him. The colonel glanced briefly at his sergeant major. "Max . . . What the hell . . ."

"I don't know, sir," Kennedy replied. Like his wife, Max figured Camp Supply would be the last place Sarah would show up with her child.

Jason eyed the reception committee that had gathered before the headquarters tent. He didn't relish the confrontation he was about to have but he had made up his mind that it was best to get it out in the open. He didn't know what was in Sarah's mind as to what she planned to tell her father about the events that had followed her departure from this camp a year ago. He had recently come to the opinion that he didn't give a damn anymore. Stone Hand's death had changed his mind about a lot of things and one of them was to let Sarah choose her own life . . . and settle it with her father herself. He had not failed to notice that the closer they had come to Supply, the more she seemed to come out of the shell that had engulfed her back in the canyon.

They rode straight up to the small gathering of people in front of the tent, Jason, leading a spare horse, followed by Sarah, followed by Magpie, carrying the baby. Not a word was spoken until Jason pulled up before them.

"I brought you your daughter. She's a little hard for wear but I reckon she'll be all right."

"Coles . . ." Holder stammered and then turned toward his daughter. "Sarah, what . . . ?"

Sarah Holder made her decision at that point, before her father became totally lost in the confusion of his daughter's sudden and unexpected appearance. He had been content for many months, knowing that Sarah was safely back East and completely removed from the area of his concern. Then after receiving word that she had never reached Baltimore, he had searched the prairies and settlements for one hundred miles around, all in vain. For no one could give him a clue as to her whereabouts. It was as if she had vanished from the earth. Now, to have her appear like this, in the accompaniment of Jason Coles and an Indian woman, was beyond his comprehension. Before Jason had a chance to speak, Sarah greeted her father. Her manner was almost casual as she explained the situation. The colonel was eager to embrace her explanation.

"Father," she gushed, "it looks like we owe Mr. Coles another debt of thanks for saving me again."

Jason looked sharply in her direction, finding it surprising, to say the least, that her attitude had turned so miraculously. All traces of the almost trancelike gloom that had cloaked her for days seemed to have been swept away. The fury that had consumed her when she stabbed the body of Stone Hand again and again had vanished without leaving a trace. Once again she was in control and appeared to know exactly where she was heading. Jason backed away and let her tell the story the way she wanted it told.

Cora Kennedy and the colonel arrived at Sarah's stirrup at almost the same time. She smiled as she accepted their assistance in dismounting. Father and daughter embraced. Holder glanced up at Jason, still in the saddle. "What happened, Coles?"

Again, before Jason could answer. Sarah responded to her father's question. "I was abducted again by that savage. I'll tell you about it later. Just know that although I was held captive, I was not seriously harmed, Jason rescued me and now I'm back safe and sound and no harm done."

"My God!" Holder gasped. "Stone Hand? I thought he was dead!" He looked quickly at Jason. "You said you . . ."

Jason interrupted. "I know—I thought I did at

the time. But the devil wouldn't die even though I cut him plumb near in two." He shook his head in apology. "But, like she said, Colonel, no harm done."

"No harm done?" Holder was still confused. "No harm done?" He turned to his daughter and then back to Jason. "What the hell happened?"

Jason paused, hesitant to embellish.

"What happened to the scout who went with you? Long Foot wasn't it?" This from Max Kennedy.

"Went under," Jason replied, "him and his wife, too."

"Stone Hand?"

Jason nodded in reply. Max swore softly.

Further questioning was interrupted by the sudden crying of the baby. All eyes turned to the Indian girl on the horse beside Jason.

Before the question could be asked, Sarah spoke up once more. "This is Magpie, Raven's sister. And this is her baby." She stole a quick glance in Jason's direction when she said it but he showed no emotion whatsoever. Had not all eyes been fixed on Sarah they might have noticed the flicker of surprise that registered on the face of the Osage girl. It was gone in an instant, replaced by a subtle smile. There was a brief twinkle in Cora's eye, however, and she stepped forward and took Sarah by the arm.

"Come, dear, you must be exhausted." Turning

to the colonel, she said, "I'll take her to my tent so she can rest up a bit. Then she can answer all your questions."

They stood silent for a few moments and watched Cora and Sarah disappear into the tent. Colonel Holder looked visibly relieved to have Cora take charge of his daughter. Jason couldn't help but smile inwardly. The colonel never did know what to do about Sarah. She appeared to be bouncing back to the same self-confidence she had exhibited when he first met her crawling out from behind the wheel of an ambulance. If he were a betting man he'd lay odds the story she cooked up for her daddy, about where she had spent the last year of her life, would sure be a corker.

When Cora and Sarah had gone, Jason stepped down and went around to the packhorse he had been leading. "I brought you something else, Colonel." He untied the bundle from the saddle pack. "You can do what you want with it. Me, I'd stick it on a pole in the middle of the reservation." He handed the bundle to Max Kennedy.

"Merciful God!" Max exclaimed, almost dropping the grisly package. He glanced up at Jason, a trace of anger in his eyes. "What the hell is this?"

"That," replied Jason without emotion, "is Stone Hand."

Colonel Holder was stunned for a moment only before realizing the significance of the gruesome remains before him. "Sergeant Major, get this over to the reservation and get it up on a pole. Coles is right. Get it up on a pole and mount a guard around it. I want all those young bucks to see that damn thing." He turned back to Jason. "And, Coles, well done. I'll see that you receive additional scout pay for this."

Magpie had an uncle who lived on the reservation and after some deliberation Jason decided it best to take the girl there. Magpie was not pleased with the decision but she said nothing. After seeing her settled, Jason made camp off by himself, near the horse herd, close to the creek. He assured Magpie that it wasn't necessary, still the young Osage maiden came to his camp daily to prepare food for him, even when he did not eat it. She was never without the baby. He noticed a definite change in Magpie's disposition since he had taken her to her uncle's lodge. He couldn't define it, it was almost chilly toward him . . . and yet she never failed to come to his camp each day. He found himself missing the affectionate, almost fawning little maiden she had been on the trail. Maybe she feels differently now that she is back among her own people, he told himself. Maybe, now that the baby is hers, that is all she needs.

Sitting by his campfire in the evening, Jason thought more about the way things had turned out. In the few days since he had returned to Supply, he had had barely more than a glimpse or two of

Sarah. From what he could see, she had adapted beautifully, looking for all the world like the Sarah Holder who had first taken Camp Supply in a tidal wave of charm. He smiled to himself when he thought about how quickly that baby had become Magpie's. He was even chagrined to notice that Captain John Welch had called on Sarah several times. Jason no longer cared . . . and he found that rather interesting. He thought more and more about his little valley in the Colorado Territory, and finally one day he decided it was time to return there. Upon making his intentions known to Colonel Holder, the colonel insisted that he join them for dinner that night before pulling out the next morning.

When Jason entered the colonel's tent that night, the first person he met was Captain John Welch. The two men eyed each other coldly for a long moment before Welch broke the silence.

"Mr. Coles," he acknowledged stiffly.

"Doctor," Jason returned.

There followed an uneasy silence, mercifully broken when Sarah swept in from the other end of the tent and immediately took charge. "Why, Mr. Coles, I wasn't sure you were coming," she teased. "Another minute and we'd have started without you." John offered his arm and she took it. Jason followed them in to dinner.

"Well, Coles, so you're going back out in the Colorado wilderness," Colonel Holder stated when the meal was finished and coffee was being served. "That's mighty lonesome territory for a man alone. I'd be happy to keep you on the payroll here. The army always needs scouts."

"I appreciate it, Colonel, but I reckon it's time for me to get back to ranching." The thought struck him that it was odd, the colonel referring to Colorado Territory as wilderness. In his mind, Camp Supply was wilderness. Colorado Territory had to be paradise.

"Well, we shall miss you, Mr. Coles," Sarah said cheerfully.

Jason did not reply. He found the situation amusing. Here they were, sitting around the dinner table, and it was Mr. Coles this and Miss Holder that, a world apart from the beaten wretch that had fought for her life like an animal . . . and John Welch doting upon her every word, his aloof attitude of before completely forgotten. Jason marveled at the transformation. What could have brought about such a change in attitude? Maybe the ambitious young officer had truly had a change of heart and come to realize that Sarah should not be blamed for what had befallen her. Jason doubted it. More likely the young man reconsidered his possibilities for advancement if he married the colonel's daughter. This line of reasoning made even more sense when Holder confided to the dinner guests that he had received word of his coming promotion in rank to that of general.

"Does this mean a new assignment?" Jason inquired.

"Yes, it does. I'm being reassigned to Fort Lincoln."

"I suppose you'll be taking Max Kennedy with you."

"Yes, indeed. Sergeant Major Kennedy will go with me. Captain Welch has requested to accompany me as my staff surgeon. We'll be leaving as soon as replacements arrive."

"Well, congratulations, sir. I reckon you'll make a helluva general." He glanced at Sarah. The question in his eyes must have been obvious for she answered.

"And I'll be going to Fort Lincoln with Father. From there I suppose I'll continue on to Baltimore." She smiled sweetly at Jason.

"Perhaps we can persuade you to linger awhile in Fort Lincoln," John Welch inserted.

Jason studied the faces of the two young people across the table from him. Well, he decided. I reckon they deserve each other. He had a suspicion there might be a wedding in Fort Lincoln. It was time for him to go. "Well, folks, I'll be leaving now. Colonel, thanks for the victuals. Miss Holder, best of luck to you, ma'am."

A few moments later he was outside in the clear starlight of the evening. It felt good to be out under the stars. He glanced back at the tent flap. He thought about Colonel Holder's offer to keep him on the army payroll. Maybe it would have been the smart thing to do. He could sure use the extra money. It was hard to explain—he just didn't have the stomach for it anymore. Deep down he didn't feel the Indian was getting a fair shake. All the army was doing now was running the poor devils into the ground, sending them off to reservations on land so sorry it wouldn't sustain life of any kind. He didn't want any part of it anymore. He couldn't really say he was sorry to close this chapter in his life. There was a loneliness in his heart but it was not a painful thing and he looked forward to the morning that was to come. He still had a few of his horses and with a little luck maybe a few head more were still grazing in the sweet grass of his little valley.

CHAPTER 20

Magpie did not come to his camp that morning. He could not deny the feeling of disappointment that resulted. Still, why should he have expected her? She knew he was leaving to go back to his ranch in the mountains. Too bad, he should have said his good-byes to her the day before. He was afraid he was going to miss her. But he'd soon get over it, he told himself as he tightened the girth strap one more time before stepping up into the saddle. Satisfied that he was done with Camp Supply for good, he turned the Appaloosa's head to the north and urged him forward.

He was passing the sergeant major's tent when the flap was suddenly thrown back and Max stepped out. On his heels was Cora and she called out in mock indignation, "Did you think you were going to just ride out without saying good-bye to your friends?"

Jason grinned and reined up before them. "Why, Cora, I figured you would still be asleep."

"No such thing, Jason Coles. Get down off that horse and give me a proper hug."

"I reckon you heard we'll be going to Lincoln," Max said.

"Yeah, I heard. I don't suppose you'll shed too many tears over leaving this place."

Max laughed. "I reckon not."

He spent a few minutes more saying good-bye to Max and Cora and then he was back in the saddle and moving off to the north at a brisk pace, anxious to get the dust of Camp Supply behind him. Still he could not shake a feeling of loneliness, even when the sun caught the tips of the far hills and bathed them in a golden wash, a sight that normally cheered him. He rode on for a quarter of an hour, something worrying in his mind. Finally, without stopping, he swung the Appaloosa's head sharply around to the west and headed toward the Cheyenne reservation.

It was still early when he reined up in front of Magpie's uncle's tipi. She was sitting outside before the fire, holding the baby, dressed in a buckskin dress and leggings—like she was ready to travel, he thought. He glanced over at her horse, hobbled beside the tipi. It was packed with all her belongings.

He smiled. "Looks like you're going on a trip."

She got to her feet, a look of impatience fixed on her face. "I am going on a trip," she said and went over to untie her horse.

"Where you going?"

She fixed him with a stern look. "You know where I'm going, Jason Coles. I'm going with you."

"Damn!" he chuckled. "I don't remember asking. You sound mighty damn sure of yourself."

She was struggling hard to maintain the no-nonsense facade she had so carefully constructed but his smile was infectious and she could not avoid the embarrassed grin that pushed the corners of her mouth up. "Enough talk! Time to go." She handed him the baby while she jumped up on her horse. Reaching for the infant again, she could not avoid his eyes. They were laughing at her. "You dumb man. If I wait for you to ask me, I'd be an old woman."

They rode out of the reservation toward the hills. As they passed the trading post, he paused for a brief moment to look at the grotesque monument atop a lone pole near the hitching post. As he stared at it, the wind caught in a hollow of the already badly decomposed head, turning it slightly on the pole so that the vacant eye sockets came to rest on Jason. He felt a chill run the length of his spine. It was not fear. Jason didn't fear anything that was dead. It went deeper than that. Stone Hand had touched Jason's soul with a cold finger.

He was unaware that he was still staring at the disembodied head until Magpie touched his arm lightly. "All right," he said, nudging his horse with his heels. "Let's go. I thought we'd let the little one say good-bye to his daddy." Magpie replied something but she spoke too softly for him to hear. "What did you say?"

"I said, not Stone Hand's baby," she said, this time in her elementary English. "Baby white baby."

He drew back sharply on the reins, pulling his horse up short. "What?" He moved over beside her and pulled the blanket away from the infant's face. He stared hard at the child for really the first time ever. "Well, I'll be damned . . ." He could not suppress a laugh. "After all this we went through, it ain't even Stone Hand's son." Then he realized the significance of Magpie's startling report. "So you and me are going off to Colorado territory with John Welch's son."

She nodded. The look on her face told him that she was chagrined that it took him so long to figure it out. "Our baby now."

He smiled at her. "Our baby now," he repeated. "It's a start," he added and urged the Appaloosa forward. After a few minutes, he looked back again and said, "We've got to find you a new name. You're too damned pretty to be called Magpie."

Her face was aglow. "How about Jason Coles' wife?"

"That ain't bad but maybe we can come up with something shorter."